MARDI GRAS MURDER

D0951154

MARDI GRAS MURDER

ELLEN BYRON

W✺RLDWIDE

TORONTO • NEW YORK • LONDON
AMSTERDAM • PARIS • SYDNEY • HAMBURG
STOCKHOLM • ATHENS • TOKYO • MILAN
MADRID • WARSAW • BUDAPEST • AUCKLAND

Mardi Gras Murder is dedicated to my readers.
Without you, this wouldn't be a book.
It would just be a file in my computer.

WORLDWIDE™

ISBN-13: 978-1-335-40542-5

Mardi Gras Murder

First published in 2018 by Crooked Lane Books, an imprint of The Quick Brown Fox & Company LLC. This edition published in 2021.

Copyright © 2018 by Ellen Byron

Recycling programs for this product may not exist in your area.

This edition published by arrangement with Harlequin Books S.A.

For questions and comments about the quality of this book, please contact us at CustomerService@Harlequin.com.

Harlequin Enterprises ULC
22 Adelaide St. West, 40th Floor
Toronto, Ontario M5H 4E3, Canada
www.ReaderService.com

Printed in U.S.A.

MARDI GRAS
MURDER

The People of Mardi Gras Murder

The Crozat Family

Magnolia Marie ("Maggie") Crozat—our heroine
Thibault ("Tug") Crozat—Maggie's father
Ninette Crozat—Maggie's mother
Grand-mère—Maggie's grandmother on her dad's side
Lia Tienne Bruner—Maggie's cousin
Kyle Bruner—Lia's husband

Law Enforcement

Bo Durand—detective and Maggie's boyfriend
Rufus Durand—on leave as Pelican PD police chief; currently a detective; father of baby Charli
Hank Perske—acting police chief
Cal Vichet—officer
Artie Belloise—officer
Regine Armitage—EMT
Cody Pugh—EMT

Friends, Frenemies, and Some Citizens

Gaynell Bourgeois—friend and coworker
Ione Savreau—friend and coworker
Whitney—Bo's ex-wife and Xander's mother
Xander—Bo and Whitney's seven-year-old son with Asperger's syndrome
Vanessa Fleer—frenemy turned kind-of friend, Ru's ex-fiancée and mother of Charli
Quentin MacIlhoney—defense attorney, Vanessa's fiancé

Lee Bertrand—Grand-mère's boyfriend

Chret Bertrand—Gaynell's boyfriend

Jayden Jones—Chret's friend and fellow vet

JJ—proprietor of Junie's Oyster Bar and Dance Hall

Old Shari—nonagenarian bartender at Junie's Oyster Bar and Dance Hall

Little Earlie Waddell—publisher, editor, and jack-of-all-trades at the *Pelican Penny Clipper*

Eula Banks—civil servant, Hall of Records

Mayor Beaufils—mayor of Pelican

Fay Labadie—senior citizen

Stacy Metz—wife of Robbie Metz, pageant judge

Contestants for the Title of Miss Pelican Mardi Gras Gumbo Queen

Belle Tremblay—the perfect contestant

Allouette ("Allie") Randall—the reluctant contestant

Kaity Bertrand—the enthusiastic contest

Parents and Guardians of the Contestants

Pauline and Jules Tremblay—Belle's parents

Denise and Mike Randall—Allie's parents

Gin Bertrand—Kaity's grandmother and guardian

The Judges

Gerard Damboise—head judge

Constance Damboise—his wife

Robbie Metz—owner of several Park 'n' Shop convenience stores

Mo Heedles—multitier marketing skin care maven

PROLOGUE

THE RAIN CAME. Came in a way no one in St. Pierre Parish had ever seen before. Bayous and rivers exploded their banks, turning small towns into lakes. Some residents escaping the deluge had to dodge alligators that the rushing water swept onto their flooded front porches. "It was like the good Lord took all his showers on one day," Claude Fauchon muttered to the Cajun Navy as the hardy volunteers rescued him and his ancient mutt from the submerged Creole cottage Claude had owned for sixty of his eighty years.

The rain sent a torrent of water raging down the usually placid Bayou Beurre. And with it came a community's rubbish: worn-out tires, a ringer washer, an out-of-date infant's car seat, even a suitcase full of 1960s-era women's wigs. The junk backed up against the single lane bridge behind Crozat Plantation Bed and Breakfast, blocking the bayou's path to the Gulf of Mexico. The bayou overflowed, threatening the B and B's outbuildings. But an intrepid crew of Crozat family members and volunteers let the relentless rain soak them as they hauled away the detritus of small town life. It wasn't until they'd almost reached the bottom of the pile that they found the body.

The body of a stranger to Pelican, Louisiana.

ONE

Three weeks later...

"I'M GONNA MISS your mama's cooking something fierce," Fay Labadie told Maggie as she hugged her goodbye.

Maggie grinned. "Words I'll never hear about my own cooking, that's for sure."

She placed a small suitcase into the trunk of a waiting cab. It contained the few belongings Fay had been able to salvage from her flood-ravaged cottage. Following the weather catastrophe, the Crozats had closed their B and B to paying guests so they could house locals like Fay, whose home lay in the vulnerable, low-lying outskirts of Pelican. The Crozats had taken a financial hit from their generous act, but at least their home still stood. Wary of the mighty Mississippi, Maggie's ancestors had built their plantation on the highest ground they could find. As this was Louisiana, high ground was barely above sea level, yet that was enough to protect the plantation's manor house. Some of the outbuildings hadn't been so lucky. The 1920s garage, sitting closest to Bayou Beurre, took on three feet of water when the bayou breached its banks, putting on hold the family's plan to turn it into a spa that might lure more guests to Crozat Plantation's lovely but simple facilities.

Weeks after the storm dropped fifteen inches of rain

in twenty-four hours, the streets of St. Pierre Parish were still lined with piles of debris people pulled from their homes—ruined furniture, toys, photo albums. Every road seemed a funeral procession of memories. But the Crozats' personal rescue mission was winding down. Some of their displaced guests were returning to houses patched up through the state's Shelter at Home program, which aimed for quick fixes that could make at least a few rooms habitable until major reconstruction began. Others left the B and B for short-term rentals or to bunk with family members. Fay Labadie had succumbed to her son's entreaties that she move in with his family in Oregon. "It's temporary," the retired librarian insisted as Maggie helped her into the back of the cab.

"I'm sure it is." And knowing Fay, Maggie was sure it would be. Like so many seniors—and not so seniors—Fay's emotional attachment to Cajun Country was stronger than the steel bridges spanning the Mississippi. As Maggie's beloved Gran' once put it, "I'll be in Pelican from cradle to crypt."

Maggie watched Fay's cab make its way down the B and B's hard-packed, decomposed granite driveway and turn onto the River Road toward New Orleans. She flashed on the body of the old man found under the bridge over Bayou Beurre at the far end of the Crozats' property. He hadn't been far from her thoughts since then. When she tried to push the image away, it returned like a recurring nightmare. The man was Pelican's only storm fatality. But found without a wallet or ID, he had yet to be identified. No one in town seemed to know him. This was unusual for a community so close-knit that residents occasionally discovered they accidentally married distant cousins.

Maggie forced herself to focus. Mardi Gras was coming, and to the Crozats' surprise, none of their guests had been scared off by news reports about the storm damage in St. Pierre Parish, which many of them felt paled compared to the destruction wrought by Hurricane Katrina. Come the weekend before Mardi Gras, the B and B would be full of New Orleanians eager to trade the chaotic partying in their own city for Pelican's down-home festivities, so Pelican had to be ready for the revelers. The motto, "Yes, we Peli-CAN" was now a rallying cry, inspiring citizens to show the world the flood was no match for the town's Mardi Gras celebrations.

"Hey there, you."

Maggie started and then smiled. She turned to see her boyfriend, Pelican Police Department Detective Bo Durand. They took a step toward each other and embraced.

"You're a fair sight prettier than moldy drywall," Bo said.

"Why, sir, you flatter me." Maggie, doing her best Southern belle imitation, pretended to fan herself. "How are repairs going?" The guesthouse Bo rented was uninhabitable, forcing him to bunk with his cousin Rufus Durand, currently on leave from his job as Pelican PD police chief, thanks to an altercation with the town mayor over a parking space.

"I got the place almost down to the studs, but my landlady doesn't want to put any money into repairs until she knows how much help she's going to get from the government. Place could be a total loss. On top of that, it's crazy time with Rufus. He's celebrating because Chief Perske's given his two-week notice."

"So, Ru's going to be chief again?"

"Yeah, and he's taking advantage of his last gasp of freedom before he's back in a position where he has to be a 'role model.' I don't know what I'm gonna find when I open the door. One day he's partying like a frat boy, the next I gotta talk in whispers because it's his day to have Charli, and you know how nuts he is over that baby."

"She's the best thing that ever happened to Ru. The way he cares for her is enough to take the quotes off of 'role model.'"

"I know, I know. But now that he's baby-proofed the place, I can't open a dang cabinet."

"You don't remember from when Xander was a baby?" Maggie said with a grin. Xander was the seven-year-old son Bo shared with his ex-wife, Whitney.

Bo frowned and shook his head. "I was never too good with those locks when it was my own kid." He made a face. "The last couple of days Vanessa's had Charli, so Chez Ru's been rocking. Music blasting, trash and laundry piling up. I smell like stale beer and gym socks."

"You don't." Maggie pulled Bo to her and kissed him. "Okay, you do a little."

"I think I'm gonna have to burn my clothes and take a bath in one of those industrial washing machines."

Maggie laughed. She then grew serious. "I keep thinking about the flood victim. Has the department had any luck identifying him?"

"Not yet. To be honest, we haven't had time to do much about it. It's a mess working out of the temporary space." Pelican PD headquarters had taken on two feet of water, compelling the force to relocate to temporary digs. "Let's talk about something besides flood stuff.

I need a break from it. You haven't had the chance to fill me in on Pelican Mardi Gras."

Maggie smiled. "Alrighty, my little Pelican Mardi Gras virgin. The day starts with a Courir de Mardi Gras, aka the Mardi Gras Run. That's where people dress in these unique costumes and go door-to-door, singing and begging for ingredients to use in the big communal gumbo. It's a chance to drink and act goofy without anyone knowing who you are because you're wearing a mask. It used to be only men, but in the time between when I moved to New York and came back, two other runs started, one for women and one for families. I've never done the Run before. I'm looking forward to it. There's also the big gumbo cook-off—"

"Your dad told me about that."

"Oh, my dad is all about the gumbo cook-off. He gets a little crazy, let me tell you. And the whole day ends with a fais do-do, so no matter how tired you are from being a Mardi Gras, you *will* be dancing."

"Being *a* Mardi Gras?"

"That's right; here in Pelican, *Mardi Gras* is a proper noun. You not only go to Mardi Gras, you *are* a Mardi Gras."

"What about a parade?"

"Oh, there's a parade. It's not Mardi Gras without at least a little 'Throw me something, mister.'"

"Isn't there some kind of beauty contest as part of the festivities?"

Maggie groaned and rolled her eyes. "My least favorite part of the day. Forgetting to mention it must have been a Freudian slip. Yes, there's the legendary Miss Pelican Mardi Gras Gumbo Queen Pageant. Gran' is a judge every year, and I bless her and Mama for never making me enter. They must've known I'd sooner pack a hobo stick and run away. Although the winner does get to wear a wonderfully kitschy crown with a gumbo pot centerpiece made from rhinestones."

Bo raised an eyebrow. "Getting an image of you in a bathing suit, high heels, and a crown...and liking it." Bo's cell phone rang. He pulled the phone out of his back pocket and checked it. "Chief Perske," he said. "I have to take this."

He stepped away, and Maggie entertained herself by admiring how the detective's jeans hugged his long, lean frame. Bo ended his call and stood rooted in place.

"Everything okay?" Maggie asked.

Bo frowned. "Something I didn't see coming. The coroner's home was flooded, so he hasn't been at work. He went back to the morgue today, and the first order of business was examining our mysterious drowning victim. Only...it turns out he didn't drown."

"Wait—the man from the bayou?" Maggie asked, confused. "The man found under our bridge? He didn't drown?"

"No." Bo's voice was grim. "He was murdered."

TWO

Maggie stared at Bo.

"Murdered?"

He nodded. "Shot to death. Which you don't know, because Perske specifically said not to tell you anything about it."

"Of course he did." Being an artist, Maggie possessed a visual acuity that enabled her to pick up clues others missed in past murder investigations. This thoroughly annoyed the outgoing police chief.

Maggie rubbed her forehead. "It makes no sense. No one seems to know the victim. But somebody killed him."

"Well, that means somebody's lying."

Maggie started up the whitewashed cypress steps of the manor house, and Bo followed her inside. They walked down the wide hall into the kitchen, where they were greeted by the rich aroma created by a confluence of flavors wafting up from a cast iron pot of seafood gumbo on the stove. The scent of the Cajun-seasoned broth, filled with crab, oysters, shrimp, and crawfish, made Maggie's mouth water. She ladled two bowls full and topped them off with thick slices of French bread she cut from a baguette straight out of the oven. She handed a bowl to Bo, and they sat down at the trestle table that doubled as a workspace for Maggie's mother, Ninette, the B and B's legendary cook. Ninette was at the far end of the table, making notations on a list la-beled "Groceries."

"Do you think the man's wallet washed down the bayou?" Maggie asked as she and Bo tucked into their dinner.

"We're looking for it, but I don't think so. My guess is whoever killed the guy removed anything that could ID him."

"I didn't check him out too closely, needless to say. But I did notice his clothes looked worn. Who would want to kill some poor old man?"

"I know someone who might want to kill a middle-aged one," Ninette muttered.

Maggie and Bo shared a look, amused by this flash of attitude from Maggie's kindhearted mother. "Dad and the gumbo contest?" Maggie asked.

Ninette sighed. "Oh yes. I should warn you, nothing's changed about your dad and that cook-off in the years you were away in New York. He still gets all het about it and starts banging around my kitchen and getting in my way and using up all my ingredients."

"I'll talk to him, Mama."

"Oh, *chére*, you know there's no talking to him when it comes to his gumbo."

"So the competition's that stiff, huh?" Bo said. "I better give my own gumbo recipe a test run before Mardi Gras." Bo motioned to his bowl. "And if your dad is making seafood, I'm going with chicken and sausage. I can't see anyone beating this."

"You better not beat him, period, or it could be the end of our relationship," Maggie joked.

"I'd be some kind of fool to put a gumbo cook-off

ahead of a beautiful girl." Bo kissed her forehead. "I best be going." He nodded to Ninette. "Ma'am."

"'Night, *chér*." She gave Bo a warm smile. "I'm impressed by your priorities. By the way, that happens to be *my* seafood gumbo. And you're right. If I bothered entering it in a contest, no one would beat it."

Bo left through the kitchen's back door, and Maggie set off to track down her father. She found Tug crouched in front of the family's ancient black safe in the back parlor-turned-office. His face was a study in concentration as he turned the tumblers.

"Dad, any chance you can go a little easy on the gumbo competition this year?" Maggie asked.

"Tell your mother no." Tug shoved aside a pearl tiara and other family heirlooms. "She's got to make a King Cake for our guests, and you know how much she loves coming up with new recipes for those. So she should stop fussing about my gumbo and focus on that." Tug gently extricated a tattered recipe housed in a plastic page protector. "Hold this." He handed the recipe to Maggie, reached deep into the safe, and pulled out a beat-up cast iron pot. He addressed the pot fondly. "Hello, old friend."

Maggie, bemused, shook her head. "Some kids have to compete with siblings for attention. I had to compete with a black pot."

"This pot never told me it was borrowing the car to go on a church youth group retreat when it was really going to a party in New Orleans."

"It was a party *at* a church." Tug shot his daughter a skeptical look. "Okay, a church turned into a club," she admitted.

"Where the only prayer was 'Dear Lord, don't let

my parents find out where I really am.'" Tug turned his attention back to the pot. He stuck his head inside, reveling in the lingering bouquet of herbs and spices.

"You know, Dad, you're making Mom kind of crazy."

"Some men make their wives crazy all year. I save it for Mardi Gras."

Maggie started to rebut but stopped herself. "When you put it that way, it's hard to argue."

"Now if you could just convince your mama of that."

MAGGIE LEFT TUG murmuring sweet nothings to his pot and made her way to the shotgun cottage she shared with her beloved Grand-mère. She found Gran' at the living room's antique desk, separating a small stack of documents into two piles. "Pageant applications?"

Gran' nodded. "It's mind-boggling how few people bother to read instructions. The application clearly states contestants for Miss Pelican Mardi Gras Gumbo Queen must be between fourteen and seventeen years of age. And yet"—she pointed at the larger stack—"thirteen, eighteen, even one hopeful twenty-four-year-old contestant. At least I'm winnowing down the pool of potential gumbo queens." Gran' reached for a tissue. She sneezed, coughed, and sneezed again.

"You need water." Maggie went into the small shotgun kitchen and retrieved a bottle from the refrigerator. She brought it to her *grand-mère* and then sat on the arm of the sofa. "You won't believe this. The man found in our bayou after the flood? He didn't drown. He was murdered."

Gran' gasped and crossed herself. "That's dreadful. Why?"

"Nobody knows. I can't stop thinking about him,

Gran'. The man died on our land. What if he has family out there, wondering where he is? They deserve to know what happened. And the poor guy deserves better than being Pelican's mysterious, murdered John Doe."

"I'm sure once Pelican PD is operating at full capacity, they'll identify him and bring closure to his family." Gran' grabbed another tissue and let loose with a flurry of sneezes. "Oh dear."

"That's not good. You don't sound well." Maggie placed a hand on her *grand-mère*'s forehead and frowned. "You're warm too. I'm worried about you."

"It's nothing—merely a late winter cold. A good night's sleep and I'll be fine."

Maggie hugged Gran' and started for her bedroom. Gopher, the family's basset hound rescue, and Jolie, the cute mutt the Crozats were fostering for a family on an extended Hawaiian sabbatical, padded along with her. Jolie's cat companion, Brooke, preferred the comforts of the manor house, where the family was tending to both her and Jolie's litters until they were old enough to go to new homes.

Maggie changed into a tee shirt and pajama bottoms, then picked up the forty-five-pound Gopher, with a grunt, and placed him on the bed. His short, stubby legs made leaping onto it impossible. Jolie had no such problem. Within a minute, she was also on the bed, snuggled up next to Gopher. Maggie joined them and struggled to get comfortable in the foot of space the pups left her. Jolie recalibrated, curling up in the small of Maggie's back while Gopher stretched his entire body the length of her legs and pressed up against them.

Gran' appeared in the doorway. "I wanted to say goodnight. By the way, I know the current housing situation with Bo has been rough on…aspects of your relationship. If you ever need me to make myself scarce…"

"No, no, no," Maggie said with a vehement shake of her head. She and Bo had yet to christen the shotgun with their romance because both were discomfited by the thought of displacing her *grand-mère* for a booty call. "Thanks anyway, Gran'."

"Alright, *chére*. But the offer remains on the table." Gran' shook her head affectionately as she took in the picture of Maggie squeezed to the edge of the bed by her canine companions. "I do hope that handsome boyfriend of yours knows that when you tie the knot, he'll be sharing his matrimonial bed with critters."

"The 'M' word hasn't come up yet, Gran'. I mean, not *yet*—scratch that, it was presumptuous. No marriage talk. We're just dating, being in the moment, taking things a day at a time, and… I've run out of clichés."

"Well, when it does happen—and notice my commitment to the word *when*—my wedding gift to you will be a king-size bed."

Gran' blew Maggie a kiss and closed the door behind her. Maggie heard a hacking cough as Gran' set off to bed, and vowed to take her to the doctor first thing in the morning.

MAGGIE LOOKED AT her clock and yelped. "Nine a.m.?" She jumped out of bed, but not before scolding the pooches still sacked out on it. "What kind of alarm clocks are you?"

Fifteen minutes later, she was showered and ready to take Gran' to the doctor before reporting to her job as a tour guide at Doucet, a plantation once owned by Ninette's family and now serving as a nonprofit historical site. Gran' wasn't in the cottage, so Maggie walked toward the manor house. Gopher and Jolie tagged along, occasionally stopping to sniff a bush and mark their territory. Maggie stopped short when she reached the family's gravel parking area. Tug and Ninette were helping Gran' out of Tug's old SUV.

"We're getting you straight to bed in the Rose Room so I can keep an eye on you, Charlotte," Ninette told her mother-in-law.

"Where were you?" Maggie asked, worried.

"Your father heard me coughing in the early a.m. and insisted on taking me to the Emergency Room," Gran' said. "It appears I have a case of walking pneumonia."

Tug wagged a finger at his mother. "You're gonna take care of yourself so it doesn't turn into the real thing. At your—"

Gran' held up her hand. "Oh no you don't. Anyone who utters the phrase 'at your age' will be subjected to an onslaught of my germs."

Tug and Ninette brought Gran' to the manor house while Maggie returned to the shotgun cottage. She picked out a nightgown for her *grand-mère* and put together a bag of sundries, then dashed back to the others and helped her parents tuck Gran' under a downy, deep-pink duvet cover in the Rose Room, the B and B's loveliest lodging. "I feel like the Queen of England," Gran' said. "Oh, speaking of queens, I need the pile of Gumbo Queen entry forms from the desk. I can use this time to go over them."

"Oh no you don't," Tug declared. "The only thing you're going to do right now is rest."

"I can't forsake my judging duties," Gran' protested.

"Can and will, Mama."

Tug and his mother both folded their arms over their chests and faced each other in a standoff. "My money's on Gran'," Maggie whispered to Ninette.

"Five dollars says your father takes this," Ninette whispered back. Gran' finally threw up her hands, and Ninette chuckled. "I win."

"Oh, for heaven's sake, Thibault, if you're going to be stubborn about this," Gran' said. "But a Crozat must replace me as judge. It's a family tradition. Ninette's going to have her hands full with guests soon, and you've got to represent the family in the gumbo cook-off. So…"

Gran' turned her attention to Maggie. "Magnolia, dear, I'm afraid you'll have to take my place as a judge for the Miss Pelican Mardi Gras Gumbo Queen contest."

THREE

"No," Maggie protested. "You know how I feel about that contest."

"After the flood, our little town needs to celebrate Mardi Gras in the grandest way possible, and that means including the pageant," Gran' said. "It's a way of reclaiming the spirit of Pelican. You'll have to put your progressive views aside and take one for the team, *chére*."

Both of Maggie's parents nodded in agreement. Resistance was futile and, if she was completely honest with herself, selfish. Gran' was right. Maggie's hometown needed her to step up. "Okay," she said. "I'll do it."

"That's our girl," Gran' said. "I know you'll bring a fresh, youthful eye to the judging. Our precious spot on earth will bounce back better than ever. Like the town motto says, 'Yes, We Peli-CAN!'"

Gran' finished her pep talk with a loud sneeze, and the others discreetly backed away from her germs.

A light rain fell as Maggie drove to Doucet in the 1964 black Ford Falcon convertible with the red ragtop roof she'd inherited from her late grandfather. On the seat next to her lay a small pile of applications from finalists for the title of Miss Pelican Mardi Gras Gumbo Queen. The other judges had been notified she would be replacing Gran', who had recommended particular contestants for them to focus on. Maggie planned on reading their entry forms on her lunch break and dreaded the task of choosing one teen hopeful over another.

She parked in the small employees' lot behind the plantation's manor house. Maggie opened her umbrella and hopped out of the car, negotiating puddles as she made her way to the staff room housed in the old overseer's house. Once there, she struggled into the uncomfortable pink polyester, ersatz antebellum gown that served as her tour guide uniform. Ione Savreau, her close friend and boss, was already there, along with young coworker Gaynell Bourgeois, who completed the trio of work buddies. Maggie noticed Gaynell was changing out of her gown instead of into it.

"Guess what?" Gaynell pulled off a wig designed to resemble a nineteenth-century hairstyle, releasing a cascade of her own blonde curls. "Ione said that until Mardi Gras, instead of being a guide, she wants me to set up a room where guests can watch me make costumes and masks for the Courir." The Bourgeois family had played an important role in Pelican's Courir de Mardi Gras for generations, channeling their innate artistic talent into the Run's colorful costumes and masks. This year, Gaynell had the added honor of being chosen as a *capitaine* of the women's Courir.

"That's fantastic," Maggie said. "Yet another great idea from our beloved head honcho."

"Just milking the talents of my staff for some freebie entertainment," Ione, always modest, said.

"Okay, I'm now on a mission to come up with a talent that will get me out of this ball gown." Maggie yanked up her dress, trying to cover more cleavage. "Nineteenth-century hoop skirt is so not my look."

But when she finished the last tour of the day,

knowing that judging for the Miss Pelican Mardi Gras
Gumbo contest awaited her at home, Maggie didn't rush
to change. She frittered around the Doucet office until
Ione shooed her away. "Go," Ione said. "Your community needs you. And I need to lock up this dang place."

Maggie stopped at the shotgun cottage and changed
into a teal V-neck cotton tee shirt and black jeans, an
outfit she deemed conventional enough for the occasion. She stopped in to see Gran' and have the outfit
approved. "Put on a skirt," Gran' ordered her.

"I spent the day trapped in a sweaty, corseted ball
gown. Please, oh please, let me wear pants."

Gran' shook her head. "This is not a pants-and-jeans
group. The head judge, Gerard Damboise, is your pro-
verbial old fart. You need to wear the kind of conservative outfit he would deem appropriate attire for any
representative of the Miss Pelican Mardi Gras Gumbo
contest. Otherwise, he won't respect you, which will
render you useless as a judge. Go change."

"I really have to?"

"Yes, you really have to."

Maggie groaned but did what she was told. Digging
an appropriate outfit out of her wardrobe of jeans and
tee shirts wasn't easy. She settled on what she wore to
funerals: a black pencil skirt and a silky dark green tee
that almost passed as a blouse.

She then ambled over to the main house's parlor office, where she fluffed up the needlepoint pillows decorating the intricately carved walnut Victorian settees
facing each other across an ornate coffee table topped
with Italian gray marble. The table hosted carafes of
coffee and hot water, a small wicker basket containing
an array of tea bags, and a platter of Ninette's home-

made pralines, whose sugary scent permeated the air. Maggie heard cars making their way down the plantation's drive. This was followed a few moments later by the sonorous bong of Crozat's doorbell.

Her fellow judges had arrived.

SMALL TALK BEFORE the meeting gave Maggie time to size up the other judges. Robbie Metz, owner of several Park 'n' Shop convenience stores in the area, had a slight build, wiry dark hair clinging to his scalp in tight curls, and the harried expression of a man in his midthirties who had four children under the age of five. Maureen "Mo" Heedles, an African American woman of either forty or fifty-that-looked-like-forty, was the vivacious saleswoman of a multi-tier marketing skincare line called Veevay Beauty. "I'm the number one rep in southern Louisiana, and I've got the purple Mitsubishi Galant to prove it," Mo declared as she shook hands with Maggie, using a sales sleight of hand to deposit product samples in Maggie's palm. "Call me 'the black Martha Stewart of skin care.'"

The other two judges were a couple in the early days of their senior years, Constance Damboise and her husband, the infamous Gerard. Constance was reserved. She wore her gray hair in a meticulous bob and dressed in the kind of elegant Chanel-ish suit Maggie associated with ladies who lunched at traditional establishments like Galatoire's in New Orleans. She was half a head taller than her husband, Gerard, who introduced himself with pride as the president of the St. Pierre Parish Historical Society. A small man with a compact build, the shape of his bald head reminded Maggie of an incandescent lightbulb. She understood why Gran' insisted she don a different outfit; Gerard was the kind of old-fashioned dresser who wouldn't be caught dead without a sport coat, even on Louisiana's most humid days.

It didn't take long for Maggie to notice that none of the other judges seemed to like Gerard very much—including his wife. "I keep telling you, I agree with Robbie," Constance said to her husband in an exasperated tone. "An exhibit about the orphan train would be wonderful. I don't know why you've suddenly turned against it."

"I've heard of the orphan train, but I don't know anything about it, really," Maggie said. Gerard looked none too happy she'd inserted herself into the conversation.

"You see?" Robbie pointed out, a note of triumph in his voice. "We could educate people about an important but little-known chapter in our local history." He addressed Maggie directly. "The orphan train ran from 1854 until the last train came in 1929. It brought orphaned or unwanted infants and children from the New York Foundling Hospital to be adopted by families and couples in southern Louisiana parishes. Lots of people know about the orphan trains that ran from the East Coast to the West Coast, but hardly anyone knows about our own Cajun orphan train. That's how my great-greats came here," he said with pride. "Mo, help us talk Gerard back into it. He's bailed for no good reason."

"Don't drag me into this," Mo said, holding up a hand and shaking her head. "I'm still waiting on an exhibit about my people, who were here way before those orphans."

Gerard released an exaggerated sigh. "Robert, when you're planning an exhibit, you must think of its appeal to visitors, especially in light of our need to raise funds to buy a decent home for the society and move it from its current sad location. It occurred to me, what are we going to display? The grimy undergarments of poor immigrant children? Most of them came from New York's Lower East Side tenements."

"You mean they were Jewish," Robbie said. "Like me."

"And Irish and Italian and Polish and—"

"It sounds fascinating," Maggie said, interrupting Gerard's list of ethnicities, none of which seemed to impress him. "I'm an artist. And I lived in New York. I could help create appealing displays. I already have ideas for—"

"It's not happening," Gerard snapped.

"Don't let him scare you," Mo told Maggie. "When you're the big dog, you get to bark."

Gerard collected himself. "I'm concerned some people may not want their past dredged up. It's a rather inauspicious entrée into our society."

"Those are my ancestors you're talking about," Robbie said, irate.

"For some it was a welcome fresh start," Gerard backtracked. "Be that as it may…"

"Constance, talk to him," Robbie pleaded. "Get him back on board."

"Robbie, dear, I think it's obvious my husband doesn't listen to me." Constance added a laugh to make the comment sound like a joke, but her eyes were cold and angry.

"Let's table any discussion of future exhibits and get to the business at hand," Gerard said. "Finding our next Miss Pelican Mardi Gras Gumbo Queen."

Two hours later, Maggie knew more than she ever

wanted to about the pageant and its rules. She had objected to one in particular. "'Applicants must be between the ages of fourteen and seventeen years old by Mardi Gras, single, have never married or cohabitated with a boyfriend, have no children, and have never given birth.' The last one is rather judgy."

"It's been in the rules since the contest started."

"Yes, but now it's the twenty-first century. And a girl shouldn't be punished because she got into trouble."

"The rule does its job of ferreting out contestants with poor judgment."

"I don't think—"

Gerard, losing his patience, threw a hand up in the air to stop Maggie from arguing. "It's a moot point because we all know Belle Tremblay will be our pageant queen."

"Wha-wha-what?" Maggie, outraged, sputtered. "Are you telling me the winner is predetermined, and this whole thing is a farce?"

Gerard sucked in a breath. "No, I'm saying, given Belle's accomplishments and pedigree, I can't imagine a better contestant."

"Excuse me, but—"

"Ignore him, Maggie," Robbie said. He glared at Gerard. "The rest of us will make sure every contestant gets a fair shot."

"I'm not saying they won't," Gerard replied. "But you'll see I'm right. She's lovely and talented. Plus, her pedigree is impeccable."

"You make her sound like a schnauzer at a dog show," Maggie said. Mo held a napkin over her mouth to cover a laugh.

"Nooo." Gerard elongated the word in a show of exaggerated patience. "She's a Tremblay and Savoy on her

father's side and her great-great-grandparents were a Boudreau and a Favrot on her maternal grandfather's side,
descended from two of the founding families of Pelican."

"Names from a hundred years ago shouldn't mean
anything now."

"Spoken like an infernal millennium, or whatever
you're calling yourselves these days. Your entire generation needs a good spanking."

Maggie glared at him and pulled at her skirt, which
had attached itself to the brocade upholstery of the sofa
upon which she was seated. Her traditional getup hadn't
deflected the man's dismissive attitude. Mo put a hand
on her knee. "A little advice, my new friend. Never get
in a pissing match with a skunk."

Gerard pursed his lips. "I'll choose to ignore that
tasteless remark." He adjusted his reading glasses as he
perused a list attached to a clipboard. "All we have left
to do tonight is a group photo for that beast known as
social media. Maggie, you're the youngest—"

"Not by much," Mo hastily interjected.

Gerard ignored her. "So you're in charge of making sure the Historical Society gets some press from
this event."

"You do know I'm only filling in for Gran' until she
gets better," Maggie reminded him. "And she's getting
better every minute." *I hope, I hope.*

"Please," Robbie said. "It's one less chore he'll dump
on the rest of us."

"All right," she said, caving out of sympathy for the beleaguered businessman. "But I don't have a selfie stick."

"I do." Mo pulled one out of her purse. "I got my
own PR to worry about, so I never miss a chance for
some self-promo."

Maggie attached her phone to the selfie stick, and the other judges huddled around her. "One, two, three—smile." The judges did so, and Maggie snapped a photo burst. As soon as she finished, the judges dropped their smiles and broke apart.

"I'm officially adjourning tonight's meeting," Gerard said. "Tomorrow we have interviews with contestants scheduled at the end of the school day. Please be on time."

"Before everyone goes," Constance said, "I have a picture of this year's crown. I think it's particularly lovely."

Constance pulled a photo from a folder and passed it around, to murmurs of approval. "It's spectacular," Maggie had to admit. And it was. The front of the crown rose a majestic eight inches from its base. It was festooned with a rhinestone gumbo-filled black pot resting on a log fire made of sparkling yellow and orange rhinestones. For the first time in her life, Maggie imagined herself wearing such a fancy headpiece. She pulled out her cell and snapped a photo of the crown, then texted it to Bo with the message "Now I want one." A few seconds later, he texted her back: *"Lol! Hypocrite."*

Post-meeting chatter between the judges was interrupted by the arrival of Ninette, who carried a frosted King Cake on a platter. "I was testing a new filling for my King Cake and would love some volunteers to let me know how it is."

There was a chorus of eager yeses. While Ninette cut the cake, Mo handed postcards to Maggie and Constance. "I'm having a Veevay Vivacious You Party. We'll drink champagne, try products, and get all pretty. Tell your friends. It's the perfect girls' night out."

"Sounds fun," Maggie said. "I'm a bit of a sucker for beauty products."

"Then you are my new best friend," Mo declared. She threw an arm around Maggie's shoulder and gave her a squeeze.

As the judges enjoyed their cake, Maggie wandered over to her mother. She was a prisoner of Gerard, who was fawning over Ninette. "Absolutely delicious. This has to be one of the Crozats' most treasured heirloom recipes."

"Actually, I clipped it from one of those celebrity chef magazines they sell at the market," Ninette said politely. "I'd best be putting the rest away before it goes stale."

Ninette extricated herself from the unctuous judge, leaving him to Maggie, who searched for a topic that might be of mutual interest and drew a blank. She finally blurted out, "So, they still haven't identified the man who died in the bayou behind our house. Have you heard about that?"

Gerard's whole body tightened. "Only gossip."

"It's sad no one knows who he is. The police are working on it, though."

"Seems like a waste of time. I'm sure he's simply some transient from New Orleans. Pelican PD must have more important things to do." Gerard checked his watch. "Constance, we need to go."

The judges said perfunctory goodbyes, and then Mo and Robbie followed the Damboises out of the manor house. Maggie replayed her exchange with Gerard in her mind. She closed her eyes and painted a mental picture of his body language. Then she picked up her phone and texted another message to Bo: "Gerard Damboise knows something about the murder victim."

FOUR

SECONDS AFTER THE text went through, Maggie's phone rang. "Talk to me," Bo said. "What did you pick up from this guy indicating he might be a lead?"

"It's only an instinct—"

"And yours are pretty good."

"He got very uncomfortable when I brought up the mystery man. Then he tried to end the conversation as fast as possible."

"I'll bring him in for questioning."

"Do me a favor and wait a little while. I don't want Gerard connecting me to this in any way. I'm picking up a lot of hostility among these judges. The way things are going, you might end up with a few more murders on your hands."

"Oh man, I do not have time for that. I'll give this Damboise guy a call in the morning and have him in about lunchtime. Hey, buddy, that black pot's not an ashtray—it's an heirloom. Flick your cigarette somewhere else. Sorry. Ru has his deadbeat friends over."

"I'm more concerned about something else. Tell me you don't have your own black pot."

"Of course I do. Me and every gumbo- and jambalaya-lovin' man in Louisiana has one. My baby's been handed down through generations, just like your dad's."

"Your baby?" Maggie whimpered.

"What's wrong?"

"Nothing. Except I just got a bleak vision of my future."

Bo chuckled. "I can guarantee you it will include some fine cast iron cooking."

Bo signed off, and Maggie decided to check on Grand-mère. She made her way to the Rose Room, where she found Gran' being tended to by her octogenarian boyfriend, Lee Bertrand, proprietor of Pelican's lone service station. "Look, *chére*. Lee brought me flowers and chocolates, like it was Valentine's Day." Gran' proudly showed off both.

"Every day I spend with you is Valentine's Day," Lee said.

"Coming from anyone else, that line would engender an eye roll," Gran' said with a laugh.

"I'll try to stick to flowers and not flowery language," Lee responded. "Hey, Maggie, I hear you're a pageant judge now."

"Only until Gran' gets better," Maggie said, adding hopefully, "which will probably be any day now, right?" Gran' answered Maggie's question with a sneeze and a phlegmy cough.

"Guess who entered the contest?" Lee said. "My great-granddaughter Kaity. Since she and her grandmama, my daughter Ginnevra—we call her Gin cuz it's short for her name, and it's her beverage of choice... Where was I?"

"You were saying that since Gin and Kaity have been living with you," Gran' gently prompted.

"Right. Since they moved in with me on account of the flood, they're considered residents, and she's eligible. Gin's super excited."

"What about Kaity?" Maggie was wary of the mothers Gran' referred to as "momtestants."

"Oh, she's excited too. She hears the crown is 'to die for.'" Lee stood up. "I'll be back tomorrow, Charlotte. You make sure and get your rest."

Lee blew Gran' a kiss, gave Maggie a small salute, and took off. Maggie sat on the edge of the bed and leaned in to give Gran' a hug. Gran' gently pushed her back. "Oh no you don't," she said. "I get what you're doing...trolling for germs."

Maggie opened her mouth to protest and then stopped. "Busted," she admitted. "This judging gig is rough. I don't know if I can make it through without blowing up at Gerard Damboise. He's already trying to force a winner down our throats."

"Who?"

"Some girl named Belle Tremblay."

Gran' nodded. "Ah, she's a Tremblay. Now I see what's happening. Gerard is obsessed with growing the Historical Society into an actual museum housed in an impressive historical location, and he's constantly trying to raise funds for that. He once tried to pressure old Adella Poche into bequeathing the Society her Creole cottage, which has been in the Poche family for generations. Adella's son Rex threatened to clock Gerard, which put a stop to that, although I think Rex might reconsider Gerard's offer when Adella passes, because I can't imagine he'd give up the glamour of life in New Orleans for a homestead in our quiet little village."

Gran' stopped to take a breath. "Anyhoo, Gerard's been cozying up to Jules and Pauline Tremblay for years. He's desperate to have them donate memorabilia and antiques to the Historical Society, especially items from Pauline's ancestors, who were Boudreaux and Favrots. Artifacts from founding families like that are particularly important in terms of attracting donors who like to feel they're hobnobbing with the gentry."

"Aren't the Crozats and Doucets founding families too?"

"Yes, and we've donated, of course, and will again. But Gerard knows better than to keep bothering me. In fact, I know a way to prevent him from bothering you as well. I'll give him a call. I doubt he'd want the town to know that in his off hours he tries on the clothes displayed at the Society. Particularly the Confederate general's uniform."

Maggie gaped at her *grand-mère*. "How do you know that?"

Gran' fluffed a pillow behind her and affected regal stature. "*Chére*, I'm the town doyenne. It's my job to know everything. And equally important to know when to use it."

BEFORE HEADING TO work the next morning, Maggie stopped at the Crozat's garage. Chret Bertrand, her friend Gaynell's boyfriend and Lee's great-nephew, had started a small construction business employing his fellow military veterans. She found him surveying the building's flood damage with his friend Jayden Jones. Maggie exchanged a hug with Chret and gave Jayden a warm greeting. Jayden, a reserved African American man who seemed older than his twenty-two years, returned her greeting with a small smile and a nod. When the Crozats found out Jayden had been left homeless by the flood, they'd invited him to stay with them in the manor house. He'd refused but accepted their loan of a tent and a spot to pitch it.

"I'm sorry we haven't been around. We've had a lot of maydays since the flood," Chret said. He placed his hand on the lower half of the garage wall, right below the damp line marking where the floodwaters had stopped their rise. "This has hardly dried at all. We're gonna have to take the walls down to the studs. I'll also rent industrial fans to dry out the wood. Last thing I want is to trap any moisture inside the walls."

"Amen to that," said Maggie, who'd grown up with the moldy aroma of a centuries-old home.

"We'll go ahead and order what we need, since it'll take time to get everything here. I'm putting Jayden in charge of this project."

"If that's all right with you, ma'am," Jayden said.

"The only thing that's not right about it is you calling me 'ma'am.'"

For the first time since Maggie met the former soldier, he looked flustered. "I'm so sorry, ma'am—I mean—"

"Maggie," she said, smiling to reassure him.

"Yes, ma'am—Maggie."

Maggie glanced around the damaged building and frowned. "We're really strapped for cash, so all we can afford is the most basic work to keep this place from being a total loss. Turning it into a spa is a pipe dream for now."

"It'll happen," Chret said, expressing a confidence Maggie didn't feel.

"I hope so. It's so hard for us to compete with the bigger operations around here like Belle Vista. And the flood sure hasn't helped. Anyway, I better get to work. See y'all later."

"Tell Gaynell we're gonna celebrate her new position at Doucet," Chret said. I'll give Bo a call, and we can all celebrate together." He motioned to Jayden. "Maybe we'll even get this guy a date."

Jayden looked down at the ground. Maggie felt a stab of sympathy for the young man. "We don't have to make it a dating thing," she said. "Just a group of friends going out to pass a good time."

Chret, who was working through his own post-service issues, had the sensitivity to pick up on Maggie's cue. "Exactly. Just friends hanging out." He gave Jayden a fond clap on the shoulder. "We best get back to what we were doing."

Maggie said goodbye to the vets and took off for Doucet. But her mind was on Jayden. She knew nothing about his past, but it was clear to her the former soldier harbored pain.

WHEN A STEAMBOAT dislodged a tour group twice as large as originally expected, Maggie had to split her time between giving tours and running the busy gift shop register. Ione let her leave early for the pageant interviews, but she still bounded into Crozat's front parlor with only moments to spare.

Gerard eyed her casual clothes with distaste. "We can't expect our contestants to maintain a grooming standard if we don't adhere to one ourselves," he scolded her.

"I'm sorry, I didn't have time to change," Maggie said, somehow managing to temper her annoyance. Then she had a brainstorm. "And I learned last night the great-granddaughter of my *grand-mère*'s boyfriend is a contestant. So, I'm afraid I'm going to have recuse myself from judging due to conflict of interest."

Maggie gave herself an imaginary pat on the back for sounding so official, but Mo laughed. "Oh, honey, if we disqualified judges who had a connection to contestants, there wouldn't be anyone left to judge." She patted a spot on the sofa next to her. "Pull up a sit." Maggie, deflated, plopped down next to Mo.

"Besides," Robbie said, "Gin has been one of my Park 'n' Shop cashiers for years. If anyone was looking for a way out due to conflict of interest, it'd be me. Not that I am," he added hastily.

"I want to go over the structure for this afternoon," Gerard said. "The contestants and their mothers will wait in the hallway. We'll go out and greet them to put everyone at ease. It can be an extremely tense situation. Then we'll the contestants, one by one, for a five-minute interview. We've narrowed the field to six young women, of which we'll choose three as finalists. Constance will lead the interviews. The rest of us will focus on evaluating the contestants. Any questions?" The others shook their heads. Gerard checked his watch. "It's go time."

The judges left the parlor and entered the hallway as a group. Mothers nudged their daughters to put away their cell phones and adopt good posture. "Hello, and welcome to the ninety-third annual Miss Pelican Mardi Gras Gumbo Queen contest," Gerard intoned. "This year's queen is sitting among you. The rest of you impressive young ladies will be her court. The Miss Pelican Mardi Gras Gumbo Queen Pageant is a glorious tradition in our historic town…"

While Gerard droned on, Maggie studied the women and teens perched or slouched in their seats. She recognized Gin from her similarity to her father, Lee. The woman's smoker's cough and heavily lined face attested to some hard living. She'd been married so many times that she'd given up taking her husbands' surnames and gone back to Bertrand. Her granddaughter Kaity, who'd also taken to using Bertrand as her last name, had a friendly face and the strawberry blonde hair that ran in the family. Maggie noticed the girl across from Kaity had dyed black hair pulled back behind her ears to show cartilage piercings, and looked miserable. But it was the two women next to the pierced girl who caught her attention. Mo noticed Maggie fixating on them. "The one on the right is Pauline Tremblay, mother of Gerard's pick for queen," Mo said under her breath.

"I met her once briefly," Maggie said, also keeping her voice low. "She works part-time for my friend Bibi Starke, who's an interior designer in Baton Rouge. Pauline's supervising the restoration of Grove Hall, my cousin Lia's new place."

"Pauline is fantastic; she did my house. But take a gander at the gal on Pauline's left. That's her cousin, Denise Randall. Interesting, huh?"

Maggie nodded. Denise resembled her cousin by design, not nature. Where Pauline was naturally tall, Denise wore platform stilettos to achieve a similar height. Pauline had a willowy figure; Denise's body seemed to be straining against an inclination toward curves. The most unusual difference was their hair. Pauline's was a lustrous chestnut similar to Maggie's, while Denise had blonde roots at her crown. Whereas many women dreamed of golden locks, Denise had gone in the opposite direction, covering hers with a dye that mimicked her cousin's brunette shade. The only similarity both women shared was bright green eyes.

"...and so, let us continue to honor the memory of our pageant's founding fathers by commencing with the interview portion of our contest." Gerard's speech came to a merciful close.

"Amen," said Denise, her tone fervent. Denise initiated a round of applause that the other mothers and a few contestants quickly joined. Maggie noticed Gin glaring at Denise and trying to out-clap her.

The judges adjourned to the parlor. One by one, the contestants joined them to answer a few basic questions.

"What do you like most about Pelican?"

"What are the three most important qualities a queen must possess, and why?"

"Why should you earn the honor of being the next Miss Pelican Mardi Gras Gumbo Queen?"

Maggie found the first three girls indistinguishable from one another. The fourth was the pierced girl, Allouette Randall, who she learned was Denise's daughter. Allouette was monosyllabic and seemed so deeply unhappy, Maggie ached for her. After Allouette came Kaity Bertrand, who possessed a vivaciousness that couldn't be denied. Belle Tremblay, the last contestant, was indeed the poster girl for any pageant queen. Maggie took an instant dislike to her for absolutely no good reason. *You're being a reverse snob*, she chided herself. *Get over it*.

Once the interviews were completed, the judges narrowed the field down to the three finalists. Belle was the obvious front-runner, but Kaity scored enough compliments from Robbie and Mo to make her a dark horse candidate, much to Maggie's pleasure. The only surprise came when Gerard declared Allouette the third finalist. "Pauline is very loyal to her cousin, Denise," he explained. "If we don't include her daughter in the final three, I'm concerned Pauline might pull Belle from the competition."

Mo nodded. "Sometimes you gotta play Pelican politics," she explained to Maggie.

"Constance and I will let the young women know around eight p.m. tonight, and then tomorrow—"

A shriek from the hallway interrupted Gerard, followed by the sounds of a scuffle and a cacophony of yelling.

"What the hey?" Robbie said, speaking for all the confused judges.

Maggie ran to the door, flung it open, and stepped into the hallway, where all hell had broken loose. Gin and Denise Randall were locked in a catfight as their daughters yelled at them to stop. Maggie tried to yank the women apart, only to be knocked aside. The other mothers looked on helplessly.

"Take it back!" Gin screamed. She put Denise in a chokehold.

"Never!" Denise spit out between coughs. "She doesn't belong here, and you're proving it!"

"Hey!"

The other women started at the sound of a male voice, but Gin and Denise kept at each other. Jayden, who had come into the manor house to take a shower, put down his towel and stepped between the women, struggling to keep them separated. It was at this moment Gerard appeared behind the other judges.

"He's gone crazy—he's attacking the women!" Gerard yelled, panicked. "Constance, get your purse pistol!"

"No!" Maggie yelled. "He's saving them from each other."

Maggie stepped into the fray again. She grabbed Gin and pulled her away while Jayden did the same with Denise. The hallway fell silent, the only sound coming from the women's heavy post-fight breathing.

"I. Am. *Never*. Speaking. To you. Again," Allouette spit at her mother. She turned to Pauline. "Can you take me to your house?"

Pauline snapped out of the paralysis afflicting her. "Yes." She put a hand on Denise's shoulder. "It'll be all right."

Denise, weeping, followed after her cousin. Grabbing this as an opening, the other mothers and contestants murmured excuses and rushed for the front door. Gerard made an effort to regain his composure. "Well, that was… I don't know what that was." He shook a finger at Gin. "I should disqualify both you and Mrs. Randall from this competition. But out of respect for your connection to the esteemed Crozat family, I won't."

Gin looked abashed. "Thank you, sir."

"However, if anything like that ever happens again, there *will* be consequences. We need to go, Constance. I have an appointment." Gerard proceeded down the hall to the front door, gesturing for his wife to follow, which she did.

Gin straightened her clothes and fixed her hair. "I'm sorry, baby girl," she said to Kaity. "But nobody talks smack about my loved ones."

"I thought you were awesome." Kaity took her grandmother's hand. "Let's get you a nice gin and tonic."

Gin squeezed Kaity's hand. "You know your grammy so well."

Kaity led Gin out of the manor house, leaving only Maggie and Jayden in the hallway. Maggie took a deep breath. "Wow. That was ugly. Thank you so much for helping me break it up."

Jayden didn't seem to hear her. "That man said I attacked the women." His voice was low, the tone laced with fury. "He wanted to shoot me. And he didn't even apologize."

Maggie felt terrible for letting Gerard escape without calling him out on his insulting behavior. "Oh, Jayden, I'm so sorry. Please don't let Gerard Damboise upset you. He's a pompous twit who doesn't deserve a minute—no, a *second*—of your thoughts."

Jayden continued to stare at the door without speaking or moving, unnerving Maggie. For the first time since they met, she had the ominous sensation the tightly coiled vet might be dangerous.

FIVE

As SOON AS Jayden disappeared down the hallway leading to the main-floor guest rooms, Maggie stepped outside onto the manor house veranda, hoping some fresh air might calm her. She found Denise sitting on the front steps. Her face was blotchy and wet with tears. "I owe you an apology," she said. "There's absolutely no excuse for my behavior."

Maggie sat on the steps next to Denise. She noticed the woman was trembling. "You don't have to apologize to me. Although you might want to throw a few 'I'm sorrys' Gin's way. I don't think you want her as an enemy."

"No, never. I don't want anyone as an enemy. I have no idea how I lost it like that. It's just that this pageant is so important to Allouette…"

She trailed off. Maggie debated how to phrase her response. "If it makes you feel better, I am not getting that from Allouette *at all*."

"Oh, it means a ton to her. But you know teens. It's all about looking cool, so she's hiding it."

"Well, she's doing a *really* good job of that."

Denise nervously twisted her hands together. "That Gerard Damboise is not a nice man. He doesn't respect my family. He thinks I'm not worth the time of day because I married an American, not a Cajun or Creole. But oh, how he loves my cousin Pauline. He's always sucking up to her. She hates it but puts up with it because she's a nice person. She was a Miss Pelican Mardi Gras Gumbo Queen herself, you know. Talk about setting the bar high, huh?"

Maggie, fixated on Denise's weaving and unweaving of her fingers, responded with a cursory nod. A truck bearing the logo of HomeNHearth, a local big box hardware chain, turned into the Crozat driveway and lumbered toward the manor house. Denise brightened. "My husband Mike is here. I came with Pauline, but Allouette didn't want me in the car with them." Denise tried to sound matter-of-fact, but the tears threatening to spill over her lower lids gave her away. "With her dad making deliveries, it was easy enough for him to come get me."

The truck groaned to a stop in front of the veranda, and a man hopped out of the driver's seat onto the ground. Mike Randall was in his early forties and had the bland good looks of a former high school jock. His medium brown hair was cut short on top, with a fade on the sides, and his ruddy complexion showed a macho disdain for sunblock. "Hey, babe," he addressed his wife. Then he nodded at Maggie and gave her a sly smile. "Hi there."

"Hello." Maggie's tone was cool. She instantly pegged him as the kind of guy who flirted to remind himself he was still desirable. For Denise's sake, she hoped his come-ons never moved beyond flirting.

"We've met before," Mike said. "I make a lot of deliveries to your other family manse, Doucet. Man, these old plantations are money pits. I don't know how you folks keep them up."

"It's not easy," Maggie had to acknowledge.

The front door opened, and Tug stepped onto the veranda. He had flour on his face and hands, and wore a stained apron that read "Got Gumbo?"

"What's going on?" he asked. "I heard a commotion but was in the middle of making a roux."

"Hey, you must be Mr. Crozat, the Pelican Gumbo King," Mike said.

"I don't know if I'd call myself the king," Tug said a touch coyly.

"Oh yeah, you're a legend. But I best warn you, you may have some serious competition this year. I entered the cook-off. Time folks around here got a taste of some fine Mississippi gumbo."

He winked at Tug, who glowered. Mike climbed back into the truck cab and patted the seat next to him. "Come on, babe," he said to his wife. "Pop a squat."

"Thanks for your kindness, Maggie. And again, my apologies."

Denise scampered over to the truck and hauled herself up into the passenger's side of the cab. The truck rolled down the driveway and out onto the River Road.

"I don't like that guy," Tug muttered.

"I'd say it's you feeling competitive, but something about him bothered me too."

Maggie and her father, both pensive, watched the delivery truck lumber out of view.

MUCH AS MAGGIE loved her father's gumbo, a thick concoction loaded with chicken, andouille sausage, okra, and tasso ham, she was ready for a break from it and jumped at Bo's invitation to join him for dinner. She drove into Pelican's historic business district, where four blocks of nineteenth-century buildings with ornate black wrought iron balconies ringed a village green.

When it came to decorating for a holiday in Pelican, Mardi Gras ran neck and neck with Christmas. Every building was festooned with a riotous array of purple, green, and gold flags, banners, wreaths, and garlands. Cajun and zydeco tunes played from speakers the Chamber of Commerce had set up in the green's bandstand. Maggie sang along with Clifton Chenier's *"Allons a Grand Coteau"* as she parked in an angled space. She locked up the convertible and headed into Junie's Oyster Bar and Dance Hall.

Old Shari, the restaurant's nonagenarian bartender, waved and shouted a greeting. The proprietor, JJ, greeted Maggie by enveloping her in a hug. JJ, who'd inherited the restaurant and a closet full of caftans from his late mother, Junie, never missed an opportunity to kitsch up the place. Oversized purple, green, and gold glittery balls hung from the century-old tin ceiling. A center table had been removed and replaced by a fake tree covered with Mardi Gras beads hung on it by patrons. JJ himself sported a gold lamé caftan and a bright green silk scarf decorated with purple fleur-de-lis.

"Here you go, *chére*," JJ said. He strung multiple strands of beads around her neck. "Ones you don't want, put on the Mardi Gras tree."

"My first beads of the season. I want them all." Maggie kissed JJ on the cheek. Maggie noticed a plastic cauldron next to the tree. A half dozen more cauldrons and pumpkin-shaped buckets were scattered around the room. "Are you doing some kind of holiday combining now?"

"Leaks, *chére*. The storm did a number on the old girl's roof. And we're way down the list for repairs." JJ grinned. "Shabby chic is so yesterday. I give you…

dilapidated chic." He announced this with a grand swoop of his arms.

"Maggie! Hey—over here!"

Maggie saw Gin Bertrand waving to her. Gin was sitting with a group of women Maggie recognized as mothers of Miss Pelican Mardi Gras Gumbo Queen contestants. Maggie walked over to the table.

"I want you to know I got a nice apology email from Denise, so we're good," Gin said. "We got some of that 'the enemy of my enemy is my friend' thing going on now."

Denise, who was sitting next to Gin, flashed a relieved smile. "Yes," she said with a vigorous nod. "We both figured we went after the wrong person. If anyone's to blame, it's Gerard Damboise."

Gin snorted with derision. "Him making anyone who isn't a Tremblay feel less than. It gripes a person."

The other women vigorously nodded agreement, but Denise put a finger to her lips. "Shh, Pauline's coming back from the little girl's room. I don't want her feelings getting hurt." She waved to her cousin, who was exiting the restroom. Pauline, looking perplexed, waved back as she walked toward the table.

"Maggie, before I forget, I need to tell you something." Gin rose and pulled Maggie away from the others. "I didn't want to say this in front of the ladies," she whispered, "but I got a text saying Kaity was one of the three finalists. Thank you for that."

Gin winked at Maggie, who held up her hands and shook her head. "No, no, no. I had nothing special to do with it. Kaity got the honor all on her own. I make sure I don't show favoritism to any contestant."

"No worries, *chére*—I won't breathe a word. I'm just happy for the turn things took. It wouldn't have been too good if they'd gone the other way, either for Kaity or your Gran' and my papa's relationship."

"Wait, what—?"

"Oo, my food's here. Talk at ya later."

Gin winked again and then sauntered back to her table, leaving behind a nonplussed Maggie.

The front door swung open, and Bo came into the restaurant. He wore jeans and a black sport coat over a white button-down shirt, his ersatz uniform when working a case. Pretty much every woman in the restaurant shot him a glance, which didn't escape Maggie. He ambled over and kissed her. She could have sworn she heard a disappointed sigh coming from a nearby table. "Sorry I'm late. The computers at temp headquarters keep crashing, and it's slowing everything down."

"I never mind waiting for you," she said, and returned his kiss to the sound of another disappointed sigh.

Bo took her hand and led her to a table tucked in a corner. A glass of Chardonnay and a bottle of beer sat waiting for them, along with a basket of popcorn shrimp. "JJ knows us so well." He studied Maggie. "What's wrong?"

"Nothing. Except… I think I was just threatened." She recounted her conversation with Gin.

"Yep, that's what I'd have to call a veiled threat. Man, they take that pageant seriously around here."

"I know. I can't wait until Gran' gets better so she can relieve me." Maggie sipped her wine. "Oh, I needed this tonight." Bo nodded in agreement and took a slug of beer. "Did you find out anything else about our John Doe?"

"Nothing helpful. No item of clothing on him was less than fifteen years old, down to his socks. If anything was recently purchased, we'd at least be able to

track down the store of origin and see if we could connect him to a general area in the country."

"Were you able to get anything out of Gerard?"

"He never returned my calls."

"What?" Maggie stopped drinking mid-sip. "He said
he had an appointment."

"If he did, it wasn't with me."

"Really?" Maggie frowned. "He doesn't seem the
type to dodge the police. He's a super by-the-rules guy."

"I'll let it be known at the station to keep an eye
out for him. Might be a traffic stop in his future." Bo
put a hand over Maggie's and smiled, creating a single
dimple on the right side of his mouth. "Let's put floods
and bodies and suspects out of our minds and focus on
what's important here—popcorn shrimp."

In response, Maggie picked up a shrimp, tossed it up
in the air, and caught it in her mouth. Bo laughed. "Sexy."

Then he did the same.

Bo BEGGED OFF going back to Maggie's place for a night-
cap. "Whitney and Zach are spending the night in New
Orleans," he explained, referencing his ex-wife and her
second husband. "She's got a doctor's appointment first
thing in the a.m., so I need to relieve the babysitter and
pick up Xander." He made up for his absence with a
kiss Maggie could take home with her.

Maggie drove out of Pelican and onto the River Road
toward Crozat, smiling to herself as she replayed Bo's
embrace in her mind. The road was littered with pot-
holes caused by the flooding, and she forced herself
to focus on navigating around them. She stopped for
a red light and gazed past the levee to the Mississippi.
Although it was late February, the air was warm, so

Maggie lowered the car windows. She could hear a barge engine hum as it made its way to the Crescent City and eventually the Gulf of Mexico.

The traffic light turned green. Maggie was about to go when she was suddenly thrust forward by the impact of a car hitting her back bumper. "Sonuva..." Maggie swore. She put the Falcon in park, stepped down on the emergency brake, and got out, slamming the car door. There'd been a spate of accidents lately caused by people texting behind the wheel, which infuriated her. She marched up toward the car behind her, ready for a confrontation. Then she saw the driver was slumped over his steering wheel. Anger forgotten, she ran to him.

"Are you okay?" The man lifted his head and mumbled something unintelligible. "Let me help you." Maggie fumbled in the dark for the car door, somehow managing to pull it open despite her shaking hands. The driver grabbed her wrist and she screamed. The man clinging to her was Gerard Damboise.

Gerard's face was white; spittle dripped down from the left corner of his mouth. "I—I—"

"I need to get you help." Maggie pulled away, but Gerard clung to her with a clawlike grip and garbled something that sounded like "please." He tried to form another word, but all he could manage to express was a puff of air. "Gerard, let me go! I have to call 911."

Instead of freeing her, Gerard grabbed Maggie's shirt with his other hand and yanked himself up to a sitting position. "Lies. Secrets."

He articulated the two words perfectly. Then the St. Pierre Parish Historical Society president released Maggie, made a gurgling sound, keeled over into the passenger's seat, and took his last breath.

SIX

MAGGIE REFUSED TO believe Gerard had died. "I—I'll…
I'll call for an ambulance." She ran back to the Falcon
and grabbed her purse. She rummaged through it, but
her phone wasn't there. Maggie searched the car seats
and floor. No phone. "What do I do, what do I do?"

She saw a car coming from the opposite direction,
and jumped up and down to get the driver's attention.
The car raced past her. "That's what I get for wearing
all black," she muttered. Another car drove by, and the
pattern repeated itself. Maggie, desperate, started running toward Pelican. A new-model SUV came down
the road. She threw her arms in the air and yelled as
loudly as she could. The car stopped and Maggie ran to
it. Her relief grew when she saw the driver was Pauline
Tremblay. Next to her was Allouette. "Maggie? What's
wrong? I was just driving Allouette home."

"There's an emergency." Maggie pointed to Gerard's
car. "And I can't find my phone."

Pauline pulled up behind it and jumped out of her
SUV. "Call 911 and stay in the car," she instructed Allouette. The teen, who looked terrified, nodded.

Pauline followed Maggie, and peered into the pageant judge's car. She let out a shriek. "Oh my God!
How…what…?"

"I don't know."

"Lord have mercy," Pauline murmured, crossing herself. She'd gone so pale Maggie was afraid she might pass out. "Lord have mercy."

The pageant mom, her gait unsteady, walked to a nearby tree and leaned against it. A minute later an ambulance came screaming up the road, and EMTs Cody Pugh and Regine Armitage jumped out. "Over here!" Maggie called to them as they ran to her. "But I think it's too late."

Cody pulled open the door to Gerard's car. He lifted Gerard's hand to take his pulse. "Nothing," he said after a minute. He laid the late man's hand down, and then did a double-take. Cody leaned into the car to take a closer look at Gerard's body. "Regine, call Pelican PD," he said to his partner, who immediately did so.

"Why?" Maggie asked. Her heart began beating rapidly.

"That." Cody gestured to a hole in Gerard's jacket under his shoulder blade—a small, perfectly round hole, singed around the edges.

"Is it…?"

"A gunshot wound? Looks like it." Cody bent down and sniffed the air above the hole. "And smells like it."

A Pelican PD patrol car pulled up behind the ambulance. Maggie was so absorbed in her conversation with Cody she hadn't heard its siren. Officers Cal Vichet and Artie Belloise emerged from the patrol car. Artie, who had a fondness for anything edible, held a half-eaten po' boy in one hand.

"Got your call, Cody," Cal said. "We were just around the corner, running a DUI checkpoint."

"Which we got going pretty much twenty-four/seven with Mardi Gras coming," Artie chimed in. He took the last bite of his po' boy, then noticed Maggie. "Uh-oh. If Maggie's here, there must be a murder."

"Hey," Maggie protested.

Cody motioned to the officers. "You need to take a look-see."

Cal and Artie took turns leaning into the car and giving the late Gerard a once-over. "Seems like we got a crime scene on our hands," Artie said. He headed back to the patrol car to retrieve the familiar yellow tape that would mark off Gerard's car and the area surrounding it.

"Excuse me." Pauline had recovered from her near faint and joined the group. "I'm not exactly sure what's going on, but if no one needs me, I should get my cousin's daughter home."

"Hold tight for a bit, ma'am," Cal said. His tone was polite, but firm. Cal, on the laconic side, was often the Laurel to Artie's affable Hardy.

"Really? Oh dear." The expression on Pauline's face was worry trending toward panic.

"Why don't we check on Allouette?" Maggie suggested to the anxious woman. "She's probably wondering what's going on."

She gently steered Pauline back to her SUV. Allouette stuck her head out the window. "What's the deal?" the teen asked. "Why do we need the police and an ambulance?"

"Chére," Pauline said, "there's been an accident of some kind. Mr. Damboise, the man who runs the pageant…has passed away."

"Seriously? He died?" Allouette wrinkled her brow as if trying to wrap her mind around this shocking development. "Wow." Her expression grew hopeful. "Does this mean the pageant is cancelled?"

Pauline emitted a frustrated snort. "Teenagers," she said to Maggie, shaking her head. "Allouette, we have to show some respect and not worry about superficialities like the pageant right now." Allouette, who was engaged in a flurry of texting on her cell, didn't respond.

Artie approached the women. "As they say in the movies, looks like we got ourselves a situation. The evidence van is on its way to check things out. Meanwhile, I'm going to need some statements."

"Oh my God, I didn't see anything, I swear." Pauline was close to hyperventilating. "I stopped to help Maggie. I won't say anything else without a lawyer." Pauline had obviously seen a few police procedural TV shows.

"It's true, Artie," Maggie said. "I waved her down after I found Gerard was…incapacitated."

"Alrighty. But I need your contact info."

Pauline released the breath she was holding. "Yes, Officer. Of course. Allouette, can you please pull a business card out of the glove compartment?" Allouette did as instructed, and Pauline handed the card to Artie. "Poor Gerard. Poor, poor Gerard."

"Hey, Cousin Pauline, I have homework," Allouette said.

Maggie, struck by the mundane juxtaposition of homework and death, emitted a giggle tinged with hysteria. She clapped her hand over her mouth. "I'm sorry. Nerves."

"Don't know why you're nervous," Artie said. "You've been around more of these investigations than half the department. If those other murders hadn't been solved, we'd think there was a serial killer in our midst, and her initials were MMC. Magnolia Marie—"

"We get it, Artie," Maggie said, gritting her teeth.

Artie turned to Pauline. "You're free to go, but make sure you're available if needed."

"Yes, of course, will do. What a night. I should have taken I-10." Pauline hoisted herself into the SUV and screeched off like a NASCAR car driver racing away from his pit crew. Maggie spit out the dust the SUV kicked up.

Cal, a serious look on his long face, approached her. "Won't know for sure what all's up until Ferdie Chauvin gets Gerard on the coroner's table, but evidence indicates his death wasn't an accident. Maggie, walk us through how you came on him."

Maggie shared the story of how she discovered Gerard, before saying, "You can check my rear fender and see if there's any damage that would support my story."

"For your sake, I hope there's not," Artie said. "I knew you well enough to assume you didn't kill Gerard, even if he was the town pain. And vintage cars are pricey to repair."

Maggie, Cal, and Artie walked over to the Falcon. Artie trained his flashlight on the car's bumper while Cal got on his knees to examine it. "Nothing. Let's check out Damboise's front fender."

The three moved over to Gerard's car. Once again, Cal examined it carefully. "There," he said, pointing to a dent in the license plate frame. "That's new. If the damage was old, it wouldn't have that sheen to it. It would show the effects of weathering."

"Alright then," Artie said. "Anything else you can tell us?"

"Yes. He begged me for help, or at least tried to. And then he said two words very clearly: 'Lies. Secrets.'"

"Did he happen to say what these lies and secrets were?" Maggie shook her head. "Dang. Would make our job so much easier if he had. We'll need a written statement. We can meet you down at the station."

"I'll be there shortly."

Maggie climbed into the Falcon, turned the car around, and drove back into town. She nabbed a parking spot in front of Junie's. The restaurant had emptied out. Only a few stalwarts remained planted at the bar.

"Hey," JJ said, surprised to see her. "You forget something?"

Maggie hesitated and then decided not to share the news of Gerard's death. She wasn't ready to handle the barrage of questions that would follow. "I can't find my cell. Has anyone turned it in?"

JJ shook his head. "But that doesn't mean it's not here. Place is so dark, I walk into stuff myself." JJ turned up the lights, exposing Junie's in all its stained and faded glory. The bar regulars shielded their eyes and protested. "Oh, hush up. I'll turn 'em down soon as we find Maggie's phone."

Maggie checked around the table where she and Bo had been sitting, but found nothing. She and JJ scoured the restaurant. "This is nuts," Maggie said, frowning. "I know I had it here. It's not in my car. Maybe I dropped it when I was leaving."

"Or maybe the phone got throwed away when the tables was bussed," Old Shari piped in.

"It's worth taking a look," Maggie said.

"Lucky for you, I haven't put the trash in the dumpster yet," JJ said. He pointed to a black plastic bag by the back door. "Unlucky for you, that doesn't make it any less fragrant."

JJ left Maggie by the bag. She wrinkled her nose and tried to take shallow breaths as she donned plastic gloves and dug through the refuse from a night at Junie's. She could feel the slimy remnants of diner's meals through the gloves. Her hands landed on a flat, rectangular object. The shape and weight felt right, so Maggie carefully extricated it from the bag. She'd found her phone, reeking of old jambalaya, its screen shattered and body smashed.

"Well, that's not a pretty sight," JJ said, peering over her shoulder. He wrinkled his nose. "Or smell. If you're done, I best throw out the bag."

"I'm done." Maggie held up her phone. A chunk of glass fell off the front, clattering to the floor. "And apparently, so's my phone."

WHEN MAGGIE GOT home after giving Artie and Cal a written account of what she'd witnessed, her parents were waiting with a bourbon on the rocks, which Maggie gratefully accepted at the door. "We were worried about you," her father said. "We called Junie's, and JJ told us about your phone. But he said you seemed extra upset, like something else was going on."

"It's been…a night." Maggie downed the drink. "Gerard Damboise is dead."

Tug and Ninette exchanged a shocked look. She held up a hand to prevent them from asking questions, and strode down the hall to the B and B's parlor office. "I need to call the other judges. I know the police are with Constance, but I don't want Robbie or Mo to find out from gossip."

"What a terrible loss," Ninette murmured. "Well, to be honest, Gerard wasn't a very nice man. But it's a loss to Constance. I assume. Although I never picked up on her being passionately in love with him. I'm going to stop talking now."

Ninette freshened Maggie's glass from a bottle she held, and then she and Tug retreated. After another belt of bourbon, Maggie called Mo, whose voicemail sang a jingle raving about the anti-aging benefits of Veevay Beauty products. Maggie left a carefully worded message and then moved on to Robbie. Sounds of a hectic family life with four kids accompanied the call.

"Dead? Holy— *Jonathan, get to bed—you were supposed to be asleep an hour ago!* What do we do now?"

"That's up to Constance. I think she's our main concern at the moment."

"Right, sure." Robbie, ever the Chamber of Commerce president, slipped into businessman mode. "We need to honor him. Maybe rename the pageant for him. Or add another scholarship—you know, the Gerard Damboise Memorial Award. *Jonathan, I told you, get to bed!* I gotta go."

Maggie hung up the landline phone. She picked up her purse and dragged herself to the kitchen, where she washed out her drink glass. There was a light knock, and Maggie looked up to see Bo standing in the doorway. "I heard about Gerard Damboise. Xander's asleep and Rufus is keeping an eye on him so I could come over and check on you."

"Words I never thought I'd say: Rufus is my hero."

Bo took her in his arms. "Did Artie and Cal tell you they think Gerard was murdered?" she asked.

"Yes."

"It was awful. He was trying to tell me something. He said, 'Lies. Secrets.' And then he was gone. I feel terrible. I thought of him as some pretentious bore, but when he was holding on to me, begging for help..."

Maggie couldn't finish the sentence. Bo held her tighter. "I hate you had to go through that. I tried calling you as soon as Artie and Cal told me what happened, but your cell went straight to voicemail."

"There's no way you could have reached me. My cell's gone to phone heaven."

Maggie reluctantly left the comfort of Bo's arms and pulled the damaged phone out of her purse. She and Bo sat down at the kitchen table. "I can get the screen replaced, but it's so shattered that I think the phone's a total loss. It must have fallen out of my purse or something. But I have a screen protector on it. I'm surprised there was this much damage."

Bo studied the cell, his face grim. "That's because this wasn't an accident, Maggie. Someone purposely destroyed your cell phone. On the same night Gerard Damboise was killed."

SEVEN

MAGGIE TRIED TO wrap her mind around Bo's statement. "Why would someone destroy my phone? And how could it have anything to do with Gerard? I just met him."

"I have to believe there's a connection." Bo pointed to the screen. "If this was accidentally damaged, there'd most likely be one central break with a few smaller breaks jutting out from it. And the body of the phone would be okay, maybe wonky. But this thing is trashed. The way the screen shattered tells me someone took a heel to it."

"Stiletto or loafer?"

"That's for the crime scene investigators to figure out. Sorry, but this is now evidence. You got a napkin and a bag?"

Maggie retrieved both for Bo. He carefully wrapped the phone in the napkin and then dropped it in the plastic bag. "I'll have to send it to Baton Rouge PD; they've got the techs for the job. Pelican PD's rudimentary at best in that area. We're understaffed to begin with, and the flood really knocked us out. Now, take a minute and think about anything you have on here connecting to Gerard. It'll help Baton Rouge if I can steer them in a direction."

Maggie concentrated. "There are the photos Gerard made me take of all the judges...emails between us...

texts too." Maggie opened her eyes. "I can't think of anything else."

"It's a good start. I'll tell them to focus on those areas. I'll also give JJ a call in the morning and ask him to come up with a list of everyone who was at Junie's last night around the time you were there."

"Bo...do you think Gerard's death has anything to do with our victim?"

"Maybe. And a strong maybe if someone found out Pelican PD was looking for a link between the two men. Which is impossible to establish when you don't know who one of the guys is." Bo stood up. "Much as I hate to leave you for a bunch of reasons—the main one being concern for your safety—I need to get back home to Xander." He leaned down and kissed Maggie. "Be careful, *chère*. I got a bad feeling about what all's going on around here."

"Me too," Maggie said. She wrapped her arms around herself and shuddered.

First thing in the morning, Maggie called Constance Damboise. Bo advised her not to share Gerard's last words with anyone outside law enforcement, so she kept the conversation purposefully vague. "I'm deeply sorry about your loss," she told the newly minted widow.

"Oh yes, it's terribly sad. It's sweet of you to call."

"Of course. And I'm sure I speak for all of us judges when I say we're here for you in any way you need us."

"Thank you, that's so kind. I was actually hoping you and the other judges could stop by this morning. I have some thoughts about how we should proceed with the pageant."

The pageant? Maggie was taken aback by Constance's matter-of-fact response. *Must be shock.* "Please don't worry about the pageant. It hasn't been twenty-four hours since Gerard…passed away. I'm sure you need time to process what happened."

"I've always found focusing on work to be a useful distraction. See you at six, say? I'll confirm with the others. Bring a notepad."

Constance ended the call. "Well, that couldn't have been weirder," Maggie said to Gopher and Jolie, both of whom lay snoring at her feet. Maggie sat back in her chair and folded her arms, thinking. Then she sprung to her feet and left the shotgun cottage for the manor house. She fixed Gran' a tray of croissants and tea, and delivered it to her in the Rose Room.

"I'm blessed to have such a thoughtful grandchild," Gran' said. Her cloud of white hair fluffed up against the stack of pillows supporting her, and her cheeks showed a blush of color for the first time since she'd taken ill.

"I also wanted to talk to you about Constance Damboise."

"Ah, an ulterior motive to breakfast in bed. Somewhat less thoughtful. But much more intriguing."

Maggie recounted her conversation with Constance. "She may not know yet that Gerard was probably murdered. Still, her tone was pretty light for a woman who suffered a shocking loss."

"Well, you see," Gran' said, delicately pulling apart her croissant, "I'm not sure how much of a loss it was."

Maggie raised an eyebrow. "Really."

"It was a second marriage for both Gerard and Constance. Gerard's first wife decamped rather quickly, and he was single for years. Constance shared his passion for history and tradition, but I always got the sense that was all they had in common. Also, genealogically, Constance was a bit of a mutt in Gerard's eyes. One side of her family is from a northern state. And they've only been in Louisiana since the 1920s."

"Only?"

"Yes, 'only' to someone obsessed with lineage like Gerard. He often implied Constance married up when she married a Damboise, and I think she grew to resent it."

"I'm impressed she had any patience to begin with. I would have resented it the minute he opened his mouth."

"Because you're from another generation, *chére*, one that puts far less stock in frivolities like an outdated class system. But many older than you still cling to the old social order. Like that Philip Charbonnet."

Maggie shuddered. "Ugh, don't remind me." Only months before, the repugnant Charbonnet had proposed to Maggie for no other reason than her family's Louisiana lineage. The last she'd heard of the slimy operator, he was working in a menial capacity at a New Orleans assisted living facility, trying to find a moneyed senior who'd lost enough of her wits to marry him. "I'm curious about Gerard. Was there anything to him besides his obsession with old-timey lineage?"

"Not really, sad to say. I know he worked for years in some capacity at the state library in Baton Rouge. I could never pinpoint exactly what he did there; he was vague when you asked him. He made himself sound important, but it came across as someone trying very hard to inflate a small balloon. Gerard Damboise struck me as an undistinguished man looking for a way to distinguish himself. And he found it when he got the job of running the Historical Society."

Gran' polished off her croissant, and Maggie picked up the breakfast tray. "Thanks for the intel. I need to get going. I have to buy a new cell phone."

She shared the story of her phone's demise with Gran', who looked perturbed. "Well, things have taken an ugly turn, haven't they?"

"Yes," Maggie said, her tone grim. "I think whoever killed my phone also murdered Gerard. And possibly our John Doe. Hopefully, they'll assume any incriminating evidence I might have is gone with my cell. But still, I'll have to keep my nosing around on the down low. And I *will* be nosing around. Gerard Damboise practically begged me to with his last dying breath."

"A normal grandmother would say, 'No nosing around, for heaven's sake! Stay out of this.'"

Maggie smiled affectionately at Gran'. "But you're far from normal."

"And proud of it," Gran' said with a wink.

AN HOUR AFTER her conversation with Gran', Maggie emerged from the Pelican phone outlet with a new cell, although thanks to the salesman's rapid-fire loop-de-loop of a pitch, she had to take it on faith she'd signed up for the best data plan. She arrived at work and joined Ione in the staff room to change into their antebellum ball gowns. "Do you know anything about art restoration?" the general manager asked.

The question came out of the blue, but Maggie answered, "As a matter of fact, I do. I minored in it at art school. It was a way of studying the materials artists used in past centuries."

"Good," Ione said. "Meet me in the nursery in fifteen minutes."

Ione finished putting on her own costume, a camel-colored day gown that complemented her dark brown skin tone, and left the staff room to open the plantation for business. Maggie put her thick chestnut hair into a ponytail she stuffed under a banana-curled wig, lifted up her hoop skirt to make walking easier, and beelined to the nursery, which was housed on the second floor of the manor house. The room, still painted in its original pale yellow, featured a beautiful cypress cradle, where generations of Maggie's ancestors on her mother's side had been rocked to sleep. Antique toys that hadn't been broken in play lined the walls. The air, like that of so many centuries-old homes, was perfumed with mildew, and Maggie noticed a green stain dripping down the wall above the fireplace.

Ione was already there. She pointed to a painting hanging above the fireplace mantel. It was a primitive rendering of a toddler on a rocking horse that still sat in a corner of the nursery. Below the image were the words *Grata sit calidum, et de fisco.* "We had flood damage from the rains in this room. The moisture must have affected the painting, because pieces of it are coming off. I know it's not one of the best pieces of artwork in the plantation's collection, but it's sweet, and I'm sure the little boy is one of your ancestors. I wondered if you'd be interested in restoring it instead of leading tours."

"Absolutely. I'd love to."

"Great. I thought I'd set you up in one of the rooms off the gift shop so visitors can watch your progress, like they do with Gaynell. They're loving that. Oh, and I want to give you a new title: Doucet Art Collection Specialist."

Maggie bit her lip, trying to control her excitement. "It would be unprofessional to jump up and down."

"Go for it."

"Thank you, thank you, thank you!" Maggie said, jumping up and down. She hugged Ione, who laughed and hugged her back. Then Maggie reached for the painting and gently touched a corner. Flakes of paint clung to her fingers. She stepped back and studied the artwork from a distance. "I've always been curious about this particular painting. It's unsigned and there's something about the strokes that indicates it was painted in a hurry. Was that the artist's style? Or was there another reason for the rush?"

Ione smiled. "I knew you were my girl. If there's a mystery to this painting, you're the one to solve it."

"It'll also take my mind off the mysteries I can't solve. Like the murders of John Doe and Gerard Damboise."

IONE AND MAGGIE agreed her new job would begin the next day. After her last tour, Maggie retreated to the staff lounge and changed into her street clothes, reveling in the fact that her days of stuffing herself into a polyester nightmare of a knockoff antebellum ball gown were over, at least temporarily. She checked her phone and saw texts from fellow judges Mo and Robbie confirming the meeting with Constance. Her new phone also showed Maggie she was already five minutes late, so she hopped in the Falcon and drove the short distance to the Damboise home.

The home of Constance and the late Gerard was a white raised Creole cottage on a side street not far from Pelican's village center. Magnolia trees flanked the four steps leading to the home's front door. Maggie parked and hurried up the stairs. The door swung open before she could knock. "We heard you parking that old beater of yours," Mo said. She gestured for Maggie to follow her inside.

The living room was an immaculate shrine to Damboise genealogy. Oil portraits of ancestors graced the walls, each frame boasting a nameplate identifying the subject. Old black-and-white photographs crowded the cypress mantle of the fireplace. Maggie searched for an image of Constance in the collection, but found none. She did, however, spot several photos of Gerard posing with men and women Maggie recognized as being members of Louisiana's aristocracy.

"Maggie." Mo nudged her in the ribs.

"Sorry. I was admiring your home, Constance. So much history."

"Yes." Constance didn't seem too enthusiastic about it. "Why don't we get started? And please help yourself to some snacks." She gestured to a spread of desserts on the antique coffee table. "People have been so generous."

Maggie ID'd a plate of pecan sticky buns as a donation from her cousin Lia's bakery, Fais Dough Dough, and helped herself to one. She sat down between Robbie and Mo on the Damboises' Victorian settee, which, judging from the itchy texture, was still covered in its original horsehair. "History sure ain't comfortable," Mo said under her breath.

"I'd like to go over the pageant schedule," Constance said, popping open her laptop. "I want to make a few adjustments to Gerard's original plans. Maggie, I don't see your notepad."

"I forgot one," Maggie said meekly. "I'll have to take

notes on my phone. But Constance, are you sure you still want to be a judge? You've suffered a great loss."

"I can't imagine not being a judge," Constance said, affronted. "Dropping out would be an insult to my late husband. He lived for the Miss Pelican Mardi Gras Gumbo Queen Pageant and wouldn't dream of letting the young ladies down. I can assure you, if the roles were reversed, Gerard would insist the contest not be affected in the slightest bit."

"No argument there," Mo said.

"Now to the schedule," Constance said. "I want to flip it around so that the evening gown contest comes after the talent portion of the competition, not before it. This will give the girls more time to get dressed in their evening wear, something Gerard didn't consider when he mapped out the events."

Maggie swallowed her opposition to judging teen girls, never the most confident, on their looks and clothing choices. Her primary concern remained the newly widowed Constance. "Um…"

"Yes, dear?" Constance said, striving to be patient.

"Even given your admirable devotion to the contest" —Maggie decided to lay it on thick—"it might be a good idea if we took a day off from pageant events. For one thing, I think you need a little downtime." Constance opened her mouth to respond, but Maggie rushed on. "Plus, it would be the appearance of propriety. People might think we were insensitive if we kept plowing ahead."

Constance considered this. "That's a legitimate point. We'll take tomorrow off. Then the contest will resume as normal. In honor of my late husband. But there will continue to be changes now that I've taken over for him."

Maggie, disquieted by the hint of vitriol in Constance's voice, simply nodded. "I had an idea, Constance," Robbie said, sounding like an eager student. "I thought we could turn the essay portion of the contest into the Gerard Damboise Memorial Award, sponsored by the Chamber of Commerce. Since Gerard was such a nut—expert—about local history, we would make that the essay's theme. Whichever finalist writes the best piece about Pelican's past wins a two-hundred-dollar scholarship."

"That's a wonderful idea, Robbie. I love it."

"Suck up," Mo muttered.

Robbie ignored her. "Glad you like it," he said, looking pleased with himself. "I'll notify the contestants right now." He pulled out his cell phone and began texting.

"Alright then." Constance said. "I think we accomplished quite a bit. I'll type up notes from the meeting and email them to you, along with a few other thoughts."

Maggie and Mo stood up. Robbie hit "Send" on his phone and joined them. "We'll see you day after tomorrow," Maggie said to Constance. "But if you need anything before then, please let us know."

"There is one thing you could do for me, dear. My purse pistol has gone missing. Would you mind checking around Crozat for it? It may have dropped out of my purse during our meeting."

Maggie wanted to say, *A loaded gun may be lying around our home, and you're saying it as casually as if an eyeglass case fell out of your purse?* Instead, she politely responded, "Of course." And planned to let Bo know of this new development as quickly as possible.

EIGHT

MAGGIE TEXTED Bo about the missing purse pistol the instant she, Mo, and Robbie stepped out of the Damboise home. Then she alerted her father, who responded with a promise to hunt for it, laced with expletives about people who were careless with their firearms.

Maggie put away her phone and focused on Mo and Robbie, who were in mid-conversation. "I'm telling you, that woman only has one oar in the water," Mo was insisting to the convenience store owner. "What do you think, Maggie?"

Maggie was about to respond when Little Earlie Waddell—the *Pelican Penny Clipper*'s publisher, editor-in-chief, reporter, and occasional maintenance man—zoomed into a parking spot in front of the Damboise home and practically fell out of his PT Cruiser. "I heard y'all were meeting for the first time since the murder, and raced over to get some quotes," he gasped, out of breath.

"Murder?" Robbie was dumbfounded.

"My sources tell me Gerard Damboise was found shot to death by a certain Magnolia Marie Crozat."

Robbie, Mo, and Earlie all turned to Maggie. "Your 'source' is a police scanner, Little Earlie," she said, fuming. "And my comment is 'no comment.'"

"How could you not tell your fellow judges this?"

Robbie demanded of Maggie while Mo nodded vigorously.

"For two good reasons. One, it hasn't been confirmed, has it?" Maggie glared at Little Earlie, who had the decency to look uncomfortable. "And two, it's up to Constance whether or not that information is shared. Would either of you want me shooting my mouth off if something like this happened to one of your loved ones?" Robbie and Mo sheepishly shook their heads. "Now that we've settled this, Little E, I like you, and you've done some good reporting in the past, but it's time to go *away*."

"I got what I need," Little Earlie said. "But y'all will be hearing from me." The *Penny Clipper* jack-of-all-trades hopped into his car and peeled out.

Robbie smoothed the sides of his hair, something Maggie deemed a nervous habit. "I signed on to this judging gig because I felt it was my duty as president of the Chamber of Commerce. But it's getting scary-crazy."

"It's very stress inducing," Mo said. "Thank goodness Veevay Beauty makes an anti-stress balm with all-natural ingredients. I'll make sure you get a sample when you come to my party, Maggie."

Maggie marveled at Mo's slick sales tactics. "Wow, no wonder you score that purple Mitsubishi every year."

Mo pumped her arms up and down in a "raise the roof" gesture. "Veevay all the way, baby!"

The judges headed off in different directions. Maggie was about to get in her car when a late-nineties pickup truck stopped mid-street. Gin Bertrand leaned out of the driver's window. "Hey, Maggie, what's the deal with this essay? How's Kaity gonna write about this dang town's history? We've only been here but a few weeks."

"It's a way of memorializing Gerard Damboise," Maggie explained. *Ugh, I sound like I'm parroting some party line.* "I'll tell you what. I'll help Kaity find a topic. And I'll make the same offer to all three finalists so no one can complain about favoritism."

"I appreciate that. Glad you're on our side."

"I just said—" Maggie Gin's truck screeched off before Maggie could finish the sentence. She took a deep breath to quell her increasing annoyance with Gin, then texted her offer of help to both Pauline and Denise. Her phone pinged. She was relieved to see it was a non-Miss Pelican Mardi Gras Gumbo Queen-related message from her cousin Lia Tienne Bruner, who was pregnant with triplets and currently on bed rest: "You around? Need a small favor."

Moments later, Maggie was on her way to Grove Hall, the Durand family ancestral plantation home now owned and being restored by Lia and her husband, Kyle. Maggie parked in front of the classic example of Greek Revival architecture, which gleamed with a coat of fresh white paint after decades of neglect. She maneuvered around stacks of lumber and construction equipment, and then dashed up the front steps into the house. Kyle, who Lia affectionately liked to call her "tall drink of Texas water," turned off the floor sander he was operating and came over to give Maggie a hug. "We lost a lot of our crew to flood repair, so I'm taking on some of the work myself," he explained, lifting up his safety goggles so they sat on top of his head.

"You're doing a great job. This floor will be gorgeous. Lia asked me to pick up a book of wallpaper samples for the babies' room."

"Yeah, she texted me you'd be by. The sample book's by the front door. But first, I have to show you something."

Kyle led Maggie up the home's curved oak staircase and took a right at the second-floor landing. They walked into a large, empty room facing a thicket of woods behind the house. "Pauline, our decorator, and I were looking at the house from the back, and she noticed something interesting. How many windows do you see in this room?"

"Three."

"Yes. But when you look at the house from outside, there's a fourth window. It doesn't belong to this room, or the one next to it. So, we did some exploring..." Kyle motioned to the wall next to him, which was still covered with century-old, peacock feather-patterned wallpaper. He placed his hand on a spot and pressed. A door hidden in the wall opened. Kyle gestured for Maggie to follow him, and they stepped inside a small, shadowed room. "A secret space," Kyle said. "Pauline told me these were built into homes for a couple of reasons. Sometimes it was for safety, sort of an early panic room. And sometimes it was to hide a family member from society. A relative with mental or physical issues they didn't want the world to know about."

"That's awful." Maggie glanced around the spare room. The walls of the secret room, originally white, had grayed with time. Paint flaked and bubbled where water had seeped in. The air was stultifying despite the cool mid-winter temperature outside. Maggie could only imagine how miserable the space, with no cross breeze, was during summer months, especially in the days before central air conditioning. "It's like a family's own personal insane asylum."

"We don't know it was used for that, although given the number of reprobates on the Durand family tree, it wouldn't surprise me. But I bet it made a great hiding place during the Civil War. No one would ever know you were here."

Despite the room's oppressive heat, Maggie shivered. "I get a bad feeling from this place. Are you going to keep it as a secret room?"

"For now. I hate to mess with the architectural integrity of the house. But if we do keep it, we'll have to have some sort of cleansing ceremony."

"Amen to that."

Kyle escorted Maggie back to her car. He deposited the book of wallpaper samples in her back seat, and returned to his tasks inside Grove Hall. Rather than drive away, Maggie took a walk to the back of the plantation manor house and studied the mysterious fourth window. She had no idea why the Durand family needed a hidden room, although based on the family's lineage of ne'er-do-wells—Bo excepted, of course—she assumed it was to hide from both Union troops and a Confederate Army looking to conscript male Durands. But Maggie realized the room could provide Kaity Bertrand with a good essay topic, and returned to her car to call the teen and let her know.

"You look so...super pregnant."

Maggie sat on the bed next to Lia, who lay flat on her back with a single pillow under her head. Lia laughed. "I am carrying three of these critters. But I'll tell you one thing. You know how you sometimes think it would be heaven to spend a week in bed? I am here to say, be careful what you wish for. It's incredibly boring."

"Do you have to spend the rest of the pregnancy on bed rest?"

"No, thank the Lord. In about a week, I'll be able to spend a couple of hours up and about, but with extremely limited activity. So, talk to me. Is it true Gerard Damboise was murdered?"

"Wow, there are no secrets in Pelican, are there? It appears so." Maggie's phone chimed. She pulled it from her pocket and read the new message. "And his wife's 'purse pistol' has gone missing. She thought she might have dropped it at our house during a pageant meeting, but my dad just texted to say he didn't find it."

"The endless hours of TV I've watched while stuck in this bed have taught me the spouse is always suspect number one."

"I don't know. Constance doesn't seem too devastated by her loss, but I don't get she was miserable enough to kill Gerard. I better let Bo know about the gun."

Maggie typed a quick message. Her phone erupted with a flurry of texts. She read them and groaned. "One of the loony pageant moms. Denise. She's hypercompetitive. Robbie Metz had the brilliant idea—and I mean brilliant in the most sarcastic way—of turning the essay portion of the contest into the Gerard Damboise Memorial Award, where the finalists have to write an essay about Pelican history for a two-hundred-dollar scholarship prize."

"Sounds like an idea Robbie would come up with. He wants to run for mayor during the next election."

"Really?"

"Yup. You can add gossip to the short list of things I get to do while on bed rest."

"Anyway, now this mom, Denise, is trying to find an angle that would give her poor daughter a winning edge." Maggie read the text thread, ending with *"...Since Cousin Belle doing essay on Crozat Plantation and its place in Pelican, Allouette doing essay on Doucet."* She held up the phone to Lia. "See how Denise followed that with a string of happy face and thumbs-up emojis? I should tell her sucking up to me is the worst way to go. The sad thing is she's way more obsessed with the pageant than her daughter is. I think Allouette would drop out in a heartbeat. It must kill Denise that Belle snatched up Crozat as a subject first. And from what I've seen of Belle, the idea came from her, not her mother." Maggie squinted as she thought for a moment. "I'm starting to think word got out that Gerard favored Belle as the Miss Pelican Mardi Gras Gumbo Queen. A couple of the pageant moms seem close to the edge mentally. Could something like that push them over it?"

"Well, in this TV movie I saw—twice because they reran it and I have nothing better to do than lie here—the mom of a gymnast was so competitive, she secretly hired a hit man to bump off a judge who was keeping the girl from Olympic tryouts."

"Denise may be jealous of Belle, but I can't imagine her doing anything to hurt her. She adores Belle's mother, Pauline. They're cousins." Maggie smiled at Lia. "And you know how close cousins can be."

Lia returned Maggie's smile. "I do indeed. But

maybe there's a nutty mom who's going to kill any judge who doesn't vote for her daughter."

"It does seem like these pageants can become dangerously competitive, whether it's between the girls or the 'momtestants.'"

"Exactly. There was another movie about the mother of a cheerleader—"

"Okay, tomorrow I'm going to the library and coming back here with a stack of books because you need to stop watching TV."

"TV's not nearly as interesting as what's happening around here. The gossip hotline leaked the news that the man who died in the flood didn't drown—he was murdered. Could the same person who killed Gerard have killed him?"

"I did wonder about that. But the more I think about it, the harder it is to connect Gerard, a scion of the community and lifetime Pelican resident, to a stranger no one in town seems to know."

"When you look at it that way, it does seem to be a reach."

"But you mentioned secrets. I wonder…"

"What?"

Maggie flashed on Gerard's final words. "Turning the Historical Society into a museum was an obsession with Gerard. I wonder if he collected secrets he could use to manipulate or blackmail people—a parent, a contestant, maybe even a judge. I think I need to find out more about everyone involved with this pageant."

Lia struggled to pull herself up to a sitting position. "You could be working with the next victim or the killer. I'm worried about you."

Maggie gently eased Lia back down to a prone position. "You're not allowed to gossip anymore *or* to worry, mama-to-be. I promise I won't do anything dangerous. That's what the heroes of Pelican PD are for."

"Alright." Lia yawned. "I feel better. A little."

Lia drifted off to sleep. Maggie quietly left the house, double- and triple-checking the front door to make sure it was locked.

The last thing Maggie would admit to her beloved and very pregnant cousin was that she was worried too.

NINE

Maggie slept fitfully that night, awoken by each creak and groan emanating from the ancient shotgun cottage. She dreamt about discovering a dying Gerard Damboise. His face appeared to her in vivid, almost hallucinogenic colors. *What is my weird place in the universe where I'm always the one finding dead bodies?* she wondered when she gave up trying to get a decent night's sleep. It felt like the definition of a rhetorical question.

In the morning, she took a cold shower, hoping the shock to the system would snap her out of her sleep-deprivation fog. She covered the dark circles under her hazel eyes with extra concealer, poured herself a thirty-two-ounce mug of coffee to go, and headed over to Doucet.

She parked and pulled a plastic bin of art supplies out of the Falcon convertible's trunk. Maggie bypassed the overseer's house, reveling in the fact that for the first time since she began working at Doucet, she wouldn't have to force on an antebellum hoop skirt. On her way to the small room Ione had assigned her, she passed a throng of visitors watching in fascination as Gaynell worked her sewing machine magic, bringing riotously colored Mardi Gras costumes to life.

Maggie's new workroom was a nondescript space added to the plantation by the state when it managed the property. The building, designed as a petite version of the manor house, contained Doucet's gift shop and various staff offices. But it was full of natural light accentuating the deterioration of the painting she was tasked to restore, which sat on an easel in the middle of the room. Maggie pulled a camera out of her supply box and snapped numerous shots of the artwork to serve as reference points. She printed them out on the gift shop printer and taped them to the easel and workroom wall. Then Maggie collected chips the painting had shed onto the floor. She held them up to the light, examining them closely.

Ione stuck her head in. "How's it going? You got everything you need?"

Maggie nodded, still focused on the chips in her hand. "This is strange. I thought the paint used here was watercolor. But these chips are made of more than paint. They seem to be a mix of watercolor with glue and paper. Like a collage. But the overall image doesn't seem like a collage."

Ione stepped in the room. She and Maggie studied the painting. "I don't know anything about art," Ione said, "but I do see the artist dated this piece 1861. Around the time the Civil War broke out. Maybe the artist couldn't get the paint he needed, so he improvised with whatever materials he had."

Ione left, and Maggie forged on with the restoration. Yet the painting continued to crumble with every touch, and she groaned in frustration. Then she made a discovery that dispelled all exhaustion.

She ran to the gift shop, where Ione was arranging a display of Mardi Gras ornaments. "You have to see this," she said, beckoning for Ione to follow her. The two women set off down the hallway to Maggie's workroom.

"Look." Maggie pointed to the upper-right corner of the artwork, where a large section of paint had peeled off. What lay underneath was a revelation. "There's a reason why the portrait seemed so simple and like someone created it quickly. It's hiding another painting."

Ione peered at the painting. "You're right. Wow."

"I know. My goal now is to carefully remove the overlay without damaging whatever's underneath. I'll research the best way to do this."

Ione stood up. "If you need any special supplies, let me know. This is exciting."

She returned to the gift shop, and Maggie pulled out her tablet to search art restoration websites for ways of handling the delicate task ahead. She learned all she needed to proceed was the small scalpel she already owned and warm water to dissolve the centuries-old animal glue serving as an adhesive. Maggie ran her fingers over the corner where the hidden picture had been revealed. "Oil, not watercolor," she murmured. This was good news. If she worked with the utmost care, she could remove one painting without damaging the other.

She was about to begin work when she received a text from Mo: "FYI, judges all being interviewed by Pelican PD. See you tonight at my Veevay party!" Maggie, who'd been formulating excuses to get out of the sales party, changed her mind. It offered her a chance to dig up information on the pageant mothers, who, she assumed, wouldn't pass up a great opportunity to brown-nose.

Maggie's stomach growled; it was time for lunch. She locked the workroom door behind her and went to see if Gaynell wanted to take a break. She found her coworker madly sewing away. "No time," Gaynell said, gesturing to the piles of colorful fabric surrounding her. "I don't know how I'm going to get the costumes *and* masks finished in time for the Courir."

Maggie picked up a wire mesh mask. Many Courir mask makers prided themselves on using found objects and recycled material as decoration. Gaynell had turned a milk jug handle into the mask's nose. "That's as far as I got." Gaynell pushed back a blonde curl that fell in front of her eyes. "I need to finish that one, six more, and five costumes."

"There's no deadline for the project I'm working on. How about I take over the masks? That way all you have to worry about are the costumes."

"Would you? Oh, I love you so much right now." Gaynell ran from behind her sewing machine to hug Maggie. "Now I can stop for a super-quick lunch."

Since the weather was chilly and drizzly, the women opted to eat lunch in the staff lounge. Maggie told Gaynell about the hidden painting, and the two spent a few minutes musing about what the story behind it might be. Gaynell then pressed Maggie for details about Gerard's demise. Maggie shared what she could, hoping that articulating the circumstances might reveal some missed clue to his murder. But there were no new revelations. "I wonder if there's some bigger reason why you keep happening on people who've met an untimely end," Gaynell mused.

"I had the same thought this morning."

Gaynell studied her friend. "I think there is. Somehow the Lord, or a Higher Power—whatever you want to call it—knows you'll help the victims. You have a gift for it, Maggie. You're like the murder whisperer or something."

Maggie made a face. "Oh, that sounds *awful*. I think it's more like the universe has figured out a way to use the fact that I'm incredibly nosy." Her phone rang and she answered the call. "Hey, *chér*." She addressed Gaynell: "It's Bo."

"You guys talk. I gotta get back to work. Mama's dropping off a couple of capuchons for me to use as models. You know, the hats that look like dunce caps that the Mardi Gras wear. You'll get to wear one in my Run."

"Looking forward to it. I think."

Gaynell chuckled and then took off. Maggie turned her attention to Bo. "Sorry."

"No worries. For the record, I think you're going to make a hot Mardi Gras."

"Thanks, but have you seen the costumes? They're basically giant pajamas. 'Hot' is going to be a stretch for me in one of those outfits. What's up?"

"I need a favor. Whitney's at a doctor's appointment, and I'm at the station with an IT guy, trying to figure out what we can and can't save from the water-damaged computers. Thanks a lot, flood," he said sarcastically. "Ru offered to pick up Xander from school. Would it be okay if he dropped him off with you for a couple of hours?"

"Absolutely. He can be my assistant."

"He'll love that."

"Is everything okay with Whitney?"

"Yeah…yeah." Maggie picked up the hesitation in Bo's voice. "I gotta run. We'll talk later."

"Love you," Maggie said to a dial tone. She finished her lunch, which consisted of French bread, cheese, and yet more of Tug's gumbo, and then returned to her workspace.

Tour guides stopped by with their groups, who watched Maggie with fascination. The guests peppered her with questions, and she patiently shared her process and goal over and over again. As the day went on, Maggie became so adept at delivering the explanation, she was able to continue working while she talked. By late afternoon, a few more inches of the hidden painting had been revealed, but no hint as to its subject. Ready for a break, she welcomed the arrival of Rufus and Xander.

"How do, Miss Magnolia Marie," Rufus greeted her. He held Xander by the hand and wore his daughter Charli strapped to his chest in a baby carrier.

"Hey, Ru. You're looking good. I'm impressed by the gut shrinkage."

"You and the rest of the ladies in town can thank Sandy for that. She's got me working out and eating like a fashion model." With Bo and Maggie's encouragement, Rufus had bounced back from a doomed relationship with Vanessa Fleer, Maggie's former coworker and the mother of his child. He was dating Sandy Sechrest, the sweet ex-pole dancer who owned DanceBod, Pelican's sole exercise outlet. The romance had softened Ru and helped heal a centuries-old feud between the Crozat and Durand families.

Maggie noticed Xander eyeing the room with curiosity. "Buddy, I could use some help making the Courir masks, if you're interested." Xander gave a vigorous nod. Maggie took his hand from Rufus and led the boy to the box of odds and ends meant for decorating masks. "Why don't you start picking out the decorations? I'll show you how to use a hot glue gun when Rufus and I are done talking."

Xander plopped down on the floor and began a highly focused sorting of material. Loose beads, pipe cleaners, wax lips, old buttons, rattan, plastic bugs, stray pom-poms, even fake mustaches were all doo-dads which could be transformed into a mask's facial features. As the boy organized the scraps-turned-art supplies into piles that meant something only to him, Maggie turned her attention back to Rufus. She pulled him out of earshot from Xander. "Have you learned anything new about Gerard's death that you're okay sharing with me?"

"I'm okay telling you whatever I think will help us, whether soon-to-be-gone Chief Penske cares or not. What's my motto?"

Maggie grinned. "'In Louisiana, we only follow the rules we like.'"

"Exactly. So, Damboise was shot by a small-caliber pistol. That's not what did him in, though, which is why he still had the strength to spit out a few words to you. The loss of blood and stress triggered a massive heart attack."

"Then technically, whoever shot him is guilty of *attempted* murder."

"He's not any less dead cuz of that."

"I was thinking about the man found on our property—"

"And wondering if his being murdered had anything to do with Gerard being sent to his maker? We had the same thought because us law enforcement types are not fans of coincidences. But until we get more deets on your guy, we're focusing on Gerard's death."

"Any luck tracking down Constance Damboise's purse pistol?"

Rufus shook his head. "Don't know if it was tossed, lost, or stolen. Her alibi checks out. She was at that new needlecraft store, A Stitch in Wine, where they do craft parties and wine tastings together. And Constance was doing a whole lot more wining and 'whining' than stitching," he said, making air quotes on "whining."

"Not only can witnesses testify she was there during the time Gerard would have been killed, she was too drunk to get behind the wheel, so one of the ticked-off stitchers had to drive her home. She didn't retrieve her car until the next day. But she's not completely in the clear. Always the chance she hired someone to bump off her hubby. Still, at least she's got an alibi. All Mo Heedles can tell us about her own alibi is that she was home testing some of that tutti-frutti face stuff she sells. Robbie Metz says he was driving between his stores. Given that big old brood of his, I wouldn't be surprised if he was driving around to avoid going home."

"And then there are the pageant moms."

"Yeah, that group o' crazies. We're still sifting through their stories."

Charli fussed and Rufus pulled a baby bottle out of his back pocket. He cooed to his infant daughter as he fed her. "I hope there's not this much drama when my Charli runs for Miss Pelican Mardi Gras Gumbo Queen. Speaking of which, what do you know about your squatter, Jayden Jones?"

"He's not a squatter—he's an invited guest. And he's been nothing but polite as a person and professional as a construction worker."

Rufus eyed her. "You're not the only one around here who can sense stuff. What are you holding back?"

Maggie was torn—share her instinct about Jayden's short fuse or wait? Deciding the instinct was closer to gossip than fact, she opted to wait. "I'm not holding back anything concrete. I promise I'll let you know if anything specific comes up. Charli's dribbling."

"Way to throw me off track." Rufus pulled a spit towel from his back pocket and cooed to Charli as he patted her face, "Who's daddy's little princess?" Charli chortled and grabbed his hair. "Alrighty, Maggie, we're off. Sandy's starting a new class called BabyDance. She left off the 'bod' because calling it 'Baby DanceBod' didn't sound right."

Maggie laughed. "Good call on her part."

"Whitney will be by for Xander when she's done at the doctor's. If you need anything before then, let me know."

"Thanks, Ru." Maggie glanced over at Xander, who had already laid out objects that would create fantastical Mardi Gras masks. "I think we'll be fine."

MAGGIE TAUGHT XANDER how to safely use a glue gun and shared a bit of the history behind the masks with him. "They started as a way for people to go crazy on Mardi Gras, but not get in trouble, because no one could tell who they were. The masks hid their identity. These days they're worn more for fun, although some people still like ones that are such good disguises their own family members don't know it's them underneath."

Maggie picked up one of Xander's creations and held it over her face. "Whoo-hoo, *laissez les bons temps rouler*," she said, lowering her voice an octave and doing her best Cajun accent as she danced around the room. "I don't believe we've met before, young fella." She lifted the mask. "See? Would you have recognized me?" Xander shook his head and giggled, which made Maggie's day. It was evidence of her growing relationship with the boy, who had Asperger's syndrome and found social interaction uncomfortable.

Maggie returned the mask to its resting place and called up some pictures on her cell phone. "I'd love to make a needlepoint mask like this someday." She showed Xander an image of a cartoonishly angry expression stitched in a rainbow of wool colors. "But these take a lot of time, and according to my friend Gaynell, it's easier to breathe through the screen ones like you're making. So keep going, my friend, and make 'em as scary-fun as ya want." She laid her Cajun accent on top of the last sentence, earning another chuckle from Xander.

She spent the next few hours with one eye on her own work and the other on her young charge, taking a brief break to show Xander photos her parents texted of the kitten and puppy the boy was set to adopt from Brooke's and Jolie's litters. He'd already developed such a strong bond with the furbabies that it inspired a breakthrough in his case of selective mutism. Toward the end of the day, the room filled with a group of tourists eager to learn about Maggie's genealogical link to Doucet on Ninette's side, and she only got to wave at Whitney when Bo's ex-wife came to pick up their son. The tourists left shortly after Whitney and Xander. Maggie checked the time on her cell phone and saw she was running late for Mo's skin care party.

She hastily cleaned up, then dashed to her car. She

didn't want to sacrifice a minute of uncovering potential clues to Gerard's murder. As she slid into the Falcon's front seat, Maggie caught a glimpse of herself in the rearview mirror and noticed a tiny new wrinkle on her forehead. Picking up a few new skin care items might not be a bad idea either.

TEN

Maggie made it home in time to change, once again opting for her funeral garb. "I really have to expand my wardrobe beyond mourning wear," she said to Gopher, who responded by rolling onto his back for a tummy rub. Jolie copied his move, and Maggie couldn't resist giving both dogs quick rubs. By the time she arrived at Mo's, all of the parking spots in front of the skin care saleswoman's shotgun home were taken. Maggie parked a block away and tottered to the party in her rarely worn black heels. If she had any doubt she was in the wrong location, the giant promotional sign for Veevay Beauty on Mo's front lawn, featuring a glamour shot of the saleswoman herself, dispelled it. The white noise of women's chatter wafted through the windows and onto the street. It grew close to a cacophony when Maggie opened the unlocked front door and entered the house.

With bright purple walls, a couch upholstered in fabric the color of navel oranges, and green, purple, and yellow accent pillows everywhere, Mo's living room was a vibrant riot of color. *It's like a bag of Mardi Gras beads magically transformed into furniture*, Maggie thought as she took in the sight. The party was peopled with pageant contest moms, which was no surprise. The event afforded them a can't-miss opportunity to curry favor with the judges—at least the two present, Maggie and Mo. The Veevay magnate was the life of her own party, passing appetizers, guffawing at a comment one guest made, giving a bear hug to another. Maggie found herself enveloped in Mo's arms and a cloud of her gardenia-scented perfume. "Maggie, you made it! Way to go!"

At the sound of Maggie's name, a half-dozen women's heads turned as if choreographed, and she was instantly the center of a small group of momtestants. This year's daughter might not be a finalist, but that didn't rule out a younger daughter getting a shot at the title. She couldn't get a word in as they chattered obsequious sentiments and bounced between self-serving questions and genuine fear.

"That was terrible, what happened to Gerard. Are you okay?"

"Why would the police need to interview me? I don't know anything."

"I dropped off a tray of my jambalaya with Constance. It was the least I could do."

"Is it true he was murdered? That was all over the laundromat this morning."

"Is there anything we need to know about how this will affect the pageant?"

Maggie's unlikely rescuer was Gin Bertrand. "Now, y'all, give the woman a break." Gin put a hand under Maggie's elbow and steered her out of the gaggle to the one empty corner of the room. "I need you to tell me something." Gin's voice was low, her tone intense. "Do the police have a suspect?"

"I honestly don't know, Gin."

"Because the police always go straight to anyone with a bit of bad in their past and then ignore everyone else."

Gin balled up her hands into fists. Maggie took a

small step away from her. "I'm assuming you have some bad in your past?"

Gin attempted a casual shrug. "I have a little record."

"I think that's like being 'a little' pregnant, Gin. You either have a record or you don't."

Gin's shoulders sagged. "It was your basic bar fight between two gals over who got to ride on the back of a cute guy's hog. But I was convicted of simple assault. I did thirty days in jail and two years' probation."

"I'm sure that was a long time ago."

"Nope, just last year. I'm kinda still on probation."

Maggie's eyes widened, but she managed not to blurt out, "Are you kidding?" Instead, she said, "Pelican PD is good about treating everyone equally. And you wouldn't be the first or last person who walked into an investigation with a record."

This engendered a cackle from Gin. "Ain't that the truth. Thank you, Maggie. You've gone a long way to easing my fears. Let's get back to the party."

Maggie was only too happy to end the conversation, which had unnerved her. She threaded her way through the women, passing Denise and Pauline, who both gave small waves of greeting. She stopped in front of the bar, where Mo was chatting with a petite, almost painfully thin woman in her mid-thirties. "Maggie, this is Stacy Metz, Robbie's wife. She's probably the only person here for the actual products. She doesn't have a horse in this pageant race."

"Yet." Stacy smiled a greeting. "Three of my four kids are girls, so I'm sure there's a contest in my future. It's lovely to meet you, Maggie. Robbie says such nice things about you."

Maggie was about to respond when Mo put two fingers in her mouth and emitted an ear-piercing whistle. Maggie winced and covered her ears, which were ringing. "Ladies, thank y'all so much for coming. Now find yourself a seat." Everyone who could find a seat did so, leaving half a dozen women, including Maggie, standing. "Before we begin exploring an exciting new beauty regimen," Mo said, "I'd like to take a moment of silence in honor of an esteemed Pelican citizen who was taken from our community too soon: Gerard Damboise."

The crowd murmured agreement. Maggie had barely closed her eyes and lowered her head before "Thus Spake Zarathustra" rumbled, then blasted from a wireless speaker. "Prepare to be transported back to a time when your skin was at its most youthful and beautiful," Mo intoned.

"All I want is skin as gorgeous as yours, Mo," Gin said.

Other women laughed and applauded, although Maggie sensed a few might be aggravated they hadn't flattered the pageant judge first.

"Oh no, no, no," Mo said, waving her arms dramatically. "You don't want my skin—you want yours. My job is to enhance what the good Lord gave you. So let's talk about how each and every one of you can use the Veevay line of skin care and beauty products to do exactly that."

For the next hour, Maggie divided her attention between observing the guests in action and experimenting with creams, lotions, and makeup made from "nature's own beauty products." She allowed Mo to cover her face with a five-minute mask loaded with lavender petals. "Wash it off, and tell me your skin doesn't feel as smooth as the day you popped out of your mama," Mo said.

The small guest bathroom was occupied, so Maggie walked down the hallway until she found a bathroom secreted away in a corner of Mo's home office. Maggie washed off the mask and ran her hands over her face, impressed her skin felt as soft as Mo claimed it would. *Hey, snap out of it and focus on investigating*, Maggie's inner voice chided.

She stepped out of the bathroom into the office. Affecting a casual attitude she didn't feel, Maggie wandered over to Mo's desk. There she lucked out. Mo was no fan of "Power Save," because her online calendar was lit up on her computer's twenty-six-inch screen. Maggie scanned the open page, chuckling at the poop emoji Mo used to highlight the next pageant meeting, happy to know she wasn't alone in finding pageant judging an onerous task. She listened to see if anyone was coming down the hallway, heard no one, and then clicked the mouse. The screen swiped to the next week's list of activities. Again, Maggie scanned the page. She stopped at nine a.m. on Tuesday. "Appointment, Dr. Petit." *Why does that name sound so familiar?* She closed her eyes and took a few deep breaths to center herself. An image of a commercial floated into her mind—a fit, slick doctor motioning to a surgically perfect woman standing next to him as he told the camera, "At Petit Plastic Surgery, we make what's good even better."

Maggie pulled her cell out of her purse and did a quick search for Dr. Petit's in the area. There was only one, the Dr. Petit of commercial fame. Which led to a question: Why would the queen of skin care, who built a business on the great dermis "the good Lord gave her" need to see a plastic surgeon? *Don't jump to conclusions,*

Maggie cautioned herself. People saw plastic surgeons for many reasons besides bodily beautification. Still, she snapped a quick picture of the calendar page, tamping down the guilt she felt about her clandestine behavior. She genuinely liked Mo and hoped whatever secrets she held wouldn't prove to be a motive for murder.

Maggie put away her phone, clicked the calendar back to its original page, and returned to the party. She was once again impressed by Mo's sales savvy. Her guests bought products for themselves, their husbands, their teenagers. Maggie herself filled a Veevay bag with enough skin care and beauty supplies to merit a few extra shifts at Doucet. Mo even signed up five women to her multitier marketing team. Pelican was on track to claim the title of Town with the Best Complexions in Louisiana.

"Y'all, this is the best Veevay party *ever*," Mo said, somehow managing to sound like she didn't say this at every Veevay party. "I saved a big surprise for the end. Guess what? Veevay's launching its own jewelry line and it is bling-tastic!" The guests collectively oohed and aahed. "Y'all will get special prizes if you preorder. Here's the catalog."

Maggie, who limited her jewelry to small hoop earrings and a gold crawdaddy charm that had been a gift from her parents when she graduated high school, passed on checking out the catalog. As the other women pored over the copies Mo handed out, Maggie took a final visual sweep of the room. She noticed Stacy Metz picking up a sample jar of Veevay Age Reversal Night Cream. Stacy then surreptitiously dropped the jar into her purse. Gin walked over to her boss's wife and handed Stacy a jewelry catalog. "Stacy, *chére*, you've gotta see this. There's one pretty item after another."

"Oh. Alright."

Stacy took the catalog and began perusing it. Maggie watched as Gin, unseen by Stacy, removed the stolen jar from the woman's purse and returned it to the table. Gin's eyes met Maggie's. She telegraphed a plea to keep the moment between them. Maggie gave a subtle nod and purposefully turned her attention elsewhere.

A moment later, there was a tap on her shoulder. She turned and found herself face to face with Gin. "Can we talk a quick minute?" Maggie nodded, and Gin gestured to the front porch. The women stepped outside, where the night was dense with humidity. Gin wiped a few drops of perspiration from her forehead with her forefinger. "I wanted you to know Stacy Metz is a good woman who happens to have a problem."

"Has she gotten help?"

"Yes. She does okay for a while and then starts again. But we take care of her."

"It's wonderful you look out for each other like that."

"We do. Park 'n' Shop is family. Anyway, just wanted to let you know what all was up. I best be getting back."

Gin hurried into the house. Maggie, pensive, remained on the porch. She thought of Robbie Metz, a hardworking businessman with political aspirations and a deeply troubled wife. And she realized Maureen "Mo" Heedles wasn't the only pageant judge harboring secrets someone might kill to keep.

ELEVEN

AFTER A HALF hour of goodbyes, Maggie managed to extricate herself from the party. She was walking to her car when she heard someone call her name. She turned to see Denise Randall. The pageant mom, slightly out of breath, caught up to her. "Boy, I had a bad case of SDS back there," Denise said. She saw the puzzled expression on Maggie's face. "Southern Door Syndrome, where you take almost as long to say goodbye as you stayed at the party."

"I've never heard that before. Funny. And oh so true."

"Anyhoo, I wanted to give you a heads-up that Allouette already sent you her essay for the Gerard Damboise Memorial Award. I'm guessing she's the first?" Denise tried and failed to sound casual.

Maggie took pity on her. She pulled out her phone and checked. "Yup, her essay is here. She's the first."

"Oh good. I mean, not that it makes a difference. Although it does show how enthusiastic she is. She wouldn't let me read it. Teenagers, huh?" Denise gave a comically exaggerated eye roll. "Anyway, I hope you enjoy the essay. And appreciate the time and effort Allouette put into it. Bye-yee."

Denise beeped open the door on her nondescript silver compact sedan, hopped in, and drove off. Now curious about Allouette's opus, Maggie opened the document on her phone. "Unbelievable," she muttered. She shot an email to the teen; if Allouette was done with homework, she needed to get her teen tush to a meeting with Maggie at Junie's.

"HERE YOU GO." Maggie deposited a Diet Dr. Pepper in front of the sullen girl sharing her table.

"Thanks." Allouette looked down at the drink but didn't pick it up.

"I'm going to read your essay back to you." Maggie picked up her phone. "'Stuff happened.'" She put down the phone, folded her arms across her chest, and waited for Allouette to respond.

"Well, it did."

"Allouette—"

"Allie. I hate my name. It's so stupid and fakey and not me."

"O-kaaay. Allie, I can't accept this 'essay.'"

Allie perked up for the first time since Maggie had met her. "Does that mean I'm disqualified?"

"It's not that easy. Believe me, I've tried."

Allie's look of misery returned. "Ugh. I hate it here. I hate Pelican. How could you come back? You were in New York, the coolest place ever. Don't you miss it? How could you leave?"

"There are things I miss about my life there," Maggie acknowledged. "Friends, the city's energy. When I first came back to Pelican, I came back as a coward. I was running away from a bad relationship. I never planned to stay. But now—and it's been a slow journey, believe me—I think it's where I'm meant to be. Professionally and personally."

"No offense, but I hope I'm never you."

"Ouch. A little offensive." Maggie leaned in to Allie.

"But I get it. Look, if you want to get out of Pelican so badly, winning this contest could help you. There's a little bit of scholarship money attached to it. And maybe you can reuse what you write on a college application. Try again, Allie. And write the truth. The good and bad of life on Doucet Plantation. That won't offend me, I promise."

Allie looked wary. "Really? You won't be pissed off if I write bad stuff? Or are you doing that thing where adults say something they don't really mean and suck you in? You think you're not going to get in trouble, and then you do."

"Boy, I really hope I'm not that dysfunctional."

A tiny smile appeared on Allie's face, which she instantly tried to quell. "Okay. I'll rewrite the stupid essay if I have to." She hesitated and then added sincerely, "Thank you."

Allie took off, almost crossing paths with Bo, who gave Maggie a kiss, then took a seat. JJ walked a beer and a cocktail over to their table. "Your regular, monsieur. And Old Shari feels you for a Pimm's Cup tonight, Maggie."

"That woman is a cocktail psychic," Maggie said with fervor.

"She is indeed." JJ winked and walked away.

Bo took a swig of beer as Maggie sipped her perfectly mixed Pimm's Cup, a refreshing blend of Pimm's Number One, ginger ale, and lemonade. "How was Mo's party? Did you pick up any other intel?"

"Well… Robbie Metz's wife, Stacy, has issues." Maggie relayed her impression of the convenience store owner's wife and the brief moment of kleptomania she'd witnessed. "Gin was right there to put the stolen jar back. Like it was routine for her."

"Stacy's condition doesn't appear to be public knowledge. So the Metzes have a secret. And secrets and murder are often not-so-strange bedfellows."

"And 'secrets' was Gerard's last word to me. Back to the party: there's Denise, who's got a schizy situation where she adores her cousin Pauline yet is obsessed with one-upping her. There's nothing secret about that drive of hers. And she sure wasn't a fan of Gerard's."

Bo took a few more swigs of beer. "Okay, so we have Denise, possibly Mo or Robbie Metz. And Gin, who's got a temper on her. Can't leave out Constance, because she's the spouse. I almost forgot Denise's cousin Pauline. We don't know much about her."

"She's the lead decorator on Lia and Kyle's house, and they have nothing but positive things to say about her."

"Then maybe she can give us some insight into Denise and whether or not she might ever go off the rails. And we can't rule out your tent guest, Jayden."

"Oh, I so don't want it to be him."

"You have a soft spot for vets, don't you?"

"Yes, I do, and I'm proud of it. I'm also proud of the fact you trust me enough to have a conversation like this."

"You've proven yourself to have great instincts. Even Rufus admits that. Plus, you can insinuate yourself into situations I can't. You're welcomed at venues where we're guests non grata, which gives you a shot at hearing and seeing things people hide from me, and the police in general. So if I have to take a dodgy route to finger a suspect, well, *c'est la vie.*"

"I like the way you think." Maggie noticed his bottle was empty. "You finished your beer. Want another one?"

"No. I don't know. Maybe."

Bo winced and rubbed his forehead. Maggie placed a soft hand on his callused one. "What's bothering you?"

"That dang artist's eye of yours. Don't miss a thing, do you?"

"This was pretty much a gimme."

"It's Whitney." Bo paused. "She had a miscarriage."

"Oh. Poor thing—that's terrible."

"It was early on. They're going to keep trying."

"I assume this means she and Zach worked through their problems. I hope it happens soon for them."

"Right, me too. But…"

"But?"

"It's a lot to throw at Xander."

"There's nothing to throw at him yet. And…" —Maggie searched for a way to put her next thought delicately—"it wouldn't hurt to start getting him used to the idea of having siblings."

Bo massaged his temples. "It's complicated. Way too complicated to talk about when I have a bruiser of a headache."

"So, not a good night to invite you home with me?" Maggie said, keeping her tone suggestive but light.

"Gran' is sleeping in the manor house while she's recuperating."

Bo shook his head regretfully and stood up. "I think I need about twenty hours of sleep." Maggie rose from her chair, and Bo put his arms around her waist. "I'm sorry I'm such crappy company. I love you."

"I love you too."

They kissed. Then he pulled away. "I gotta take off. Rufus is having his gang of miscreants over again tonight, and I can't remember if I locked the guest room door. Last thing I need is to find one of them passed out on my bed, which has been happening on a regular basis. I'll call you."

Bo left and Maggie moved from the table to the bar. Old Shari studied her and then announced, "I feel you for a double shot." She poured bourbon into a shot glass and pushed it toward Maggie, who downed it.

"You're glum, *chére*," JJ said.

"I got an 'I'll call you.'"

"From Bo? No worries there. You know he will."

"Yes. But there's weirdness." Maggie shared their conversation with JJ. "I'm trying to understand exactly why it's complicated. I'm glad Bo and Whitney have a strong relationship for exes—but is that what's complicating our relationship? Or is this purely about Xander? I know if Whitney and Zach had a baby, a sibling might be difficult for him to adjust to, at least at first. But I think he would eventually—and even benefit emotionally and socially because of it."

JJ motioned to Old Shari, who added a shot to Maggie's glass. "It's not just about Whitney and Zach having a baby, is it? You want your own someday."

"Yes." Maggie looked down at her drink. "I do. I was an only child. It's lonely. And sometimes you play catch-up emotionally. A kid on the playground says something nasty or pushes you, and you take it to heart. It stays there. You don't know that's what siblings do sometimes and then quickly brush off. I want a couple of kids, and if Bo doesn't, we need to have that conversation."

"But at the right time," JJ said. "Which may not be right now with what all's going on in his life."

"I know. But I can't put it off too much longer, says the gal who's taken to tweezing her gray hairs. Why is it always the woman who has to bring up the baby thing?"

Maggie groaned and knocked back her shot.

THE NEXT MORNING, Maggie woke up, showered, and went into the cottage kitchen, where she found her mother sitting at the table with a cup of coffee and a copy of the *Pelican Penny Clipper*. "Your father's in *my* kitchen, doing yet more tinkering with his gumbo recipe. Good thing we don't have guests right now; I might have scared them away yelling at him."

"Your yelling is everyone else's conversational tone, so I wouldn't worry about that." Maggie poured herself a cup of coffee and motioned to the newspaper. "Anything salacious in there today?"

"No. Non-update updates on Gerard's murder. A plea for information on our John Doe. Little Earlie's in his serious journalist mode, which is good for the rest of us. I made banana pecan pancakes with brown sugar butter."

"I thought I smelled something incredibly delicious." Maggie took a plate from the drying rack and piled pancakes onto it. She'd need sustenance for the lie she was about to tell.

After polishing off the stack of pancakes on her plate and resisting the urge to go back for seconds, Maggie retreated to the living room. She took a deep breath and tapped a number into her cell phone. "Petit Plastic Surgery," a chipper young woman's voice answered. "We make what's good even better. Can I help you?"

Maggie ramped up her best ditzy Southern belle accent. "I sure hope so. I messed up. I made an appointment for my boss but forgot to write it down. She's gonna be soooo mad at me if I don't get it onto her calendar."

"No problem, I can do a search for it. What's her name?"

"Maureen 'Mo' Heedles."

Maggie heard the sound of tapping on a computer keyboard, and then silence. "I'm sorry. I show nothing under that name."

"Really?" This was unexpected. Had Mo somehow figured out her appointment was exposed and cancelled it? "I think it was next Tuesday maybe?"

More keyboard tapping. "Nope. Nothing. Are you sure you have the right doctor?"

"Totally sure." Maggie had a brainstorm. "Can you check under the name 'Martha Stewart?'"

"Oh, I don't have to look that up. I remember the name because it's the same as the famous lady's. To confirm, the visit's a follow-up to her liquid facelift procedure. How does she look? The bruising should have gone away by now."

"She looks great. You'd never know she had any work done."

"That's the goal."

Maggie thanked the receptionist and ended the call. She now knew Mo's secret. The question was, did Gerard? And if so, had he somehow been using it to blackmail her?

TWELVE

ALTHOUGH THE HOLIDAY was still days away, several Doucet guides called in sick with Mardi Gras Fever, Louisiana's most contagious disease. Maggie put her art restoration project on hold and once again struggled into her antebellum gown to lead tours. At the end of the day, she hustled into town for the talent portion of the pageant contest, which was being held in the St. Pierre Parish Historical Society's permanent temporary home. The cavernous space offered better acoustics than the cozy environs of Crozat.

Ironically, the Historical Society's location—a former potato chip warehouse next to the Park 'n' Shop—was the ugliest building in the lovely Cajun town. Maggie sympathized with Gerard's obsession with finding a historically significant location. He must have found it frustrating to display Pelican's treasures in an industrial setting that still smelled like lard.

Maggie yawned as she parked, and decided she needed coffee. She went into the convenience store and picked up a large one, black. She poked around the aisles for a snack that wasn't two-thirds artificial ingredients, settling on a bag of pretzels. As she stepped up to the cash register to pay, a voice behind her said, "I'll get that." She turned to see Jayden Jones standing behind her with a container holding four coffees. "Oh hey, Jayden."

Jayden met her greeting with a slight smile and nod. "I'm getting coffee for the guys I'm working with. We're doing flood repairs at the Pelican police station." He put down the coffee and pulled out his wallet.

"You don't have to pick up my tab."

"I should be doing more than that for all the kindness your family's shown me."

Jayden paid, and then he and Maggie left the store. Pageant contestant Kaity waved from the parking lot, where she was exiting Gin's car from the passenger side. "Hey, Maggie," she said. Then her eyes lit on Jayden. "Hello," she said. Her voice had the come-hither tone Maggie imagined a phone sex operator would have.

"Hello," Jayden responded politely.

Kaity sauntered over. "I'm Kaity. We almost met at Crozat, and then all heck broke loose when my grammy got dissed by that other lady."

"Jayden Jones."

Kaity extended her hand with a flirtatious smile Jayden ignored. He gave her hand a hardy shake and dropped it, which Kaity didn't seem too happy about. But she persevered. "I never did get to thank you for helping Gram and breaking up the fight."

"No thanks needed."

"Oh, I disagree." Kaity amped up the flirt wattage on her smile.

"Hey!" Gin's voice crackled like a gun report. She jumped out of the car and pointed a finger at Jayden. "No consorting with a minor."

"I have no intention of doing so, ma'am." Jayden's response was polite, but a vein twitch in his neck told Maggie he felt otherwise. "Have a nice day, Maggie."

Jayden started for the police station. As he passed Gin, he gave her a small salute. "Ma'am."

Kaity gave her grandmother an angry look. "Thanks for embarrassing me to death."

"Put boys outta your head for two minutes, and go practice your talent."

Kaity harrumphed and stomped off. Maggie faced Gin. "You had no right going off on Jayden like that. It was—"

"Racist?" Gin gave a mirthless laugh. "Two of my husbands were black. So were a couple of my daughter's. Our husbands were good men who had the bad luck of marrying not so good women. It ain't about race, Maggie. It's about hoping and praying Kaity finds a better path than me and her mother. Who's in jail for selling the opioids she got addicted to."

Maggie felt terrible. *For someone with vaunted visual skills, you totally whiffed this.* "Gin, I'm so sorry."

"No worries. Wavin' it off." Gin waved her hands in the air like she was chasing away a bee. "But that's why this pageant is so important to us. So really, *really* important."

Gin ambled over to the warehouse, leaving Maggie feeling unsettled. What did Gin expect from her? And how far was she willing to go to get it?

O mio babbino caro, mi piace, è bello, bello.
Vo'andare in Porta Rossa a comperar l'anello...

Belle was in the middle of singing *"O Caro Bambino,"* the aria from Puccini's *Giani Schicchi* that was every soprano's go-to showpiece. Maggie couldn't deny the teen was technically perfect, but her mind drifted between replaying the conversation with Gin and debating the best way to extract information from Mo about her appointment with Petit Plastic Surgery.

Mi struggo e mi tormento! O Dio, vorrei morir!
Babbo, pietà, pietà! Babbo, pietà, pietà!

Belle finished the aria. The other judges burst into applause and a few "bravas." Maggie noticed Mo wipe a tear from her eye and Robbie restrain himself from jumping up for a standing ovation. She pitied Allouette for having to follow this act. Then again, Allie had grown up with a mother who both basked in and resented the shadow of her more glamorous cousin, so maybe she was used to it.

"Are we all settled after that bravura performance?" Constance asked. The judges nodded. "Magnolia, would you show in the next contestant?"

Maggie left the audition area and headed to the waiting room. Allie and Belle were in the middle of what appeared to be an intense conversation. Maggie cleared her throat, but the girls didn't notice. "Allie?"

"Oh. Sorry."

Allie turned away from her cousin to Maggie, then turned back. A look Maggie couldn't identify passed between the girls. "Everything okay?"

"Yes, fine. Belle was giving me some advice on my talent portion." Allie hugged her cousin, and Maggie could swear she saw Belle's eyes glimmer with tears. "I love you."

"I love you too."

Allie followed Maggie into the audition room. Maggie took her seat with the other judges and gave the teen an encouraging smile.

"Um, I don't really have a talent like Belle does. But I do write stuff. So, I thought I'd read one of my poems. This one's called 'The Magic of Yes.'" Allie pulled a piece of paper from the back pocket of her jeans, unfolded it, and began to read.

There was magic in this room.
When a song sang through the ceiling
Like a sad garden of crystal played by the wind…

The poem continued. It was beautiful, and Allie finished to a round of enthusiastic applause. She seemed surprised but happy by the positive response. "Thanks a lot—'bye," she said, and ducked out of the room.

"Alright, let's choose a winner of the talent portion," Constance said. "I think we can agree Kaity didn't 'bring it,' as the kids say." Kaity had already come and gone with her talent, which began as a monologue she'd memorized from a TV cop show and devolved into a much more interesting soliloquy about how she'd decorate the warehouse for a *Harry Potter*–themed wedding.

"Yes, although I loved her party ideas," Mo said. "She'll be getting a call from me when I throw my Spring Veevay bash."

Maggie had to agree. "I think event planning may be her talent."

"So, it's between Belle and Allouette," Constance continued. "All in favor of Belle."

Three hands went up. Only Maggie's didn't. "Belle's got a lovely voice, but I thought the performance was… proficient. Allie's poem was stunning."

"I'm sure we all agree with you on that," Constance said while Robbie and Mo bobbed their heads in unison. "But I don't think we can call writing an actual talent, do you?" Robbie and Mo shook their heads.

Maggie bristled at this attitude. "Writing's not a talent? Seriously, Constance—"

"Please calm down; I'm using *talent* in the most basic sense of the word. Belle got the majority vote. She wins this portion of the contest. I'll let her know. Magnolia, you can tell the other two girls how much we enjoyed their work. We're done for today."

Constance stood up, and Robbie and Mo followed her lead. Maggie stuffed down her resentment and approached the widow. "I haven't had the chance to ask how you're doing." Constance responded with a small shrug, which gave Maggie zero information. She pressed on. "I truly admire your strength."

"That's my stoic Yankee stock. My mother's family was from New England, as Gerard never tired of reminding me." Constance didn't bother to hide the bitterness in her voice.

"Have you made funeral arrangements? Grand-mère's been asking." Grand-mère hadn't been, but Maggie needed to keep the conversation going if she was going to glean any more information from Constance.

"I've already had him interred."

"You did?" Maggie was too surprised to dissemble.

"Yes. Robbie told me how in the Jewish faith it's considered disrespectful to leave a loved one unburied, and I thought it was a marvelous sentiment. He even had his rabbi perform a service. It was the most private of ceremonies. Gerard would have wanted it that way."

Maggie's mind whirled as she tried to process this

new information. She couldn't imagine anyone who would have wanted a private ceremony less than Gerard. In the brief time she'd known him, he'd made it obvious he considered himself one of Pelican's most illustrious citizens. She also considered it a good bet that the only thing Gerard would have wanted less than a tiny funeral was a Jewish send-off. And why the rush? Did Constance have something to hide? Or did Robbie?

"Well, I guess Gerard will be honored by the essay contest," Maggie said, regaining her composure.

"Oh, he'll be honored in many ways. Tomorrow there will be a front-page story in the *Penny Clipper* announcing an upcoming Historical Society exhibit on the Pelican orphan train. Dedicated to the memory of Gerard Damboise."

Who vigorously fought the idea, Maggie thought. The toxic underbelly of the Damboise marriage was beginning to depress her.

There was a light knock at the door, and Denise Randall popped her head in. "Hi, sorry to bother y'all. I'm here to pick up Allie and needed to use the little girl's room."

"Of course," Constance said, pointing. "It's that way. Oh, but Denise, I'm glad you're here. I have some good news for you." Constance beckoned to Denise, who darted over. Maggie made a show of stepping away to give them privacy, but kept an ear on the conversation. "I know Gerard was threatening to sue your husband over those bad investments. You don't have to worry about that anymore. My late husband had a healthy insurance policy, so I won't be acting on his threats…although I'm sure he would have eventually gotten over his anger if he'd lived." Constance seemed to throw the last line in as an afterthought.

Denise impulsively took Constance's hands and squeezed them. "Oh, Mrs. Damboise, thank you so much. You have no idea what a relief this is. I'll tell Mike right away. Believe me, he learned his lesson. No more day trading for him, especially with other people's money. He'll be finding a new hobby." Denise released Constance. "So sorry. I got overexcited. Anyway, thanks again."

Denise continued her journey to the restroom as Constance took a regal walk out of the warehouse. And Maggie added another name to the list of murder suspects—the man who lost Gerard Damboise a bundle of money, Mike Randall.

THIRTEEN

MAGGIE TEXTED Bo the news about Mike Randall's financial clash with Gerard. She noticed Mo standing outside her car, on her phone; it seemed like the perfect opportunity to do a little digging into the skin queen's relationship with Gerard. After some debate, she landed on a course of action that would involve yet another bold lie, and approached Mo.

"You're still here," Mo said. "Lucky gal. Veevay texted us reps they're coming out with a new brightening mask made with all-natural ingredients, and you're the first to know before I tweet the news to my followers. In fact, if you preorder, I'll give you a twenty-five-percent discount as my first customer for the cream."

"About that…" Maggie hesitated for dramatic effect. "When we met, I felt like I'd seen you before. I was trying to remember where—Junie's? The Park 'n' Shop? And then it hit me. I was outside Petit Plastic Surgery one day, trying to decide if I should get some information on a laser facial. And I saw you go into their office."

Mo stiffened. "It wasn't me."

"It was you, Mo."

"You can't say that for sure."

"Yes, I can. Because…" Maggie hesitated for real, trapped by Mo's challenge. Then it hit her. "I recognized your walk. It's very distinctive." She held her breath, waiting for Mo's response.

The woman's confidence sagged. "I've been told that before. I blame it on the dang six-inch heels I always wear. I love 'em to death, but if I don't take tiny steps, I'm like to tip over."

Maggie hid her relief that the tack she took worked. She affected an attitude of uncertainty. "The thing is I'm concerned about the Veevay products now. If their star saleswoman is getting procedures, it makes me wonder how effective they really are."

Mo crossed her arms in front of her chest and pursed her lips. She radiated a cold anger. "How much do you want?"

"What?" Maggie was thrown by Mo's sudden shift in demeanor.

"To keep your mouth shut. How much?"

"Absolutely nothing, Mo. I shelled out a lot of money for Veevay products, and if they're some kind of scam, I deserve to know that, and so do your other customers." Maggie's forceful response was true, if convenient. She did want to know if she'd plunked down money on a useless product.

Mo's affect shifted yet again. She clapped a hand in front of her mouth in horror. "Oh, Maggie, I am so, so sorry. I don't know where that came from. Well, I do. Someone else learned about my little secret and decided to keep it in his back pocket in case he ever needed to—well, I'll say it—blackmail me."

Maggie's instincts told her who "he" was, but they also warned her not to press Mo into naming names. "How did this person find out about Dr. Petit?"

"The mailman delivered a bill to the wrong house. Unfortunately, it was the *really* wrong house. But trust me, Veevay products are terrific. There are a lot of younger Veevay reps nipping at my heels. I've already lost a few customers to them, and I can't afford to lose any more. We're our own best sales tools, so to survive in this business, I need to age backwards. And short of magic, that takes the occasional visit to Dr. Petit."

"I understand, and I do sympathize with you. But you can't lie to your customers."

"I don't. Think about my party. I never made any claims about people having my skin. It was all about health and pampering and enhancing what the good Lord gave each of us."

"I do remember you saying that at the party. But don't put yourself in a position where you could be blackmailed. It's dangerous." *And may have gotten Gerard Damboise killed*, Maggie added to herself.

"I promise. Thank you, *chére*. To show my appreciation for your kindness and honesty, that first jar of brightening mask is on me. Notice I said 'first.' Because after you try it, you'll be back for more, *I gar-on-tee*."

Mo gave Maggie a rib-crushing hug, then got into her car and drove off with a wave. Maggie watched her go. She sat on the Park 'n' Shop steps to think for a moment, then texted Bo a brief recap of her conversation with the businesswoman. Mo lived around the corner from the Damboises. Finding Mo's errant bill among their own letters probably wasn't the first time the Damboises got someone else's mail. But for Gerard, it might have been the last. She just hoped it wasn't Mo who stamped him "Return to Sender."

IT WAS STILL dark by the time Maggie got home, winter having brought nightfall early. The air was damp, but warm enough to have the car windows rolled down. As

Maggie pulled into the parking area behind the manor house, she was surprised to hear the sound of a power saw coming from the Crozats' flood-damaged garage. She parked and walked over to the building, where she found Jayden sawing two-by-fours under the glare of a jerry-rigged floodlight. He turned off the saw when he noticed her. "Isn't it quittin' time?" she asked the vet.

Jayden shook his head. "Y'all have been so generous with your hospitality, but I keep getting pulled away to other jobs. It's not fair to you, so I figure as long as you don't have guests who wouldn't take kindly to my noise, I'll put in a couple of hours at night out here and make some progress."

"Thank you. I wish I could convince you to take a room in the *garçonniére* while we're light on guests."

"I'm fine with the tent. I was a foster kid. Lived in a lot of group homes, so I'm happy for some privacy."

"No family?"

Jayden swept sawdust off the two-by-four he'd cut. "Oh, I have family. Chret and all the other men I served with."

Maggie was about to dig for more details about Jayden's life when she and Jayden were both distracted by the rumble of a truck. Maggie stuck her head out the door and saw a HomeNHearth delivery truck. The truck's brakes whined as it came to a stop in front of the garage. The driver cut the engine and jumped out of the truck cab. It was Denise's husband, Mike Randall. "Hey there," he greeted her with a wink. Maggie forced herself not to recoil. "I got a big ol' order of drywall here. Your pops around to sign for it?"

"I can do that." *Because I'm a functional adult and not some helpless ninny like you're subtly implying,*

Maggie refrained from saying. Mike handed her a tablet, and she signed for the order with her index finger.

"Where do you want it?"

"There." Maggie gestured inside the garage.

"Alrighty."

Mike began to unload the drywall. Jayden stepped outside. "I can give you a hand."

"I'll take it."

Mike and Jayden began emptying the truck of its cargo, and Maggie saw an opportunity to delve into the deliveryman's relationship with the Damboises. "It's awful about Gerard Damboise, isn't it?"

"Yeah, tough break," was his rather casual response.

"It must be hard, with the two of you being friends and all."

"Whoa," Jayden said as Mike lost his grip on a stack of drywall. The two men managed to regain control of the stack before it fell to the ground.

"Where'd you get that idea about me and Damboise?" Mike said. "I barely knew the guy."

Maggie affected the attitude of the flake Mike mistook her for. "I don't know. It was off something I heard Constance Damboise tell Denise."

"What'd she tell her?"

The man's confrontational attitude was starting to make Maggie nervous. "Might be best if you ask Denise."

"I'll be doing that."

Mike dropped his end of the last drywall stack, which landed with a large thud. He strode back to his truck, jumped into the cab, fired up the engine, punched the accelerator, and barreled off. Maggie and Jayden watched him go. "Weird," Jayden said.

"You, my friend, are the master of understatement."

There was a sudden shout from the manor house, then a string of epithets. "Oh no," Maggie said. "That's my dad."

Maggie and Jayden raced toward the manor house, leaping up the back steps and slamming the door behind them. As they ran into the kitchen, Gopher and foster dog Jolie scooted past them and disappeared down the hall. An anguished Tug paced back and forth in the middle of the room, cradling his cast iron pot.

"Dad," Maggie said, "*What* is going on?"

"Someone put my black pot on the footstool," Tug said. He pointed to a small stool that stood barely a foot off the ground. "I came in to do some fiddling with my recipe and found Gopher and Jolie with their faces in the pot, licking away. You know what that means, don't you? I have to wash it. All those years and years of seasoning. Gone. Just gone."

"Uh, Dad…" Maggie, about to delivery very bad news, grimaced. "I don't think washing is the answer."

"You're right. It would be too destructive. I'll get a rag and give it a good, hearty wipe."

"No." Maggie, perilously close to losing her patience, reminded herself of her father's almost anthropomorphic attachment to the pot. "If two dogs licked it—"

"And they were going to town on that baby, let me tell you. That's some good seasoning right there."

Maggie inhaled a deep breath through her nose, slowly exhaled, and then spoke. "Dad, I love you dearly. I'd say more than you love your pot, but I'm not sure that's possible. Anyway, if both dogs 'went to town' on the old thing, there's really only one way to go. I think you have to…throw it away."

Tug winced. He sat on the stool, the pot in his lap. "I know." His voice was husky. "I couldn't bring myself to say it."

"Sir, I'm deeply sorry for your loss," Jayden said. "I'll be going back to work now. But if you need anything, please let me know."

Jayden escaped from the kitchen, leaving Maggie with her mourning father. She knelt next to Tug. "This pot's been in the family for generations," he said. "Nobody could tell you how old it is. It's like losing a member of the family. I blame Mike Randall. I know he was here. He snuck in and moved my pot to knock me out of the gumbo competition."

"He was here to deliver drywall. The man is sketchy, to be sure, and I wouldn't dismiss him as a suspect in Gerard Damboise's murder. But I do think he's innocent of murdering your black pot." Maggie put an arm around her father's shoulder. "If it's easier on you, I can...dispose of the pot."

Tug hugged the pot tighter. "No one's 'disposing' of anything. He's getting the send-off he deserves. Right after I track down Mike Randall and clock him." He stood up and stomped out of the room, clutching the pot in his arms.

"So, it's a 'he' now," Maggie said to Gopher, who'd wandered back into the kitchen and was sniffing the floor for snacks. "That is a whole new level of crazy."

Maggie heard someone coming into the house through the back door. A moment later, the scent of fresh-baked bread wafted in, followed by Ninette carrying a bag of groceries and a baguette in a long brown bag. "I stopped at Fais Dough Dough to pick up some fresh bread to go with the millionth pot of gumbo your father's making tonight."

"No gumbo tonight, Mom." Maggie relayed the sad saga of Tug's pot.

Ninette gasped. "Oh no! It's all my fault. Dad moved everything around, and I spent an hour trying to get my kitchen back in order. I must have put the pot on the stool and forgotten about it."

"You better let him know you're the culprit before he does some serious damage to an innocent man."

"I will. After I put away these groceries."

"*Mother.* No stalling."

"Fine," Ninette grumbled. Maggie took the groceries from her mother, and Ninette slowly shuffled off to meet her fate.

Maggie put away the groceries and took a container of leftover shrimp étouffée out of the refrigerator. She checked to make sure her mother, the "microwave police," wasn't on her way back into the kitchen, and then heated up a bowl of étouffée. She placed it on a tray, with a big hunk of the baguette, and made her way to Gran' in the Rose Room.

Grand-mère, clad in a dusty rose silk nightgown, sat propped up in bed by several down pillows. Her face lit up when she saw Maggie. "I could easily get used to being so spoiled." Gran' put down the mystery she was reading and accepted the tray. "What was all the commotion about?"

Maggie filled Gran' in on the sad saga of the black pot. "Hmm," Gran' said. "I'd call that a Freudian move on your sweet mother's part. It is sad about the pot. It's been in the family for who knows how long. Your *grand-pére* used to drive me as crazy with his gumbo prep as your dad drives your mama. I'm sure the same can be said of generations of Crozat women. Now, fill me in on the pageant and investigation into Gerard's death. Any suspects?"

"Many." Maggie sat down next to her *grand-mère*. "In addition to your garden variety of contestants and momtestants, there's the almost-merry widow, of course. Mo Heedle is in the mix because Gerard threatened to expose her visits to a plastic surgeon. Robbie Metz's wife appears to be a kleptomaniac, so you have to wonder if Gerard knew about that and used it to his advantage somehow. Denise hated Gerard because her husband, Mike Randall, did some failed day trading with the old man's money, and Gerard was demanding to be reimbursed for the losses. But lucky for Mike, her husband's death cleared the way for Constance to forgive the debt. And then there's Gin Bertrand, who, I'm sorry to say, has a record."

"Lee did say she's a bit of a hot mess, but he didn't give me the specifics."

"I haven't looked into the other momtestants. But so far, of the ones I know, only perfect Pauline Tremblay and her oh-so-perfect family seem to have had a neutral relationship with the late, unlamented Gerard Damboise."

"You know the old cliché, *chére*. Ninety-nine percent of American families are dysfunctional, and the other one percent is lying about it. Maybe the Tremblays' lives are a little too perfect."

"Good point, Gran'. It's time I got to know Pauline Tremblay a little better."

FOURTEEN

FIRST THING IN the morning, Maggie texted Lia for permission to use Grove Hall's remodel as an excuse to pay Pauline a visit. She filled a to-go cup with coffee and left the cottage for her car. When she reached the convertible, she found a copy of the *Pelican Penny Clipper* had landed on the car's hood. She picked it up and saw the front-page story trumpeted an upcoming exhibit on the orphan train at the St. Pierre Parish Historical Society. Maggie almost did a spit take when she read a quote from Constance Damboise: "It was my husband's dying wish."

She made the short drive into Pelican's quaint village center and stopped at Lia's bakery, Fais Dough Dough, to pick up an "appreciation" present from client Lia for her decorator, Pauline. She was surprised to find criminal defense lawyer Quentin MacIlhoney behind the counter. He was dressed in what, for the hugely successful lawyer, passed as casual wear: perfectly pressed slacks, bespoke button-down shirt, and a bright yellow cashmere pullover sweater. A brand-new Rolex watch sparkled on one wrist, a computer watch on the other. "Hi, Quentin—didn't expect to see you here. Business slow at the office?"

"My partners forced me to take a day off," he said, retrieving her box of pastries from a cooler. "Since Vanessa's helping Lia out by managing Bon Bon, I thought

I'd give Kyle a break and man the Fais Dough Dough counter for the day."

"Hey there, Maggie," Vanessa, ex-fiancé of Rufus Durand and future wife of Quentin, called to her. Maggie craned her neck and saw Van waving to her from the open doorway between Fais Dough Dough and its sister store, Bon Bon Sweets. "That's just Quentin's excuse. My mama's been living with us since her trailer took on water during the flood, and truth be told, Quenty would rather do pretty much anything besides hang around the house with her."

Quentin threw up his hands. "Busted."

Maggie gave him a sympathetic smile. Vanessa's mother, Tookie Fleer, ran airboat swamp tours for tourists. A tiny woman whose peppery personality belied her size, she was so tough that rumor had it her hobby was wrestling alligators. "But," Quentin continued, "I could use a great excuse to work late at the office. We got ourselves the mystery flood victim and the late Gerard Damboise. I need you to solve one of these murders and deliver me a client."

"That's Pelican PD's job, not mine."

"Oh ye of the stellar track record, don't be coy. My sources tell me the death of John Doe was due to a well-placed bullet."

"I didn't know that was common knowledge."

"It's not. Remember, I am an uncommon man."

"You are indeed, Quentin." Maggie frowned. Worry creased her forehead. "I don't want to believe there's some maniac loose in town. That seems the go-to answer for too many people. But I can't stop wondering, are the murders of John Doe and Gerard Damboise connected? Or is it really just a sick, horrible coincidence?"

"Here's hoping it's the latter. I get two potential clients that way."

"I have to admire your blatant avarice. But I'm hoping for the former. Intuition tells me the murders are connected in some twisted way no one's been able to figure out yet."

"I've learned not to doubt any Pelicaner's intuition, especially yours. When you nail the perp, make sure to give him or her—or them—my card."

"Them?" Maggie couldn't help smiling. "Still shooting for maximum return on the murders, huh?"

"What can I say?" Quentin thumbed in Vanessa's direction. "The future third Mrs. Quentin MacIlhoney has expensive tastes."

"Don't lay this on me, old man," Vanessa called from Bon Bon. "I'm not the one driving that new gold Bentley."

Quentin gave a genial shrug. "Busted once again."

Maggie stepped across the threshold to Bon Bon and added an assortment of chocolates to her gift for Pauline. She left the store and drove north from the village up the River Road, eventually making a left onto a long drive similar to the one at the Crozat Plantation B and B, but made of crushed oyster shells. The drive ended in front of elegant, imposing Camellia Plantation, Pauline's ancestral home. It was one of several River Road plantations still in private hands, much to the chagrin of tourists because it was breathtaking. The white antebellum structure stood two stories high. Outdoor staircases curved to the left and right of the home's grand entrance. Wide, round columns reached from the ground to the roof's eves. In a curious twist, the original wide front lawn had been replaced with a horseback-riding rink. Maggie knew nothing about horses, but she knew enough to know Pauline was astride a beauty. The steed's gray coat gleamed, even with the sun behind clouds threatening rain.

Pauline rode with the grace and assurance of an experienced rider. Behind her galumphed her cousin Denise, who disguised her obvious discomfort every time Pauline glanced her way, which she did often, as if checking to make sure Denise was still on her mount. Pauline saw Maggie and waved to her. She cantered over with ease, Denise following with less grace. "Maggie, hi. I'm so glad you dropped by. I've been meaning to invite you over."

Pauline nimbly dismounted, then helped Denise off her horse. Pauline's daughter and pageant queen front-runner, Belle, waved to her mother from the manor house veranda. She jogged over to the women. Clad in cut-off jean shorts and devoid of makeup, Belle was almost unrecognizable. Instead of a pageant queen wannabe, she simply looked like a typical teen. "Hello, nice to see you," she greeted Maggie with her usual robotic politeness. She took the reins of both horses. "I'll walk them back to the stable," she told Pauline.

"I better get going," Denise said. "Allouette is taking three advanced placement classes, and I like to make a good, healthy dinner to fuel her. Maggie, so glad I was here when you came by." She air-kissed her cousin. "See you tomorrow. Take good care of Pepin. Allouette misses him. She'll be by this weekend for a ride. If she has time. All that AP work keeps her real busy." The last comment was directed at Maggie.

Denise hurried off to her car. Pauline watched her go,

making sure she was out of earshot. "Pepin was the Randalls' horse. We're boarding him until...temporarily."

"Were they affected by the floods?"

"No." Without articulating, the message Pauline sent was that the Randalls were victims of financial troubles. "Come inside. We'll have some tea."

Maggie realized she'd yet to explain her visit. "Lia asked me to stop by and drop off some treats from her shops. She's grateful for how much effort you've put into Oak Grove."

"That's so sweet, but totally unnecessary. I'm having the best time working with them and that gorgeous old place." She called to her daughter, "Belle, *chére*, we're going inside if you need us."

Belle, absorbed with the horses, didn't respond. She took turns nuzzling each one, stroking their manes and cooing at them. It was the most humanity Maggie had yet to see from the girl. "Belle's wonderful with the horses," she said.

"Like mother, like daughter. She lives for them. If we were down to our last dime, we'd spend it on Houmas and Pepin." She started for the manor house, and Maggie followed. Pauline, lithe and nimble in rider's attire, sailed up steps leading to the impressive carved oak door. Like the doors at Crozat, they were flanked by floor-to-ceiling windows that allowed in a river breeze. Pauline swung open the heavy door with easy familiarity, and the two women stepped into a wide hallway. Again, like at Crozat, the hallway stretched from front to back to welcome any waft of air that might cool off a humid Louisiana day or evening.

A man holding a briefcase and a carry-on bag came down the home's grand, carved staircase. "Hey, sweetie,

I'm heading to the airport," he said to Pauline, adding a polite hello to Maggie.

"Maggie, this is my husband, Jules. Jules, Maggie is Lia Bruner's cousin. She's also a judge for the Miss Pelican Mardi Gras Gumbo Queen contest."

"Really? A pleasure to meet someone so important." Jules said this with humor. He extended his hand, and Maggie shook it. Jules, like his wife, appeared to be in his late thirties. He still had a full crop of light brown hair peppered with gray, cut in a conservative style. He was handsome, but it was a tired handsome with deep worry lines. Jules kissed Pauline on the cheek she turned to him. "I better run or I'll be late for my flight. Maybe someday my company will spring for TSA pre-check, huh? Nice meeting you, Maggie."

Jules headed out the door. His wife watched him go, and then turned back to Maggie. "Where were we? Right. The parlor."

Pauline led Maggie into the front parlor. It was an exquisite combination of antique and contemporary furnishings upholstered in a range of taupe shades, with an occasional "splash of an accent color," a term Maggie had learned from the home decorating TV channel, a guilty pleasure of hers. In this case, the color was lime green, which to Maggie felt like the equivalent of splashing cold water on her face to wake up. It all somehow worked and allowed accessories she assumed were family heirlooms to take center stage.

Yet something was slightly off. It took Maggie a moment to zero in on exactly what that was. Then her artist's eye picked up worn spots on the upholstery, as well as on the baseboards and rugs. Maggie got the sense the Randalls might not be the only members of their extended family struggling financially. She debated how to broach the subject in a delicate way. "You have a beautiful home."

"It's a study in deferred maintenance." Pauline laughed and waved a hand as if to dismiss the place.

Maggie shook her head and fibbed, "No, I don't see that at all." But she was relieved, although surprised, that Pauline was so open about Camellia Plantation's condition. She'd assumed Pauline, like her daughter, valued the illusion of perfection above all else.

"Jules's company relocated its headquarters to Arkansas last year," Pauline, now a font of information, shared. "We couldn't imagine pulling up our roots here, so he took a lower-paying job with a local company that involves a lot of traveling, and I took on more design projects. Bibi Starke's been kind enough to send a few jobs my way. Like Grove Hall."

"I'm sure she's thrilled to have someone as talented as you to work with." It was time to steer the conversation toward Gerard Damboise. "I heard Gerard Damboise was thinking about hiring you to do some redecorating at his place," Maggie said. She was a little disturbed by how easily lies were coming to her.

"What?" Pauline was incredulous. "Wow, I'd love to know who started that nutty rumor."

Uh...me, Maggie thought to herself sheepishly.

"If anything, the man was a complete and total pain. He's been pestering my family for years to donate our heirlooms to the Historical Society, and we've given him an artifact whenever possible. No one's more supportive of preserving Pelican's history than a Tremblay, Boudreau, or Favrot, believe you me, but as of now we're a living history display, not a static one. The furniture stays put."

"It's a remarkable collection."

"Thank you so much. Would you like a tour?"

"I'd love one." Maggie jumped up before her hostess could retract what sounded like an obligatory invitation. Her instinct was confirmed when Pauline seemed startled by Maggie's enthusiasm.

"Wonderful," Pauline said in a tone both gracious and insincere. "Follow me."

For the next half hour, Maggie trailed behind the interior decorator as Pauline led her through beautiful room after room. There were signs of "deferred maintenance" throughout the home. Then Maggie noticed a small, circular, red sticker tucked in the corner of an elaborately carved nineteenth-century end table. "Is that for sale?" she asked.

Pauline pursed her lips almost imperceptibly. "No, why do you ask?"

"The sticker." Maggie pointed to it. She then unleashed another whopper. "I've been looking for a piece like it for Crozat's front parlor."

"Sorry, I see the confusion. We have a huge collection of furniture stored in the attic that I rotate into these rooms. I use stickers to mark the pieces I'm rotating out." Pauline pulled open a set of pocket doors. "Here's the dining room. The table dates back to the 1830s, but the chairs are contemporary..."

Maggie half-listened, her focus still on the stickers. She was convinced the red dots marked items for sale, like they did at the Brooklyn art gallery she'd owned with her ex-boyfriend in a not-too-distant lifetime. Pauline had been upfront about the Tremblays' reduced financial circumstances, yet squirrely about the furniture, which was odd. Maggie wondered if the woman had tried and failed to strike a deal with Gerard Damboise for a few pieces of her family's history. Still, Maggie wasn't picking up a sense of desperation that might lead to murder. A simpler explanation occurred to her. Perhaps Pauline's husband, Jules, was the kind of prideful man who'd want to put a spin on his demotion. That would certainly motivate his wife to hide sales generating additional income for the family.

Maggie made a show of checking her watch. "Oh wow, I've totally lost track of time. I have to get to work. Thanks so much for the tour. We should get together socially sometime—a double date with you and Jules, and Bo and me."

"I'd absolutely love that. I'll check my schedule and call you."

Oh no you won't, Maggie thought. Pauline's tone belied her words, giving the impression that a foursome with Maggie and her detective boyfriend was the last thing the decorator wanted to schedule.

ONCE AT DOUCET, Maggie resumed the painstaking task of carefully removing one work of art to reveal the painting beneath it. She barely noticed plantation guests peeking into the room to watch the process, and was so engrossed in her work that it took a minute to register someone was knocking on her workroom door. "Come in," she called. She was thrilled when the visitor proved to be Bo, with Xander at his side. "Hey, you two." Maggie put down her scalpel, brushed paint flakes from her face and hair, and went to them. Mindful of the young boy, she and Bo exchanged the most chaste of kisses.

"I gave Xander a choice between the batting cage and a petting zoo," Bo said, glancing with affection at his son, who was already pulling objects from the mask box and arranging them to form a face. "He wanted to come here."

"That makes me so happy. And I have some updates for you." Maggie led Bo to a corner of the room and in a low voice shared what she'd discovered about both the Tremblays and the Randalls.

"Interesting. And I did a little research on Stacy Metz. She's got a history of kleptomania."

"I'm not surprised. It's a compulsive behavior."

Bo nodded. "Robbie's tried to get her help, but no treatment seems to stick. They're doing their best to keep her condition quiet because it's not something an aspiring mayor would want the world to know about. When she lifts something from a local store where the shopkeeper knows Robbie, he gets an alert and returns whatever she stole. Sometimes a new merchant reports her, and whoever's on duty explains the situation. The department feels for the Metzes, who are good people in a difficult situation."

"It's hard to imagine that level of kindness anywhere but in a small town," Maggie said, moved.

"We're not all beaters and donut eaters at Pelican PD. Although now I want a donut. I'll pick up a dozen for the boys on my way to the station."

Bo started to go, but Maggie placed a hand on his arm. "Do you want to come by tonight?" she asked, her tone tentative. "I still have the cottage all to myself."

"I'd love to, but Ru's having his rascally pals over yet again. I'm afraid if I'm not there, I'll come home to who knows what all. Whitney will be by for Xander."

Bo gave Maggie a peck on the cheek and departed. *If we don't have a conversation soon, this relationship will die*, Maggie thought, fighting off a wave of nausea brought on by anxiety.

"Maggie?" Xander claimed her attention. He held up the glue gun.

"It's empty, buddy? I'll take care of it."

Relieved by the distraction, Maggie reloaded the glue gun and returned to her project, eventually exposing several more inches of the picture beneath the watercolor. She called Xander over. "What do you think this is?" she asked, pointing to the painting.

Xander studied the emerging image carefully. "A road."

"That's what I thought. And it looks like it's intersecting with another road."

The boy took a finger and slowly skimmed the painting's surface. "Could be a map."

"To buried treasure?" Maggie joked. Xander nodded, utterly serious. "You know, there are stories about pirates burying treasure at Crozat and my Doucet ancestors doing the same thing here when the Civil War broke out," she said, and grew excited. Could Xander be right? What if a nineteenth-century Doucet painted a rudimentary watercolor over a map to a family treasure chest, hiding its location until a safe time to reveal it?

The ring of her cell phone interrupted Maggie's reverie. She saw the call was from fellow judge Robbie Metz and answered it. Before she could get out a greeting, Robbie blurted, "Maggie, thank God I got you. Something terrible's happened."

"Oh no. Stacy?"

"No. Why would you say that?"

"What's wrong?" Maggie asked, sidestepping his question.

"It's Constance Damboise." There was panic in Robbie's voice. "Someone tried to kill her."

FIFTEEN

MAGGIE MANAGED TO locate Whitney, who was waiting to go into an appointment with her ob-gyn. After dropping off Xander, she raced to St. Pierre Parish Hospital. Cal Vichet stood guard at the ER entrance. "Hey, Maggie. Figure you're not here to candy-stripe. Everyone's up in Intensive Care."

The St. Pierre elevators were so slow that a few Pelican moms-to-be wound up delivering their babies in them on their way to Obstetrics. Rather than wait for one, Maggie dashed up four flights of hospital stairs. She found Bo and Rufus outside the closed door of an ICU room. "How's Constance?" she asked, winded from the run.

"They pumped her stomach, and she's resting," Bo said. "We're waiting to talk to her."

"What happened?"

"Lame attempt to make it look like she offed herself," Rufus said. "Whoever did this left a typed note, supposedly from Constance, confessing to killing Gerard. They included her missing purse pistol as so-called evidence, so at least we know where it is now. They put some kind of pill in her coffee, and by the time she figured out the bitter taste wasn't only from the chicory, she was almost passed out. Luckily, she had enough juice left in her to call 911."

"But how did they get into her house?"

"It's Pelican. Pretty much every senior in town sleeps and wakes with an unlocked front door. I imagine most of them couldn't tell you where a house key was if you put Constance's purse pistol to their head."

Bo put an arm around Maggie's shoulder. "Your fellow judges are in the waiting room. I need to talk to you." He guided her down the hall into an empty ICU room, shutting the door behind them. "Have you received any threatening letters?"

"About the pageant?" Maggie asked, confused.

"No. About the potential orphan train exhibit."

Maggie shook her head. "I never heard of the exhibit until Robbie and Gerard argued about it before one of our meetings. Why?"

"We just learned that about a week before the flood, Robbie and Constance both got anonymous letters threatening trouble if the exhibit went through. They were going to bring them to the police, but Gerard said he had an idea who sent them and would take care of it. They gave their letters to him, and since nothing happened, they figured Gerard handled the situation."

"So, the murders are tied to the orphan train, not the pageant." Maggie sat down on the edge of the room's bed, trying to process the latest development. "Someone tried to kill Constance because she supports it. But someone killed her husband, who was *against* it. This is crazy-making."

"Welcome to my job."

Maggie's stomach suddenly clutched. "Gran'. She was involved with the pageant before me. She must have heard conversations about the orphan train exhibit."

"Call her." Bo's tone was grim.

Maggie's hands shook as she pulled out her cell

phone and speed-dialed her *grand-mère*. "Hello, *chére*," Gran' greeted her. She sounded hoarse but cheerful. "I just woke up from a long, lovely nap."

"I'm so glad you're getting rest." Maggie fought to keep the anxiety she felt out of her voice. "I was wondering… did Gerard or Constance Damboise ever talk to you about a possible orphan train exhibit at the Historical Society?"

"Oh yes. I think it's a marvelous idea. Did you see the article in the *Penny Clipper*? I'm so glad Constance is going through with it. I could never understand why Gerard suddenly turned against it. His new attitude seemed rather elitist, if you ask me."

"Gran'…did you ever get a letter threatening trouble if the exhibit went through?"

"Yes, but Gerard said to give him the letter, he'd take care of it, and I never heard another word about the blessed thing. What's going on? Why are you asking about this now?"

Maggie debated whether or not to lie. Then, knowing she'd never be able to pull it off with her grandmother, she said, "Someone tried to kill Constance Damboise. The police think it's related to the exhibit and the anonymous letters."

"Oh dear. How's Constance?"

"They had to pump her stomach, but she should be okay."

"Good. She's a trooper, that one."

"Um… Can you put Dad on?"

"No, I cannot." Gran's voice was stern. "Whatever you were going to tell him, tell me."

"Fine. Have him lock every door and window in the house." There was a catch in Maggie's throat. "You may be in danger, Gran'."

"Noted. I'll make sure we take all precautions. But I'm counting on you to be careful too, *chére*. There's an ugly energy in Pelican these days."

"I know. I love you, Gran'."

"*Je t'aime aussi, belle bébé. I love you too.*"

Maggie ended the call. Someone rapped on the door, then Rufus stuck his head in. "Mrs. Damboise's ready to talk to us, coz."

Bo nodded. "I could hear what your Gran' was saying. She's right. You need to be careful. There's definitely some evil out there."

"Ain't that the truth," Rufus said. "I took a call today from Helene Brevelle, who said she could sense the bad mojo in Pelican all the way from her cruise ship. When the town voodoo priestess is getting vibes in the middle of the ocean, you know something's up." Helene Brevelle, the town's esteemed conjurer, was on an extended cruise paid for by Louisiana State University sorority girls seeking her love-and-romance gris gris bags.

"I'll never stop being amused by the fact people in Pelican put as much stock in the village priestess as the village priest," Bo said.

"Looking back at my life, the times I went off the rails were the times I ignored Helene's premonitions," Rufus said. "But I'll contemplate my navel later. We should talk to Constance before she drifts off again."

Bo and Rufus took off to interview Constance. Maggie stayed put, deep in thought as she evaluated her next move. She tapped a number into her cell phone.

"*Pelican Penny Clipper*, tomorrow's news today." Proud of the slogan he'd come up with, Little Earlie never passed up a chance to use it. Once Maggie had greeted him, he said, "Hey, Maggie, what's up?"

"I need your help." Maggie could swear she heard Earlie pant with anticipation.

"I'm listening. Real hard."

"I need you to run a front-page story saying the Historical Society's plans for an exhibit on the Pelican orphan train have been put on hold. Probably forever."

"Whaaa? I just ran a front-page story saying the exhibit's happening."

"I know, I know. But we need to cancel that story out. Lives depend on it." Maggie tossed in the last statement, hoping it would appeal to the newsman's penchant for drama.

"Hmm. Well, hard to argue with that. Is it true?"

"Pretty much."

"These days, that's good enough for me. I'll do it, but I want something in return."

"Of course you do."

"This is obviously tied to Gerard's murder and the attack on Constance—yes, I know all about that. It'll be the lead story tomorrow—"

"Second lead; my story goes first."

Little Earlie gave a disgruntled sigh. "Fine. I'll find a way to work it all in together. In exchange, I get the story when the murder's solved."

"Done. Thanks, Earlie."

"Right back at ya. All these murders lately may be bad for local real estate, but they're great for my paper."

Earlie ended the call. Maggie felt a sense of relief. By the morning, whoever was targeting proponents of the orphan train exhibit would be waylaid by the *Pelican Penny Clipper* article announcing the exhibit's demise, which would buy Pelican PD more time to apprehend the murderer.

Maggie hopped off the bed and went searching for the ICU waiting room. She found Robbie Metz there, scrolling through his cell and tapping a foot impatiently. He put away the phone when he saw her. "Mo took off for a sales meeting. Can you believe what all's going on? I blame that idiot Gerard."

"Robbie, it looks like the murders are tied to the or-phan train exhibit, not the pageant," Maggie said. "I've talked to Little Earlie, and tomorrow he's going to run a story saying the exhibit is off. But until then, anyone who supported it could be in danger. So do whatever you can to be safe. Be aware of your surroundings, and check your locks. Just be careful."

"Great. Just great." Robbie kicked a chair and then dropped into it.

Maggie sat down next to the businessman. "I have to be honest. You seem a little overwhelmed with your life. And I can understand why." *Best to go with the vaguest reference to Stacy's problem.* "I was wonder-ing how you came to volunteer as a pageant judge in the first place. It seems a burden you didn't really need to take on."

Robbie sat straight up. "It's my civic duty, Maggie. I'm an established businessman in this town." Maggie didn't respond. She found silence on her part often mo-tivated others to continue talking. Robbie slumped back in his seat. "And as long as we're being honest, it's hard being a different religion from everyone else in Pelican. Yeah, I can go up or down the river to Baton Rouge or New Orleans, and we do that when we go to synagogue. But Pelican's our home. It's where our hearts are. I love everyone here. But sometimes I feel I need to work a little harder to be accepted."

Maggie noticed Robbie's face was drawn, and the bags under his eyes were more pronounced. The poor man seemed to be aging in front of her eyes. "Well, as your basic Catholic woman, I can't pretend to feel what you feel. But I can tell you it's not easy being the local 'artsy-fartsy girl.'"

"I'm sure it's not. Welcome to the misfits club."

Maggie shook her head. "No. We're not misfits. We're different. Let's call it the Celebrate Differences Club."

Robbie managed a grin. "I like that."

Bo appeared in the doorway. "We finished interviewing Constance. She's asking to speak with both of you."

Robbie and Maggie followed Bo to the judge's hospital room. "Only two at a time are allowed in, so I'll wait outside," he told them. "But I'll be listening to the conversation."

Bo stepped back so Robbie and Maggie could enter the room. They found Constance looking pale, but she seemed alert and was sitting up in bed. "Thank you both so much for being here."

"Of course," Maggie said. "How do you feel?"

"Like I had the worst flu in the world and then took a punch in the gut. I'll be out of commission for a day or two, but I don't want that to affect the pageant judging."

Maggie was blunt. "Constance, your husband was murdered. Someone tried to kill *you*. I think the pageant is the least of everyone's concerns right now."

"Well, it shouldn't be," Constance shot back. "I refuse to give whatever psychopath did these awful things the satisfaction of seeing our lives up-ended by their despicable behavior."

"If you're going to be stubborn about this, the pageant can continue, but for everyone's safety, the orphan train exhibit is on hold." Maggie shared her conversation with Little Earlie Waddell. "Based on the anonymous letters, that seems to be the more dangerous event."

"'Dangerous event,'" Robbie parroted. He gave a mirthless laugh. "We're talking about a pageant and a historical exhibit. The only dangers should be inhaling hairspray or getting eyestrain from reading too many nineteenth-century letters. It's demented."

"Be that as it may, we now know what precautions to take," Constance said. "We'll focus all our attention on the pageant. March on, my friends. And despite the circumstances, let's try and stay as positive as we can. As the Pelican High School cheer squad says, 'Pom-poms up!' I'll check in with at least one of you tomorrow."

Robbie and Maggie said their goodbyes and left Constance. "Pom-poms up," Robbie muttered. "Is it me, or is that a strange thing for a recent widow who was almost killed to say?"

"Oh, it's so not you," Maggie said, relieved she wasn't the only one who found Constance's upbeat spirit bizarre. "I can't make sense of anything that's happening these days. All I know is if a suspect isn't caught soon, it's pom-poms down for Pelican."

SIXTEEN

BY THE TIME Maggie got home, it was late evening. She checked the manor house and saw Gran' had followed orders. The house was secured, and the rarely used security system activated. Although overwhelmed with exhaustion, Maggie somehow managed to go through her nightly ablutions, which now included applying a thick layer of Veevay Age-Away Night Crème. She'd put a lot of faith in Louisiana's humidity keeping her skin dewy, but with her thirty-third birthday approaching, it was time to seek anti-aging help from someone other than Mother Nature. She fell asleep with an arm around Gopher, and Jolie snuggled up tight against her side. As she drifted off, Maggie wondered if she was destined to spend her life sharing a bed with nothing but furry companions.

When she woke up, she could smell her mother's Holiday Brandy Pain Perdu from the shotgun cottage. She sauntered over to the manor house for French toast and black coffee. Ninette was loading the dishwasher while Tug glumly rubbed oil into a new cast iron pot. "Nice pot, Dad."

"I bought it for him to try and make up for ruining the other one," Ninette said.

"Which I appreciate, *chére*, but it'll take generations past mine to season it proper." Tug put the pot down and massaged his seasoning hand. "The gumbo prize'll be someone else's this year."

Maggie filled a plate with pain perdu, adding a dollop of sugar cane syrup. She poured a cup of coffee and sat down next to Ninette. She saw a copy of the *Pelican Penny Clipper* lying on the kitchen's trestle table and picked it up. Little Earlie had come through. A banner headline announced the orphan train exhibit was canceled.

"We didn't see you last night," Ninette said. "How is Constance?"

"Weak, but getting better. We'll be judging without her for a couple of days."

"The pageant's still happening? I thought for sure it'd be canceled."

"No. Turns out it's not the pageant that's motivating murder—it's the orphan train exhibit."

"Really? That seems such a harmless thing."

"You'd think, wouldn't you? Anyway, it's important to Constance that the pageant goes on. Oddly important, frankly."

"Well, they should cancel something out of respect for Gerard," Tug said. "If not the pageant, then the gumbo contest."

Ninette groaned, and Maggie burst out laughing. "Dad, you are such a sore loser." Tug grumbled something unintelligible and went back to seasoning his pot. "Anyway, I'm hijacking the front parlor for an hour or two. Robbie and Mo are on their way over. We have to read the finalists' essays and decide who wins the Gerard Damboise Memorial Award. It's no cancellation of the gumbo contest, but it does show respect for Gerard."

Maggie finished her breakfast, then poured a carafe

of coffee and arranged a plate of breakfast pastries on a platter. She carried both to the front parlor. Moments later, Robbie and Mo arrived. "I touched base with Constance this morning," Robbie said as he settled into a club chair. "She got a good night's rest and is feeling way better, so she's hoping they'll release her today, or at least tomorrow. In the meantime, she asked me to make copies of the Historical Society key in case any of us needs to get in there for any reason."

Robbie handed keys to Maggie and Mo. Mo refused hers. "Until that place honors the history of my people in some way, I am NI—not interested."

Maggie sympathized with Mo. "I'll help you work on Constance to get that going once she recovers from the trauma she's experienced. Has she gotten any updates from the police? Any clues about who might have done this to her?"

Robbie shook his head. Mo poured a cup of coffee. She handed the cup to Robbie, then poured herself one and picked up a croissant before taking a seat on the sofa. "It's hard to focus on anything but murder and attempted murder right now."

"I know," Maggie said. "I was thinking that hearing the finalists' essays read aloud would help us concentrate and come to a unified decision."

"I'm a fan of that idea. But would you mind doing the honors? I wouldn't be much good with my mouth full of croissant," Mo said through a mouth full of croissant.

"No problem." Maggie pulled an essay from a folder. "This is Belle Tremblay's." She took a sip of coffee, and then began to read. "'When a family has roots in a community, going back hundreds of years, like Pelican's venerated Crozat family, it creates a fervent com-

mitment to a community that cannot be challenged.'"
She continued with the essay, which Belle somehow
managed to turn into a pages-long humble brag about
her own family's history. "I am proud to be a Tremblay,
Savoy, Favrot, and Boudreau, and to carry on a legacy I
hope I will pass on to my children, as the Crozats will
pass on to theirs."

Maggie put down the page. Robbie was the first to
comment. "It's technically proficient."

"That's my general feeling about Belle," Maggie
said.

"You're not being fair to her," Mo protested. "She's
a Pelican superstar. And her complexion is flawless.
Still… I don't think this was her best category."

"Okay then, on to Kaity." Maggie picked up another
essay and began reading. "'Hidden in the depths of
Grove Hall Plantation is a secret room. What part in
Pelican's history did it play? Was it used for passion-
ate affairs of the heart and an adulterous rendezvous?'"
Maggie continued to read as Kaity painted a lustful por-
trait of a couple sneaking off for an illicit assignation.
There was silence when she finished.

"Mercy," Mo said, fanning herself.

"Yeah, I think I need a cigarette," Robbie joked.

"Whether or not she wins the contest, Kaity has a
great future career as a romance writer," Maggie said.
She put down Kaity's essay and picked up Allie's.
"'How the Past Informs the Present, by Allie Randall.
Teenagers tend to live in the moment. We may look
forward, but we rarely look back. History is something
that happened to our parents and grandparents. It has no
effect on our lives—or so we think. But history is how
we learn not to make mistakes. The legendary Ameri-

can playwright Eugene O'Neill once wrote, 'There is no present or future, only the past happening over and over again.' But in Pelican, we've learned that doesn't have to be true…'" Instead of writing an essay about Doucet, Allie had broadened the topic into an examination of Pelican itself, citing specific historical events that created change in the little village, from the ugly days of slavery to a recent spate of offensive graffiti. As Maggie neared the end, she found herself choking up and cleared her throat. "'We should never ignore the past. We should never rewrite the past. We should study it and use what we learn to build a better future.'"

Robbie and Mo burst into spontaneous applause. Mo wiped tears from her eyes. Maggie decided that if titles were bestowed upon the judges, the Veevay saleswoman was a lock for Most Emotional. "That piece of writing made me fall in love with this crazy ol' town all over again," Mo said.

Robbie nodded. "What she said," he concurred, choked up.

Maggie smiled. "Agreed. We have a winner," she said, holding up Allie's essay.

MAGGIE WAS AWARDED the task of notifying Belle and Kaity that Allie had won the essay contest. In return, Belle texted back, "Happy for her," and Kaity sent a series of confetti emojis. Allie responded with a simple "Thank you," but it was accompanied by a smiley face. Her mother, Denise, called Maggie and blubbered her happiness. "I'm so proud of my baby," she sobbed. Then she added, "And I'm sure this counts for a lot toward the title of queen." Maggie responded with a polite "We wish her the best of luck," and prided herself on coming up with such an innocuous response.

After finishing the call with Denise, Maggie hopped into her convertible for the short trip across the river to Doucet. When she got to the plantation, Maggie pulled into a parking space next to a HomeNHearth truck. On the walk to her workroom, she noticed workmen seemed to outnumber guests at the historic site. She detoured to Gaynell's workspace. After exchanging hugs, she asked her friend, "What's going on? What's with all the workmen from HomeNHearth?"

"Neighbors reported seeing flashlights around here at night. Ione's upgrading our security system. Anyway, I'm glad you stopped here—I've got a surprise for you." Gaynell retrieved what looked like a pair of baggy pajamas from her dress rack. They were fire-engine red and trimmed with rows of fringe in a riotously colored pattern. A matching hat that looked a dunce cap dangled from the hanger; its bright red base was barely visible under rows of colored fringe. "It's your Courir de Mardi Gras costume," Gaynell said. "It'll be done in a day or two. We're gonna have so much fun on the Run!"

"Laissez le Courir de Mardi Gras rouler," Maggie said, laughing.

Gaynell pumped her arms in the air and did a little dance. "Amen! Let the Run roll!"

Maggie left for her own workspace, where she readied supplies for the day. She'd arranged for Whitney to drop off Xander after being forced to cut short their last session short because of the attempt on Constance Damboise's life. A few minutes later, Whitney showed up with Xander in tow. Bo's ex looked as willowy and beautiful as ever, but Maggie saw sadness in her eyes.

Maggie ushered Xander to the mask-making area of the space. "Here you go, buddy. Your mama and I need to talk a minute." Whitney followed Maggie into the hallway. "Bo told me about what happened. I'm so sorry."

"Thank you." Whitney's lower lip quivered. "It's not the first time either. But Zach and I are going to keep trying. He's excited about growing our family. That was always a problem for Bo and me."

Maggie got a queasy feeling in her stomach, a sensation that was becoming way too familiar. "Bo didn't want more children?"

"No. He felt it would be too much for Xander, especially with the unpredictability of Bo's schedule. But that was then, Maggie. And I think the truth is that unconsciously we both knew our marriage was in trouble. I was doing the thing where you think a child will save it. He was being way smarter about it. I wouldn't worry about it in terms of your relationship. I'm sorry I said anything—it wasn't right. Really. Anyway, I'll come by for Xander in a couple of hours."

"No worries. I can drop him off when I leave work."

"Thank you. And please—forget I said anything. Your situation isn't mine."

Whitney turned and walked down the hall. Maggie knew there was no way she'd be able to forget what Bo's ex-wife had shared. *But for Xander's sake, I have to shelve it, at least for now.* She took a deep breath and returned to her studio, where she forced herself to focus on work. Stopping to take a break, she downed a bottle of water and wandered over to where Xander had finished a mask. He handed it to Maggie. Bottle caps formed the eyes, and wax lips the mouth. White carpet scraps served as bushy eyebrows, and a battered old kitchen drawer knob was the nose. Xander's creation was the perfect combination of creepy and amusing. "Xander, this is wonderful. Can I wear it on the Run?"

Xander gave a slight nod, the ever-present serious expression on his face.

"Thank you." Maggie impulsively reached down and hugged him. He tensed slightly but didn't pull away, marking more progress in their relationship. She released him and put the mask on a shelf so the adhesive could finish drying. "How about we go to the café and grab us some chewy pralines? We get them from Bon Bon Sweets, and they are delish, I *gar-on-tee.*"

She led Xander to the small Doucet café, where she bought them each a pecan praline and soda. They sat outside at a white wrought iron café table, watching swans glide across the plantation's pond. The weather was unseasonably warm, a humid harbinger of summer days to come. A blast from Trombone Shorty alerted Maggie to an incoming phone call. "We were just eating your chewy pralines," Maggie told the caller, her cousin Lia. "As usual, they're a heavenly test of my fillings."

"I'm so glad. I've been taste testing while on bed rest to make sure the substitute candy and pastry chefs at the stores are keeping up the quality. Is there a chance you could do me a small favor? Kyle's delivering a batch of pastries to Belle Vista for their weekend brunch. Pauline left me paint samples at Grove Hall, and I promised I'd pick a few today for her to try out. If there's any way you could grab them and drop them by, that'd be so helpful."

"Consider it done."

Maggie ended the call, to the effusive thanks of Lia. She and Xander followed the path to Maggie's car. "Top down?" she asked the boy. He gave a slight nod, but his eyes lit up. She pressed the button that lowered the old convertible's top, and they buckled in and then took off for Xander's house, the wind whipping their hair and faces.

After depositing Xander with his mother, Maggie drove on to Grove Hall. She took the back roads, which passed homes most affected by the floods. A few sat forlorn and semi-abandoned, but most showed at least glimmers of life. Maggie resolved to renew her volunteer efforts once Mardi Gras was over; she'd ask Jayden to teach her a few simple construction skills she could put to use in the rebuilding efforts.

She parked in the circular driveway fronting Grove Hall and let herself in. She found the paint samples in the entry foyer and picked them up. She started for the front door. Then she paused. A sudden instinct motivated her to reverse course and hasten up the mansion's cypress staircase.

When she reached the second-floor landing, she closed her eyes, trying to recall the path that led to the home's secret room. The day's fading light didn't help her task, so she resorted to feeling the walls of each bedroom until she found the outline of a hidden door. She gently pressed on it, and the door opened. Maggie stepped inside. The secret room was no longer bare. Trash and a few empty liquor bottles littered the floor. An old blanket lay rolled up in a corner. *I think I know where Kaity got the inspiration for her steamy essay*, she thought. Maggie hoped against hope that whatever assignation the girl had arranged was with someone other than Jayden. The last thing the struggling vet needed was to be caught in Gin's furious crosshairs.

Please let him be too smart to fool around with an underage, oversexed teen.

Maggie noticed a plastic bag among the trash. She picked it up and began stuffing it with fast-food wrappers and liquor bottles. She'd alert Kyle to the situation, but figured if the trespassing kids came back to a clean room before he had a chance to change the locks, they'd know they'd been busted. As she cleaned, Maggie wondered what drove people to hide aspects of their lives. She was in a room built almost two hundred years ago to shelter a family secret, now being used for clandestine assignations. There was the painting at Doucet, almost as old, hiding what might be a map. And then there was Gerard Damboise and his last words: "Lies. Secrets."

She thought about his murder and the attempt on Constance's life; evidence now pointed to the couple being victims connected to a surprisingly controversial exhibit. Robbie Metz mentioned the last orphan train had come to Cajun Country in 1929. Was there something linked to that historic event that the murderer wanted to hide?

With the only light in the room coming from the sunset's last flash, Maggie rushed to finish filling the trash bag. The dark, silent house spooked her. She dashed down the stairs and out of Grove Hall, tossing the bag into the workmen's dumpster before getting into her car. As she drove away, Maggie released a breath she didn't realize she'd been holding in. Her phone rang, and she pressed a button on her Bluetooth to answer the call.

"Hey, *chére*, it's your mama," Ninette said. "Are you on your way home?"

"Yes, I should be there in less than ten. Is everything okay?"

"Oh yes." Ninette's voice was measured. "But we're having a service for your father's pot."

"We're having a *what*?"

"A service."

"You mean like a funeral?"

"Yes."

"For a pot?"

"Just come home. And soon."

Ninette ended the call, missing Maggie's groan. Maggie speed-dialed Lia, who picked up on the first ring. "Hey, it's me. I'm dropping off your paint samples, but I can't stay for a visit. I have to go home and attend a funeral for cookware."

She relayed the saga of the ill-fated cast iron pot, and to her surprise, Lia burst into tears. "I have such great memories of your dad's gumbo," her cousin sobbed. "Then again, I also have more hormones than a mama elephant, so that could account for my being so upset about a beat-up old pot."

"Yeah, hormones would get my vote."

"But think about it, Maggie. How would you feel if Grandpa Doucet's convertible died and had to go to the junkyard?"

Maggie clutched the steering wheel of her beloved vintage Falcon. "Don't even *say* that. But I see what you mean."

"Kyle can come by for the samples. Go home. Your dad needs you."

"Okay," Maggie said, choked up. "I will." And to her surprise, *she* began to cry.

MAGGIE AND NINETTE watched solemnly as Tug dropped a final shovel of dirt on the departed cast iron pot, now resting peacefully under a centuries-old magnolia tree. "I know you both think I've gone cuckoo, but I couldn't bring myself to toss it in the garbage. Didn't seem right."

"Oh, *chér*, I know." Ninette put her arms around her husband. "I'd give anything to have that old pot back and you banging around my kitchen, getting in my way, judging my gumbo against yours."

"It'll happen. I just need time." Tug hugged his wife back. Then he picked up the lantern lighting the area.

"Dad, wait." Maggie reached into a bag by her side and pulled out a small cast iron pot. "Remember this? You got it for me when I was little so I could pretend to cook alongside you. I'd like to donate it as a marker."

"Thank you, sweet girl." Tug took the small pot from Maggie and placed it on top of the fresh mound. "I could use a drink."

"I think we all could," Ninette quickly responded.

The threesome retreated to the manor house front parlor. "Anyone hungry?" Ninette asked. "I can start a holy trinity and see where it leads." She sometimes enjoyed cooking up the Cajun trifecta of celery, green pepper, and onions, then letting inspiration strike.

"I'm having dinner with Bo," Maggie said. She checked the room's walnut grandfather clock for the time. "He was supposed to be here ten minutes ago. I better give him a call." Maggie stepped onto the veranda and speed-dialed the detective.

"Hey." Bo sounded tired and distracted.

"Hi there. Dinner tonight? Remember?"

Bo groaned. "Ugh, I'm so sorry. I've been working on the Damboise case—cases."

"Any progress?"

"There's no evidence of unexplained deposits in

Gerard's accounts, which rules out blackmail. Ballistics shows the bullet he was shot with came from Constance's pistol, but there's no evidence to show she killed him and then tried to kill herself but chickened out. And there's no evidence pointing to another suspect, so what we've got right now is a whole lotta nothin'."

Maggie heard the frustration in his voice. "*Chér*, you need a break. Instead of going out, why don't you come by here? I can mix you a drink, make you something to eat. Throw in a nice, relaxing back massage."

"I'm sorry. I'm not good company tonight. When I finish here at the station, I have a bunch of insurance paperwork for FEMA I have to go through. Maybe tomorrow night."

The *maybe* cut through Maggie's heart. "Bo... I think we need to talk."

There was a long pause and then a sigh. "I know."

Maggie ended the call before he could get out what she could only assume would be a perfunctory "I love you." The cell phone fell to the veranda floor as she dropped her face into her hands.

After a moment, she wiped away tears, picked up her phone, and went into the house. She walked down the hall to the Rose Room and gently tapped on the door. *"Venir en,"* Gran' called from inside. "Come in."

Maggie stepped into the room, where her *grand-mère* was sitting up in bed, reading. "Are you still contagious?"

"Given the amount of antibiotics I've been pumped with, I certainly hope not."

Maggie walked to the bed and kicked off her shoes. She crawled in next to Gran', who closed her book and placed it on the nightstand. She stroked Maggie's hair. "Do you hate when people say, 'This too shall pass?'"

"A thousand percent."

"Then I won't say it."

Gran' began humming a French lullaby. Maggie snuggled closer to her and was slowly lulled into a deep, deep sleep.

MAGGIE WOKE UP early in the morning next to her *grand-mère*, feeling unexpectedly refreshed. She might lack solutions to any of her dilemmas, but at least she had the energy to face down the day. Gran' was still asleep, so Maggie carefully extricated herself from the bed. She treated herself to a morning jog, returned to the shotgun cottage for a shower, and then strode back to the manor house. As she stepped inside, she heard the B and B's landline ringing, and ran into the office to answer the call. "Crozat Plantation Bed and Breakfast. May I help you?" she said in her sunniest voice.

"Uh, yeah. This is going to sound weird." The caller was male, and from the timbre of his voice, Maggie guessed he was in his late twenties or early thirties. "I'm trying to track down a guy named Ira Stein and wondered if he might be staying at your place."

"No, we don't have any guests checked in at the moment."

The caller uttered an explitive. "Sorry, my bad. I know he was going to your neighborhood, and I've tried a ton of places in the area. He was supposed to be back a week ago and never showed. I don't know how to find him. I kept telling him, it's the twenty-first century—get a cell. Even if it's one of those Jitterbug phones with big numbers for old dudes. Anyway, thanks. I'll keep looking."

"Wait—don't hang up." Maggie felt a frisson of excitement. "Mr. Stein's an old dude? Can you describe what he was wearing? I mean, generally wore?"

"I dunno. Old guy stuff. You know, ratty pants, old guy sweaters. He kind of had a 'Hey, remember the eighties look' going. Do you know him?"

"I think I do."

"Awesome. If you see Ira, tell him to find a phone and call Max. I need to know how much longer I should keep watering his plants."

Every nerve in Maggie's body pulsed. "Max, if Mr. Stein is who I think he is, you can keep the plants. He won't be coming home to water them."

SEVENTEEN

Maggie burst out of the back door and ran outside to her parents, who were weeding Ninette's organic garden. "Our John Doe has a name," she called to them.

Ninette gasped and Tug dropped his trowel. "Who—what—how?" he sputtered.

Maggie filled them in on her conversation with Max, which had continued after she'd alerted him to his neighbor's death. "Ira lived in New York on the Upper West Side. One of those five-floor walkups where millennials pay a fortune and old-timers like Ira pay practically nothing. Max said he was a total curmudgeon who worked at the lower Manhattan Department of Motor Vehicles office until he retired, and seemed to have no friends or family. But he was obsessed with genealogy. I'm sure it's our guy. I have to let Bo know."

She ran back into the house and called the Pelican PD station. "Bo's not here today," Artie Belloise told her, with a full mouth as usual. Maggie wondered if there was ever a time Artie *wasn't* eating.

"Then I need to talk to Rufus."

"Not here either. Try 'em at Ru's house. We were hanging out there last night."

"Thanks, Artie."

Maggie ended the call. Then she made a decision. She ran down the hall to the Rose Room and threw open the door, startling Gran'. "Heavens, child. I'd prefer not to add a stroke to my list of ailments."

"Sorry, but it's important. I know who the man was that we found dead in the bayou after the flood. Mom and Dad can fill you in. Tell them I ran over to Bo and Ru's."

She was gone before Gran' could respond.

MAGGIE PULLED UP in front of Rufus's home, a double-wide trailer next to the skeleton of La Plus Belle, a Mc-Mansion he and Vanessa had been building before she left him at the altar. Maggie gave the trailer door a hard knock. She heard footsteps, and a minute later, Rufus, clad in gym shorts and a grandpa tank tee, opened the door. "Hey," he said, his face registering surprise. "Why the visit? You couldn't reach Bo by phone? It's probably buried in here somewhere." Rufus gestured to the trailer's living room behind him, which looked like a party tornado had blown through.

"I need to talk to both of you," Maggie said.

"Okay." Rufus turned around and hollered down the hallway behind him. "Paul Beauregard Durand, company!"

"Hey Ru, any chance you could teach your pals how to tell the difference between a bathtub and a trash can?" Bo's cranky voice came from the trailer's bathroom. He appeared, holding a bag full of empty beer cans. Like Rufus, he was surprised to see Maggie. Unlike his cousin, the look on Bo's face also conveyed an unusual blend of pleasure and discomfort. "Maggie. Hi. What—"

"This isn't a social call," she said, cutting him off. "John Doe is Ira Stein." Rufus uttered a stunned expletive, and Bo tossed aside the trash bag. She had their full attention. "He's—was—a senior citizen from Manhattan. His neighbor, a guy named Max, has been trying to track him down. Ira told him he was coming to our area to visit family, which surprised Max since he'd always found Ira to be a loner. It was family Ira never knew he had; he tracked them down through genealogy research. Max has been watering his plants. He's got keys to Ira's apartment."

Bo and Rufus exchanged a look. "We need to go to New York," Bo said. Rufus nodded. "I'll call Perske, then NYPD and tell them to secure Stein's apartment."

Bo disappeared down the hall, leaving Maggie with Rufus. "Nice work," he said.

"It's more about luck. I happened to answer when Max called." Maggie picked up the trash bag Bo had discarded and began filling it. "Might as well make myself useful while we're waiting. By the way, Ru, if you were thinking your recent party lifestyle would be a great way to complicate my relationship with Bo, job well done."

"Hold up. That's the exact opposite of my plan." Rufus tossed more beer cans into Maggie's bag.

"Plan?"

"I mean, don't get me wrong—I'm having a great time. But I've been trying to push Bo *into* your arms, not out of them."

"Seriously?"

"Yeah. I figured if things were bad enough here, he'd be forced to move in with you."

"How romantic," Maggie said dryly.

"He's got this bug up his butt about everything being 'perfect.' That's a lotta pressure to put on a relationship. I've never tried to be perfect in a relationship."

"So I hear from all your exes," Maggie said. Rufus gave her a good-natured light punch in the arm. Their relationship had improved to the point where the two former enemies could kid with each other. "But really, thank you. Although I don't think perfection is the issue anymore. The problem is much bigger than that."

Rufus gave her a quizzical look, but any further conversation was cut short when Bo returned to the room. "NYPD is in, and Perske okayed both of us going. We've got some planning to do, coz."

"I'm on it."

Ru took off down the hall. Bo turned to Maggie. "This could be a game changer, *chére*." He gave her a quick kiss on the lips. "I'll talk to you before I go."

Maggie nodded and then left the trailer so Bo and Rufus could focus on trip preparations. She began the drive toward Crozat, stopping for a red light where the River Road intersected with the road leading to I-10. She saw Lee Bertrand's pickup truck waiting at the light, pointed in the opposite direction. She waved, but he was deep in conversation with a passenger. The light changed, and as the two vehicles passed each other, Maggie glanced at the passenger side of Lee's car and caught a glimpse of silver-white hair. She almost lost control of her car before pulling to the side of the road. *Was that Gran'?*

She executed a U-turn and followed Lee's truck, keeping as much distance as she could without losing him. Driving a beautifully detailed vintage convertible made undercover work tricky. Lee traveled down the River Road for another fifteen minutes, then crossed the Mississippi and headed west. Ten minutes later, he pulled into the parking lot of the Three Bird Café and

Dance Hall. Locals loved "The Bird" because it served a reasonably priced breakfast buffet all day and offered dancing in morning, afternoon, and evening slots. Maggie checked the time on her phone. The Bird's morning dance hour had just begun.

Maggie parked and went inside the café. Tables were filled with patrons enjoying the buffet while a few couples danced to a local zydeco band playing "Louisiana Two-Step." Lee was already on the dance floor. He nimbly executed a turn with his dance partner—Gran'. Maggie approached the twirling couple and tapped Lee on the shoulder. "Mind if I cut in?"

Lee, looking like a kid caught with his hand in the cookie jar, slunk away. Gran' stood frozen. Maggie took one of Gran's hands in hers, put her other hand around her *grand-mère*'s waist, and continued the dance. "Hello."

"Hello."

Maggie twirled her *grand-mère*. "Anything you want to tell me?"

"Not particularly."

"Oh, I think there is."

"Fine."

The song ended. Gran' marched to a nearby table, head held high, and took a seat. Maggie followed her. Lee hovered over the buffet, making a show of filling his plate while stealing glances at the women. "All right, I'll come clean," Gran' said. "I began feeling better after a day or two of the antibiotics. But every time I considered resuming judging, I began to relapse. That's when I realized it took becoming ill to get me out of that infernal pageant judging. It's a miserable business, and I simply don't want to do it. At least not this year."

"Believe me, I get that. But you could have been honest with me instead of sneaking out like a teenager."

"I have to admit, the sneaking out part was fun," Gran' said with an impish grin. "I'm sorry I didn't share this with you sooner, Magnolia. I've been properly chastised and will resume my judging duties."

"Apology accepted. But I don't want you to be a judge. For one thing, you probably need more rest, which is why Lee is to bring you home as soon as you finish brunch." Maggie ignored her *grand-mère*'s pout. "Also, it's too dangerous. Gerard dead, Constance attacked…if Little Earlie hadn't published the story about the orphan train exhibit being on hold like I asked him to, anyone who supported it could have been next, including you. Judging gives you too high a profile. It's better to keep you out of it."

"Honestly, people in a small town have way too much time on their hands if a tiny exhibit at a podunk historical society can trigger such mayhem."

"It can and it has. So no judging this year." Maggie wagged a finger at her *grand-mère*. "And no dancing either until you're completely better."

"Yes, ma'am."

Maggie stood up. "I have to go to work. I'll see you later."

Gran' took Maggie's hands and held them to her heart. Her pale blue eyes were clouded with worry. "Promise me you'll be careful, *chére*. Much as you worry about me, I worry about you."

"I promise." Maggie kissed her *grand-mère* on the cheek and then left the couple to their meal.

On her way to Doucet, Maggie got a call from Whitney. "Xander wanted to work on the masks so much, he made me take him over to Doucet early. I checked with your boss, and she said it was okay if I stayed with him until you got here. I haven't let him touch anything."

"I'm almost there. And tell him if he wants to start without me, he can. He knows what to do."

Moments later, Maggie pulled into the Doucet employee parking lot and found a spot next to the ever-present HomeNHearth truck. On the way to her workspace, she passed Mike Randall, who waved to her. She stopped to greet him. "Hi, Mike. Are you part of the HomeNHearth security crew?"

"Yup. I go where they send me. Hey, thanks for throwing that essay contest Allie's way."

"I didn't 'throw' anything anywhere. She did a great job on it. Your daughter's a talented writer."

"She is?" Maggie wasn't shocked this came as a surprise to Mike. She had a feeling there was a lot he didn't know about Allie. He struck her as the kind of man who'd always dreamed of having a son and didn't quite know what to do with a daughter. "I wasn't much for school. I check out Allie's report cards and I'm like, *holy moly*. But anyway, thanks."

Mike returned to work, and Maggie followed the path to her Doucet studio. Xander was in the middle of assembling a new mask while his mother looked on, a bemused expression on her face. "Is it me, or are these masks a little macabre?" Whitney whispered to Maggie.

Maggie chuckled. "They are. They're meant to disguise the wearer's identity and maybe scare people a little, but in a fun way."

Whitney wrinkled her nose. "I guess it's not my idea of fun."

After giving her son a kiss goodbye, Whitney took

off. Maggie filled a bowl with water and warmed it on the hot plate she'd asked Ione to install in the room for her. She dipped a rag in the water. With the rag in one hand and her scalpel in the other, she set to work on the painting. Having grown more comfortable with the restoration process, she moved quickly. Tour guides continued to stop by with their groups of plantation visitors. One guest, an art historian, shared how using a canvas twice was not uncommon among artists. "The term 'starving artist' isn't just a trope," he said. "Financially, if an artist doesn't mind sacrificing one work, it saves the cost buying a new canvas to paint over it." Having been a starving artist herself, Maggie seconded his comment.

Younger tourists gravitated toward Xander's masks. One teen, a sullen-looking boy clearly dragged on the tour by his parents, fixated on a mask that looked like a rudimentary skull. "That would make an awesome tattoo," the teen said.

"Not happening," came the instant response from his mother. She rolled her eyes and pulled him away to continue the tour.

By the time Maggie and Xander broke for lunch, she'd exposed more than a third of the hidden work of art. "We're both making good progress today, buddy," she told Xander as she pulled his *Star Wars*—themed lunch bag from the room's mini fridge. Xander didn't respond. She saw he was staring at the painting. "What?" Xander pointed at a rectangle above the end of the path Maggie's efforts had revealed. "You think that's important?" Xander nodded. She put down the lunch bag, picked a rag, and dipped it in the bowl of lukewarm water.

A half hour later, she and Xander stepped back to analyze what she'd uncovered. "Those are the front steps of the manor house," Maggie said. "That's where the path stops. You see that pattern of X's on the top step? Those aren't there on the real front steps."

A thought occurred to Maggie. She searched the photos she'd taped around the room of the original painting until she found the one she wanted. *"Grata sit calidum, et de fisco,'"* she read. "I need to look that up."

She pulled out her cell phone and found a translation app, which she quickly downloaded. She then typed in the Latin phrase and pressed "Translate."

"'A warm and welcome treasure,'" she read. "You were right, buddy. This *is* a treasure map. And I think we just discovered where that treasure might be buried."

EIGHTEEN

IONE CAME TO the studio as soon as Maggie alerted her to the possibility of treasure on the premises. She studied the painting thoughtfully. "So, you think this indicates your ancestors buried something important under the manor house front steps?" Ione asked.

"Yes. Of course I need to keep going and see what else my restoration reveals. It may mark the port of entry or the location. I won't know for sure until I reveal more of the underlying painting, but the X's are telling."

"Who knows about this?"

"Just Xander and me."

"Don't tell anyone else. Last thing we need is for word to get out. Every treasure hunter in the state will be digging up this pea patch. We're taking you off the tour. From now on, keep the door closed when you're working." Ione bent down to be eye level with Xander. "Son, you can keep a secret, can't you?" Xander gave a solemn nod, and she smiled. "I figured as much, but I wanted to be sure. No telling anyone about what all's going on here. Promise?" Xander gave another nod and crossed his heart to confirm. Ione turned to Maggie. "The timing couldn't be better regarding security. Since HomeNHearth is already here, I'll have them install extra alerts on the windows and doors of this room."

"Good idea."

Ione left to track down the HomeNHearth security

team. Maggie took a rag and handed it to Xander. "This would go faster if I had some help. You've been watching me since the beginning. But it's an important job, Xander. Tell me the truth—do you think you can do it?"

Xander's eyes lit up. "Yes," he said with authority.

He took the rag, dipped it in water, and carefully began removing the old watercolor painting with great precision, exposing more of what lay underneath. Maggie watched with affection. Naysayers might scoff at entrusting the task to a child, but she knew Xander's ability to hyper-focus made him the perfect candidate for the job.

The two worked side by side for the rest of the afternoon, stopping only for snacks. By the end of the day, they'd begun to uncover a rendering of the Doucet Manor house. Maggie intertwined her fingers and stretched her arms above her head. They ached from hours of repetitive motion. She rung out the rags and hung them over a laundry rack to dry. "Alrighty, buddy, let's get you over to your dad's. He has to go to New York for a case tonight and wants to see you before he leaves."

Maggie drove Xander over to Rufus's double-wide. When they stepped inside, the difference was astounding. Gone was all evidence of partying. The place was meticulous. Three-month-old Charlotte Elizabeth Diana Durand slept peacefully in a bassinet that rocked automatically. A lullaby tinkled from a mobile of tiny, happy wooden animals.

Bo came down the hallway from his temporary bedroom. He broke into a wide grin when he saw his son. "Hey, little buddy." Xander allowed himself to be scooped up in a hug. Bo kissed Maggie on the cheek while still holding on to his son. "Thanks for bringing him by. And yourself as well."

Maggie had to smile at this, despite the questionable state of their relationship. "How long do you think you'll be gone?"

Bo let go of Xander and gave a "you got me" shrug. "NYPD spoke to Max, the guy who called you. He warned them Stein's apartment is a hoarder's paradise. No idea how long it'll take to go through everything until we find any clue as to who killed him."

The front door opened, and Rufus came in carrying one small and one large shopping bag. "Hey there, hi there, ho there," he greeted them. "Thanks for watching Charli, coz. I did a little last-minute shopping for our trip." Rufus reached into the bigger bag and pulled out a brown leather jacket, which he put on and modeled. "Do I look like a New York hipster?"

"Think you'd have to do some searching in New York to find a hipster with a jambalaya gut," Bo said.

"You'll be sorry for that comment when I don't share these guidebooks with you." Rufus pulled two books out of the second bag. "Especially this—*Best of the City*. Best pizza, best Chinese food, best clubs. And there are so many good museums they can't pick a 'best of.' I've never been to a museum before. I'm thinking I might go to this MOMA. Although that's a little sexist if you ask me. Where's the DADA museum?" Rufus reached into the bassinet and stroked his sleeping daughter's tiny head. "Ain't that right, princess?"

"Rufus, MOMA stands for Museum of Modern Art," Maggie said, suppressing a laugh. "And there was an avant-garde movement called Dada—or Dadaism—in the early twentieth century. It rejected the increasing growth of capitalist society."

Rufus made a face. "Modern art? Forget it. That stuff's a scam. Looks like a five-year-old's finger paintings. And I'd be happy to see a little capitalist growth in my paycheck."

"This isn't a vacation," Bo admonished his cousin. "We're trying to nail a murderer."

"Yeah, well, we still gotta eat. And no more scolding me, or I won't share where the best Chinese food is."

Rufus wheeled the bassinet down the hall to his bedroom. "I better finish packing," Bo said. He leaned toward Maggie and paused. Then he gently kissed her on the lips. "I'll let you know as soon as I learn anything."

Maggie nodded, and Bo headed down the hall, holding Xander's small hand. Maggie watched until they disappeared into Bo's room, and then left the trailer. The night was dark, with the moon blacked out by clouds. She walked to her car, pulled open the Falcon's heavy door, and got in. She put the key in the ignition and began driving. But not toward home; instead, she drove to the Historical Society.

The parking lot in front of the old factory was empty and silent. Maggie quelled her nerves as she fished the spare key from Constance out of her purse. She slipped it into the door's lock and stepped inside the dark building. She flipped a switch, and a bank of fluorescent lights sputtered on, offering an unflattering glow, more interrogation room than hallowed hall.

Maggie walked toward the back office, glancing at display cases filled with Pelican ephemera. Photos, maps, and descriptions of the photos and maps hung on cushioned room dividers doing their best to separate exhibits. Despite the Society's makeshift nature, Maggie felt a surge of pride in her hometown's past, especially when she passed a display case featuring items her family had donated from Crozat and Doucet. But Mo was right. No items anywhere paid homage to the underbelly of Pelican's history. And Gerard had kept to his stubborn promise that there be no evidence of the controversial orphan train.

Maggie located the Society's office and found her key also opened its door. She stepped inside. Two old, battered desks sat facing each other in the middle of the room. Each was piled with folders. Tall file cabinets lined every wall, and on top of each was a stack of memorabilia. Maggie wilted at the thought of wading through the endless array of material.

A thought occurred to her. *One of these desks must belong to Constance Damboise.* Identifying the desk that *didn't* belong to the widow was easy. On the one facing the door, Maggie noticed a nameplate reading "Gerard Damboise, President." Maggie immediately sat down at the opposite desk, which proved to be Constance's, and began sorting through files. She found nothing. *But Gerard was against the orphan train exhibit, so maybe Constance would have kept any material on it in a less obvious place*, she mused. Maggie pulled out a bottom drawer and thumbed through alphabetically organized hanging files. She found nothing under "O," and began to think she was on a fool's errand. Then she spotted one marked "Miscellaneous." She reached into it and extracted a fat, unmarked folder. She opened the folder and smiled. Inside was a typed manuscript titled "New Beginnings: A History of the Cajun Country Orphan Train." The author was Constance Damboise. Maggie glanced at a few of the pages. Not only had Constance supported the idea of the exhibit, she'd researched the lives of the trains' young passengers. Maggie began to read.

An hour later, she was still absorbed in the foundlings' stories. Most had come from an orphanage in New York to a strange rural land where French, not their native English, was the dominant language. Many adapted and thrived. Others never made the transition and died prematurely from disease or drink. Some returned to the orphanage, eventually finding homes in the New York area. Constance had detailed the lives of most of the foundlings—marriages and divorces; spinsterhood or bachelorhood; infertility or scores of children and grandchildren, great-, and great-great-grandchildren. But a few children seemed to have arrived and disappeared, their fate a mystery. Maggie's instincts told her the clue to Gerard's death lay with the missing children. If she or Pelican PD managed to track down what happened to them, they might find the link to his killer.

She leaned back in the old rolling desk chair and wiped perspiration from her brow with the back of her hand. The office air was stultifying. Maggie thought about Ira Stein. Could he be one of the lost orphans? Then she remembered a snippet from her conversation with his neighbor Max that had slipped by her in the excitement of the moment. Ira had recently celebrated his eightieth birthday with a few of his apartment mates, who were bonded in the odd way apartment living in New York City brought strangers together. The last orphan train had rolled into St. Pierre Parish in 1929. The youngest infant foundling, should he or she still be alive, would be in the neighborhood of ninety years old. At eighty, Ira was too young to be one of the orphans.

Maggie noticed a copy machine in the far corner of the office and decided to copy the short list of children no one had traced. She turned on the ancient machine, which wheezed to life after a long wait, and began copying. The copier was so loud she didn't hear the office door open and close behind her. Maggie finished her task. She then turned around and screamed.

She was face-to-face with Constance Damboise. And Constance had a gun trained on her—one much larger than a purse pistol.

NINETEEN

"C-C-Constance," Maggie stammered. "I—I—"

"Oh my goodness, it's just you, Maggie." Constance uncocked the gun and stuck it in her purse. "This gun was Gerard's. It's much bulkier than my purse pistol. The police are still holding onto that one as evidence, but with what all's been going on, I wasn't going to be without protection. Forewarned is forearmed as they say. And I *will* be armed. Now why exactly are you here?"

Maggie collapsed into a chair, her heart thumping. "I thought you were still in the hospital."

"I despise hospitals. They're like roach motels. Seniors check in, but they don't check out. I managed to convince my medical team I was doing so much better they could release me. I wanted to stop by and check on the Society, and when I found the door unlocked, I feared we had an intruder. You still haven't told me why you're skulking around the Society office."

"I was looking for information about the orphan train." Maggie, skittish about trusting Constance, kept her explanation as vague as possible.

"Have you discovered anything?"

Maggie debated her next move. She stood up again and leaned against the desk, her pose expressing a relaxed manner diametrically opposed to what she felt. But it positioned her to knock Constance off balance should the woman try to pull the gun out of her purse. Then Maggie took a chance. "I discovered your manuscript. And I can see why you and Robbie are so committed to the exhibit. The children's stories are fascinating."

Constance smiled. "Thank you. And I'm glad you've come on board, train pun intended." She winked, and Maggie relaxed a bit. "What were you looking for specifically? I don't buy for a minute this was some casual, spur-of-the-moment visit to the Society."

"I think there's a connection between the children who came to Pelican on the train, Gerard's death, and the attempt on your life. My gut is telling me the past is affecting the present." It dawned on Maggie she was paraphrasing Allie's essay. "I'm particularly interested in the lost children. At least that's what I'm calling them. You did a wonderful job documenting the lives of the rest of them. But what happened to the ones that seem to have disappeared?"

"I've always wondered that myself. It's rather haunted me. I was going to research those children; then Gerard put the kibosh on the whole exhibit. It was originally his idea, you know. But one day, he did a complete reversal and became the exhibit's biggest adversary."

A spasm of grief crossed Constance's face. It was the first time Maggie had seen the widow express the emotion since she'd lost her husband. Maggie hated to press her, but she had to ask one more, very important question. "Constance, do you happen to remember exactly when Gerard changed his mind? It could be a clue. The police might be able to match the date with an event in his schedule that ties in to his mur—death."

Constance shook her head. "I meant 'one day' as a

figure of speech. It was more insidious than specific. You know, dismissing my plans, finding other tasks to distract me. Then a final veto."

"If you could come up with even a general time frame, it would give the police something to work with. I've found trying to recall the weather around the time of a certain event helps me remember when it happened."

Constance gave a rueful smile. "It's Louisiana. The weather's either humid or less humid, rainy or less rainy. But I'll try. Anything to stop the madness." She rubbed her forehead and winced. "I'm still a bit short on energy thanks to whatever evil brew I ingested. I always planned to visit the Hall of Records and do some research on the missing children. Why don't you hold on to my manuscript? Take it with you to the H of R and see if you can drum up anything about those wee ones based on their birth names."

Maggie clasped the manuscript folder to her chest. "Thank you. I'll do that."

"Good." Constance held the office door open for Maggie. "I'll walk out with you. Oh, and Maggie? I highly recommend getting yourself a purse pistol. You never know what might happen, do you?"

BY THE TIME Maggie got home, she was starving. She was relieved to see her family about to tuck into a late dinner. The evening air was cooled with a slight breeze off the river. On a whim, Maggie decided they should dine al fresco. She set up a folding table and chairs on the manor home's wide veranda, using an heirloom silver candelabra as the centerpiece. She, her parents, and Grand-mère dined on salad, Ninette's oyster soup, and

Fais Dough Dough French bread by the light of flickering candles. For the first time since the Great Flood, the Crozats were able to unwind. But the respite was interrupted by an unmarked police sedan making the turn into the plantation driveway and pulling up in front of the house. Bo got out of the driver's side and then extricated a large shopping bag from the back seat. "I won't be long," he told Rufus, who was sitting in the passenger seat. Bo loped up the front steps. "Evening, all."

The Crozats returned his greeting. "I thought you were flying out tonight," Maggie said.

"We are. We're on the way to the airport. But I wanted to drop something off for your dad." Bo pulled a cast iron pot out of the bag. "We'll be back for Mardi Gras, but there's no way I'm gonna have time to make gumbo and enter the cook-off. This black pot's been in my family for who knows how long. I thought it could replace the one you lost, sir. At least for this year."

Bo handed the pot to Tug, who examined it with awe. He held it up and inhaled a scent ingrained in the iron by years of seasoning. "It's a beauty," he said, his nose still in the pot. "I'll take it for a test drive with my gumbo recipe tomorrow, but I think I found a new friend. Thank you." Tug turned to Maggie but pointed at Bo. "Never let this man go," he said, his voice husky.

Maggie managed a smile. "I'll walk you to the car," she said to Bo. She and the detective stepped away from her family and down the steps for privacy. "I had an interesting meetup with Constance Damboise tonight," Maggie said.

Bo raised an eyebrow, curious. She shared her conversation with the widow. "We have Gerard's datebook," he said once she finished. "If we had an approximate date of when his attitude reversed toward the exhibit, it would be a big help."

"I'll work on it with her while you're gone."

Bo furrowed his brow and thought for a moment. "Those orphan trains left out of New York. I'm convinced there's a link between them and our Mr. Stein, and I mean to find it."

"Be careful, Bo."

"I always am. Anyway, if there's still any work to be done on the Mardi Gras masks, Whitney can bring Xander by after school."

"I'll call her."

"Good. She could use a distraction. She got some bad news. Her doctor said he doesn't think she can get pregnant. Something about her hormone levels."

"I'm so sorry to hear that. I know how much she wanted another baby." There was a brief, awkward pause. Maggie made an impulsive decision. "Bo…do you want more children?"

"Whoa," Bo said, taken aback. "We're having this conversation now?"

"Yes, because there's never a good time lately, and this is as not-a-good time as any. I want children. I do. If I ever had any doubt, the time I've spent with Xander erased it. To see him blossom, to be part of that"—Maggie's eyes welled with tears—"it means more to me than anything. I want two children, so they'll always have each other. I know I may have a romanticized version of siblings, being that I was an only child, but I'm willing to take the chance. And if you're not, I need to know that."

Bo pressed his lips together until they formed a thin line. When he spoke, he chose his words carefully. "It's easy to have a romantic vision of parenthood. The reality can be very different, especially if your child has issues. I'm not saying that would happen—or that I'd love my child any less. I'd die for Xander. He's my heart and soul. But starting again? I have to say, it gives me great pause."

It broke Maggie's heart to articulate her next thought, but she had to: "If we're in different places and there's no room for negotiation, we both need to move on."

Bo gave a frustrated grunt and ran a hand through his thick black hair, mussing it up in a way that only made him sexier, much to Maggie's own frustration. "It's a bad time for me to be making huge decisions. It feels like my life has been spiraling ever since the flood. Work is insane, my living situation is worse— although Ru did stop partying. I don't know why, but I'm grateful for that. But I can't think about the past or future right now. I can only be in the moment. I know that's a non-answer, but it's all I got."

"Okay. We can put it on hold for a little bit. But it's the elephant in the room of our relationship." Maggie shuddered. "Ugh, that sounded like it was from some book of terrible poetry."

Bo broke the tension with a small laugh. "Yeah, it kinda did." There was a pleading look in his eyes. "I do love you, Maggie. Very much."

"I know." Her voice cracked. "And I love you too. Just as muchly."

"More bad poetry."

Bo bent down to kiss Maggie but was thwarted by a car horn blast. "Hey, coz," Ru called from the car. He held up his phone. "I checked the route, and the road's down to one lane in some spots, thanks to flood repairs, so we gotta get going. I need to buy food before we board. I'm guessing they don't sell fine Cajun eats on the airplane."

"Coming." The moment with Maggie interrupted, Bo strode back to the car. He got in, gunned the engine, and drove off at a fast clip. Maggie watched them go.

"Chére," Ninette called to her from the veranda, "your dinner's getting cold."

Maggie hurried up the steps and sat down between her parents. She stared at her oyster soup, appetite gone. Ninette took one of Maggie's hands into her own and gave it a light, comforting squeeze. Tug did the same with her other hand. Gran' got up, walked behind Maggie, and embraced her. *"Tout sera comme il se doit.* Everything will be as it should."

In the morning, after a quick shower and a comfort food breakfast of Ninette's banana pecan pancakes, Maggie decided to visit the Hall of Records, an officious name for a few rooms lodged behind the town's senior center. She received an effusive greeting from village clerk Eula Banks, who was always thrilled for company at the rarely visited civil service office. After the requisite oohing and aahing over photos of Eula's latest grandbaby—"Little Felice makes an even dozen of 'em"—the clerk disappeared into a back room and reappeared with a manila folder she handed to Maggie. "Here you go, darlin'. It's a right thin one."

"Thanks, Eula." Maggie opened the file on Hans Herbig, one of the orphans listed as missing. It contained two pages, yellowed and disintegrating with age, that revealed six-year-old Hans had run away from his adoptive Cajun parents. The resourceful child made it all the way to the Mississippi border before he was recovered and returned to the foundling hospital. An addendum indicated he was subsequently adopted by a family in upstate New York. There was no indication he ever made another run for it. She used her phone camera to photograph the pages, and then handed the file back to the clerk. "Thanks, Eula. Now I need"—Maggie checked her list—"Jacob Seideman and Bridget Colleary."

"You got it."

Eula once again disappeared into the back room. While she was gone, Maggie took a seat at the Hall of Record's ancient computer, logged on to its Wi-Fi, and typed in *Hans Herbig, Amsterdam, New York*. She was rewarded with a search yielding multiple links to Herbig-related activities in the area. Buried among them was a fifty-year-old obit for the elder Herbig himself, who had gone from runaway orphan to pillar of the Amsterdam community. "Good for you, Hans," Maggie said to the computer. She hoped, for their sakes, Jacob's and Bridget's lives had had similar happy endings.

Eula returned from the back room. But instead of folders, she held two slips of paper. "I'm afraid you're out of luck on these two, Maggie. Both files were checked out to Gerard Damboise."

"I didn't know you could do that."

Eula frowned and pursed her lips. "You can't. He must've sweet-talked Delia Dulac, who filled in for me while I was in Alexandria for Little Felice's christening." Maggie had trouble imagining Gerard sweet-talking anyone. A more likely scenario was the bribe of a generous donation to Kitten and Kaboodle, Delia Dulac's feral cat rescue group. "I guess poor Gerard expired before he had a chance to return the files," Eula continued. "They're probably somewhere in his home or office."

"They may be. I'll get in touch with Constance and see if she can find them. Thanks so much, Eula."

"Just doing my job, dear. Oh, and I don't know where you and that detective stand these days, but my son Wiley is still available." Eula gave Maggie an exaggerated wink. Maggie, who had learned through mutual friends that Wiley and his live-in boyfriend were engaged, choked back a snort and politely thanked Eula.

Maggie left the Hall of Records and wandered over to the bench that sat under the ancient, massive oak tree gracing the Pelican village square. She took out her cell and called Constance. The widow wasn't home, so Maggie left a message regarding the missing files. She then texted Bo to see if the files might be in police custody for some reason. A moment later, she received a response from him: "File names not familiar. Will touch base later." Maggie leaned back against the bench and crossed her arms over her chest. *What happened to you, Jacob and Bridget? Why did you disappear?* She thought of Gerard. *What were your secrets?* No answers came to her.

Maggie's musing was disrupted by the Trombone Shorty ringtone, indicating an incoming call. She checked her phone and saw the caller was Ione. "Hi. What's up?"

"I know you're off today, but I need you to come by." Ione sounded upset. "As soon as possible."

Maggie sat up. "Something's wrong, I can hear it in your voice."

"Everyone's okay, but there's been an incident. I don't want to talk about it over the phone."

"I'm on my way."

Maggie ended the call and ran to her car. Five minutes later, she pulled into the Doucet parking lot behind the manor house. A Pelican PD police car straddled two parking spaces. Maggie got out of the Falcon and flagged down Rochelle Abady, one of the plantation's longtime guides, who was leading a group of visitors toward the manor house's back entrance. "Rochelle, have you seen Ione?"

"She's by the front steps," Rochelle said, then added in a whisper, "or what's left of them."

Rochelle herded her group away before Maggie, confused, could press her for more information. Maggie dashed to the front of the manor house and stopped short. Someone had taken an ax to the plantation home's front steps, turning them into a shattered, splintered pile of wood. Ione was in the middle of an animated conversation with Officers Artie Belloise and Cal Vichet, who were taking notes. She saw Maggie and waved her over. "You don't have to ask what happened, do you?" It was a rhetorical question asked in a sober tone.

Maggie, sickened by what she saw, shook her head. "Somebody saw the painting of the map," she said, "and then went on a treasure hunt."

TWENTY

CAL VICHET WAS on his hands and knees, examining a deep hole where the steps once were. "I've done some treasure hunting as a hobby." Cal lifted a handful of dirt to his nose and sniffed it. "I've found a few things, mostly stuff from the War Between the States. Pirate treasure's kept itself safe from me, sad to say. Anyway, I know enough to say nothing's been buried here. If anything was, there'd be elements of it, however tiny. And the soil here would be different because something rested in it for over a hundred and fifty years. Which makes this more a case of vandalism than theft."

"I guess X didn't mark the spot," Maggie said. "Which is relatively good news. Whatever's buried is still here somewhere."

"We're assuming the painting's a map," Ione pointed out.

"It is. Don't ask me why, but I know that in my heart."

"I'm with Maggie," Cal said, adding, "Ione showed us what you've been working on. You keep chipping away at that thing, and you'll find whatever it's hiding."

"In the meantime," Artie said, "we need a list of everyone who's been here the last few days. Employees, visitors, workers—every last person. And perhaps a snack. Physical labor gives me an appetite."

Cal snorted. "Hah. You've been standing there like

a lawn jockey. Only labor you'll see today is lifting a
fork to your mouth."

"Fais Dough Dough delivered fresh pastries for the
café." Ione jumped in to disrupt the sniping. "I'll have
them set up a table for both of you. With coffee." Both
officers brightened and murmured thanks. "If you need
me, I'll be in the gift shop office. Technically, it's Maggie's day off—"

"I'll be here in my studio, continuing the restoration."
The destruction of Doucet property by a greedy potential thief made Maggie more determined than ever to
uncover the painting's secret, and as quickly as possible.

Ione went off to compile the list requested by the officers. Maggie headed for her makeshift studio. As she
unlocked the door, she made a mental note to get the
lock changed. Then she had an idea. She sprinted over
to Ione's office. "I'd like to bring the painting home
and work on it there," she told her boss. "Can you ap-
prove that?"

"Can and will. But let's make sure no one sees it
leaving here. If whoever's after the treasure is still
around and knows you have the painting, you could
be in danger."

"Good point. There's a lot of that going around right
now."

Maggie left Ione's office for the gift shop, where
she grabbed a lap blanket emblazoned with the logo
she'd designed for Doucet. She then returned to her
studio, packed up the supplies she'd need to continue
the restoration, and took them to her car. When that
was done, Maggie took the lap blanket and carefully
wrapped it around the painting. She stepped into the
hallway, glancing in both directions to make sure she

was alone, then sprinted out of the building, continuing to check for curious passersby. Employees were busy leading tours, and any workmen on the property seemed to be at lunch. When she reached her car, Maggie opened the trunk of the Falcon and laid the painting flat on the trunk's floor. The car's red ragtop was down. Eager to make a fast escape, Maggie used a trick her *grand-pére* had taught her when she was a teen. Instead of opening the driver's-side door, she hurdled over it into the front seat. Then she peeled out of the parking lot and took off for home.

As soon as Maggie got to the shotgun cottage, she ran the painting inside and then dashed over to the manor house to help her family check in the guests who were arriving pre–Mardi Gras. All shared how impressed they were with Pelican's comeback from the flood, and the Crozats expressed gratitude for their support by gifting them with complimentary coffee mugs featuring a lovely illustration of the plantation manor house rendered by Maggie.

She was just returning to the kitchen, after serving the new arrivals wine and cheese in the front parlor, when her cell rang with a call from Mo. "Where the aitch-e-double hockey sticks are you?" her fellow judge demanded.

"At home helping my family. Why?"

"You're supposed to be here."

"Where's 'here'?"

"The Pelican High School auditorium. For the evening gown portion of the contest. Get your sugar buns over here. We'll wait for you."

Mo ended the call. Maggie uttered an expletive that

earned her a raised eyebrow from Tug, who was stirring yet another pot of gumbo, this time in Bo's black pot. Steam rose from the pot, and with it the scent of onions, herbs, poultry, and meats. Gran' sat at the kitchen table, sipping a hot toddy, while Ninette stirred a bowl of remoulade sauce to ladle on a shrimp and avocado appetizer. "Sorry, all—my judging duties call. I forgot I have to commit the dated and sexist act of judging how girls look in evening wear."

"Count yourself lucky," Gran' commented. "There used to be a bathing suit portion. You dodged that bullet. Oh dear, a poor choice of words these days."

"Go ahead, *chére*," Ninette said. "We'll be fine without you."

"Thanks, Mom."

Once again, Maggie ran to her car. The River Road was empty of traffic, so she flew to the high school, which lay on the outskirts of town. She parked and raced into the auditorium. It was empty save for the other judges—Constance included—who sat in the front row of the cavernous space. Although Maggie was relieved the contestants didn't have to parade in front of gawking spectators, she'd wondered why the pageant bothered to utilize such a large space. "Makes the girls stand up straight," Mo had said, to which Maggie responded, "Huh?" To which Mo said, "You'll see."

Constance patted the seat next to her. "Come. Sit." Maggie sat down and tried to catch her breath. "Before we start," Constance said, "I wanted to let you know I got your message about those files—the ones for Bridget Colleary and Jacob Seideman. I spent the day searching every location I could think of, but found nothing. I'm afraid I have no idea where they are."

Maggie sighed. "That's frustrating. But thank you for looking."

"Do you think the mur—" Constance stopped, unable to say the word *murderer*. "Do you think whoever sent Gerard to meet his fate might have them?"

Maggie's lips formed a thin line. "I think there's a very strong chance they might."

Mo climbed the stairs to the stage. "Just so y'all know, the evening gown portion is less about beauty and more about highlighting each contestant's personal style. We'll be focusing on what their choices tell us about them, as well as the grace and confidence with which they carry themselves."

Mo gave the contestants, who were in the wings, a high sign and scrambled back to her seat. Belle glided onstage with the élan of a Miss America contestant. Her blonde hair was slicked back in a soft chignon. She wore a pale-blue chiffon evening gown with a lace bodice. The gown was fitted to the waist, and then flared out in a cloud of filmy fabric. "In the days of selfies and reality stars, teens take a risk when they make a traditional choice," Belle said, reciting a prepared speech. "But it's a risk I'm proud to take. The dress I'm wearing belonged to my mother, Pauline Boudreau Tremblay. She wore it when she herself won the crown of Miss Pelican Mardi Gras Gumbo Queen. Whether or not I'm lucky enough to win that title is not the point. The point is that I honor both my mother and a Pelican tradition by wearing this gown. And I promise to take a bigger risk: as much as this moment means to me, I will *not* be taking a selfie and posting it on the Internet."

Belle turned and glided offstage to enthusiastic applause from three of the four judges. Maggie, not wanting to appear petty, joined them halfheartedly. There was a brief pause, and then Kaity Bertrand sashayed onto the stage. "Whoa," Mo couldn't help blurting. Kaity's look was the polar opposite of Belle's. Her hair, curly and wild, was dyed pink at the tips to match the Day-Glo pink of her skintight, mermaid-style satin gown, which featured a slit that ended mid-thigh and a bodice festooned with beads, rhinestones, and sequins. "Hey, y'all," she greeted the judges cheerfully. "All I wanna say is thank you *so* much for giving me an excuse to get my Grammy to buy me this totally kick-butt dress. And FYI, I *will* be taking a whole bunch of selfies and posting them all over the Internet. Hollah!"

Kaity pulled a cell phone out of her cleavage, struck a pose, and snapped a picture. She gave the judges a thumbs-up and practically skipped off stage, or at least did as much skipping as could be accomplished in six-inch, silver platform heels.

"Oh dear," Constance said.

"She gets points for honesty," Robbie said.

Maggie sympathized with Kaity's beleaguered grandmother. There was no way Gin could keep the sassy teen on a short leash.

There was another brief pause, and then Allie came on. Mo was right about the impact of a walk down the stage's pseudo runway. It even took the slouch out of pageant-averse Allie's posture. Her dark hair was styled into a 1920s-style bob. She wore a simple black gown of a shiny material Maggie couldn't place. As Allie wended her way to center stage, the stage lights bounced off her dress. Constance gasped. "Oh my Lord. Is that dress made of *trash bags*?"

"Yes, ma'am, it is," came Allie's voice from the

stage. "I created this dress from recycled trash bags. When I'm done wearing it, I can take it apart and use the bags for their original purpose. Ms. Heedles said our choices tonight were supposed to tell you about us. Belle and Kaity's gowns are both beautiful. But neither of them is me. This is." Allie gestured to the dress she'd constructed.

"Are you saying you're garbage?" Mo asked, confused.

"No. I'm saying I'm practical. And resourceful. And proud to wear something that challenges the disposable nature of today's society. Thank you."

Allie left the stage for the wings. It was Maggie's turn to clap while the other judges sat in shock. "*What* was *that*?" Constance sputtered.

"It was exactly what you asked for—a girl sharing who she is with us," Maggie said.

"Hmph. She should save it for one of those Occupy something protests."

"Let me check to make sure the girls are gone." Mo scurried up the stairs and peeked in both sides of the stage's wings. "They went back to the dressing rooms. We're good."

Mo returned to the other judges. "Let's make this quick. I have to get to a Veevay party full of women with sun damage. All in favor of Belle." She, Constance, and Robbie raised their hands. "We have a winner."

"Excuse me, but I think all the girls deserve a vote count," Maggie said.

"Seriously? Okay, fine. All in favor of Kaity." No hands went up. "All in favor of Allouette."

Maggie's arm shot straight up.

"Noted. Belle still wins. I gotta go."

The judges left the auditorium and went to their cars. Maggie's cell rang and she tapped a button to answer the call. "Hi. How's New York?"

"Loud," Bo said. "I get why it's called 'the city that never sleeps.' Considering how noisy it is every dang minute, it's an insomniac's worst nightmare. I was thinking of you and wanted to call."

"I'm glad." Maggie got into the Falcon and settled back into its bench seat. "Have you found out anything about Ira Stein?"

"I'll tell you one thing: he was a big old pack rat. There's piles of God-knows-what stacked floor to ceiling, with paths between the piles. We found a ton of notebooks, and we've been going through them, trying to find the most recent entries. Which involves deciphering the handwriting of a man who was starting to lose his wits, according to our new friend Max, who also clued us in to the fact that Stein did his genealogy research at the local library. The library won't let us near the computers without a search warrant, and even with one, they're not too happy about the whole thing. Apparently, the only people tougher than the cops in New York City are the librarians. And Ru didn't make friends with either branch of public servant when he told them all to move their butts because he needs to get home for Mardi Gras."

"Oh boy. That must've gone over real well with the NYPD."

"Yeah, I won't get specific about where the lead detective told Ru he could stick a Sazerac. But we did find a whole file folder filled with clippings about the Louisiana orphan train, so we're getting close to connecting the dots. Anything going on back home I should know about?"

"There was an incident at Doucet." Maggie told Bo about the destruction of the plantation steps.

"Huh. Sounds like some treasure-seeking vandalism. Unless there's a link between the painting and the orphans, I don't see a connection to the Damboise case. But I don't like that someone was spying on you."

"Neither do I, believe me." Maggie glanced out her car window. She saw night had fallen during the course of her phone call, and she was alone in the dark, unlit parking lot. "I better get going," she said, suddenly nervous.

"Right. Be careful, okay?" There was a pause. "I do love you."

"Please don't say it that way."

"What way?"

"Like there's an unspoken 'but' at the end of the sentence. Goodnight."

Maggie ended the call before Bo could respond. It had been a long, stressful day, and she wasn't in the mood for whatever excuse or attempt at an explanation Bo might drum up. Feeling jumpy, she double-checked her car doors to make sure they were locked. Then she pulled out of the parking lot and prayed for a safe, uneventful drive home.

TWENTY-ONE

AFTER A RESTLESS night devoid of much sleep, Maggie set up shop in the shotgun cottage living room. She placed the painting on an easel, positioning it near a window to capture the natural light. Maggie scraped and wiped away the top layer for hours, exposing more and more of the underlying scene. There was no clue about where a treasure might be buried. Nevertheless, she persisted. After a few hours, she had a breakthrough. Her meticulous work revealed that beyond the steps was a portrait of Doucet's manor house. There was a candle in a window on the second floor—a window in the room where the painting had originally hung.

Gran' strolled in carrying two coffee cups, bringing with her the rich scent of a café au lait. "You've been at that painting for hours, *chére*. I thought you might like a pick-me-up." She handed Maggie one of the cups.

"Thanks." Maggie sipped the brew and felt a renewed energy as the coffee coursed through her. "I found a clue in the painting. Look." She pointed to the candle. "I think the artist is telling us it's in the nursery." A thought occurred to Maggie. She put down her coffee cup, picked up her cell phone, and scrolled through the notes app until she found what she was looking for. *"Grata sit calidum, et de fisco,"* she read.

"'A warm and welcome treasure,'" Gran' said.

Maggie stared at her *grand-mère*. "You know what that means?"

"In my day, the young ladies of Immaculate Heart Academy had to study Latin, the theory being how could you take the message of a Latin Mass into your heart if you had no idea what the priest was saying? I continued at Newcomb and became rather fluent."

Maggie gave Gran' an affectionate smile. "I love how I can still learn something new about you."

"I'm an onion of a human being. Layer after layer. Now that I've translated for you, what does the saying mean in terms of your treasure hunt?"

"Let me think." Maggie sat down on the living room's red velvet-covered antique sofa. Gran' joined her. Maggie furrowed her brow as she called up an image of the nursery. "I think the X's on the stairs weren't marking the spot; they were a clue that the treasure's in the house. Warm and welcome…warm and welcome…" Maggie opened her eyes. "The fireplace," she said, excited. "There's a pineapple carved into the mantel, which is a symbol of wealth and hospitality. The painting hung above it. I think the treasure might be buried under the fireplace hearth."

"Bene factom," Gran' said. "That's Latin for 'well done.'"

"I'm going to let Ione know what I've discovered and see if she can get permission from the Doucet board to excavate under the hearth."

"It's a good thing the state ceded control of that old place to a nonprofit. We'd be buried six feet under ourselves if we had to wait for permission from local bureaucracy."

Maggie's cell rang. She saw it was a call from her father and pressed "Accept."

"I've got a problem," Tug said. "I want to make another test batch of gumbo in Bo's pot, but I ran out of flour for the roux. Your mama's in the middle of lunch prep for our guests. Any chance you could make a quick run to Park 'n' Shop for me?"

"Sure. I could use some fresh air."

"Thanks, *chére*. I'll reward you with a big bowl of you-know-what."

"Uh…thanks, but to be honest, I'll a little burned out on you-know-what."

Tug emitted a theatrical gasp. "Tired of gumbo? What kind of Luzianne gal are you? Don't make me report you to the cuisine police."

Maggie laughed. "Fine, I'll eat yet more of your gumbo. Now let me get to the store so I can pick up the flour."

Tug signed off with a *"Laissez les bon temps rouler."* Gran' drained the last of her coffee and then picked up Maggie's empty cup. "Between you, me, and the lamppost, I wasn't sorry to see that old pot go. I endured decades of your *grand-pére*'s obsession with the gumbo cook-off only to see it transferred to your papa. But I'm glad your gorgeous beau donated his pot so graciously. Making his once-a-year gumbo does give my sweet boy Tug such pleasure." She held up the cups. "I'll wash these. You go get that flour."

Maggie kissed Gran' on the cheek, and the octogenarian departed for the kitchen. Then Maggie cleaned off her tools and carefully rewrapped the painting. She put it back in the closet, which she locked with the door's ancient skeleton key.

AT THE PARK 'N' SHOP, Maggie quickly found the baking section. She scanned the shelves, but the spot where the flour should be was empty. Tug wasn't the only one burning through the essential roux ingredient.

"Can I help you?"

Maggie turned around to find Kaity Bertrand standing there. She wore a Park 'n' Shop smock and her usual friendly grin. "Hi, Kaity. I didn't know you worked here."

"I just started. It's part-time, a few days a week after school. Whatcha lookin' for?"

"Plain old flour."

Kaity checked the shelves. "Hmm, we must be out. But I'm sure we have some in the stockroom. Be right back."

Kaity disappeared through a swinging door. Maggie looked around and saw Gin organizing a shelf of cereal boxes. She negotiated her way around other customers toward Kaity's grandmother. "Hi, Gin. I ran into Kaity. She very helpfully offered to track down some flour for me."

"Glad to hear it. She decided she wants to go to college, so she's earning some money towards it. I have to say, I thought winning was the only way the Miss Pelican Mardi Gras Gumbo pageant might change Kaity's life. But now I see that win or lose, it's been a godsend for my grand-girl. Having to present herself in different ways made her see she wants more out of life than working here full-time"—Gin gestured to the store—"like her grammy."

Maggie was relieved by Gin's new, far less threatening attitude toward the contest. "Kaity's lucky to have a grammy like you, Gin. If she didn't know that before, I think she's figured it out by now."

Kaity came out of the stockroom, holding a five-pound bag of flour. She held the bag up triumphantly as if it were a trophy. "We have achieved flour." She handed the bag to Maggie. "Here you go, and thank you for parkin' and shoppin' at Park 'n' Shop." Kaity gave another high-wattage grin. "I'm going on break, Grammy." She kissed Gin on the cheek and bounced away.

Maggie picked up a few more items and checked out. She waved goodbye to Gin, then left the store for her car. She was about to start the convertible's engine when she heard Kaity's voice. "I'm so ticked off. I don't have time for jury duty." Maggie glanced out the car window and saw Kaity perched on the side steps of the store. The teen was in the middle of a cell phone call. "I never should've registered to vote, but my history teacher gave us extra credit if we did. I hear you can get out of jury duty if you pretend you don't speak English."

An angry Maggie started her car and backed out of the Park 'n' Shop parking lot. She made sure to dodge any eye contact with Kaity, who was still on the phone. Kaity and her grandmother had lied about the girl's age. She had to be eighteen to be eligible for jury duty—which made her ineligible for the Miss Pelican Mardi Gras Gumbo contest.

GRAN' PURSED HER lips. "Well, this is disturbing."

She'd been enjoying another café au lait at the small table in the shotgun kitchen when Maggie showed up with the news of Kaity and Gin's deception.

Maggie nodded soberly. "I have to wonder if Lee knew about it."

Gran' craned her neck to see out the kitchen window. "Why don't you ask him? He just pulled up. We were supposed to go dancing again this afternoon."

The path to the shotgun cottage crunched under heavy-soled footsteps. There was a brisk knock at the door. Maggie opened it to Lee. "A great good morning to you, pretty lady." Lee greeted them with an affable grin that brought to mind his great-granddaughter's cheery countenance. "I'm here to steal away your *grand-mère*."

"We'll see about that." Gran' marched in from the kitchen and stood in front of Lee, her arms folded in front of her chest. "Were you part of this little scam Gin and Kaity tried to pull off?"

Lee stared at Gran' blankly. "Scam? What now?"

"They were pretending Kaity's seventeen, when she's really eighteen, which makes her ineligible for the Miss Pelican Mardi Gras Gumbo Queen title," Maggie said.

"Kaity's eighteen?" Lee's surprise was genuine.

"Leland Abelard Bertrand, you appall me," Gran' said. "You don't know how old your own great-granddaughter is?"

Lee gave a sheepish shrug. "I have five kids, nine grandkids, and twenty-two great-grandkids. I think. Might be twenty-three. One of the grands was due to pop out a new great-grand sometime around now. Anyway, I do know Kaity and her mama went through such a bad patch that Kaity ran away. Gin tracked her down and took her in, but the girl lost so much school time she had to repeat a year. That's why her grades are good. Basically, it's her second year as a senior. So…would that make her eighteen?"

"Or even nineteen."

"Oh boy." Lee's shoulders sagged. "I'll talk to her and Gin."

"Don't," Maggie said. "I will."

"Whatever you think's best. I'm sorry about all this." Lee sat up straight and fixed his focus on Gran', a hopeful look in his eyes. "Dancing?"

Gran' shook her head. "No dancing."

"I understand." Lee stood up. Looking like a scolded schoolboy, Gran's boyfriend took a slow walk out the front door.

"I feel bad," Maggie said. "I don't want this to upset your relationship."

"Oh, it won't," Gran' said, waving her hand in a dismissive gesture. "He was getting a tad too comfortable anyway. It's good to keep him on his toes."

Gran' returned to the kitchen and her coffee. Maggie texted Gin and Kaity that she needed to speak to them about a matter of great importance, then picked up her car keys. "This dang contest is taking up way too much of my life," she muttered as she left for yet another trip to the Park 'n' Shop.

CONFRONTED WITH THE evidence against them, Gin and Kaity both looked abashed and were effusively apologetic. Knowing simply participating in the contest helped transform the teen's life, Maggie let go of her anger and presented the option of voluntarily withdrawing rather than being humiliated and outed as a liar, which Kaity gratefully accepted. Maggie was on her way to Junie's for a meeting about Gaynell's Mardi Gras Run when she got a text from Constance to the judges:

"Kaity dropped out. Too much schoolwork. We're down to Belle and Allouette."

One crisis solved, Maggie thought, relieved.

The crowd at Junie's was already liquored up and raucous by the time Maggie joined them. "The ladies got a head start on you," JJ informed her as he ferried two full pitchers of beer to their tables. "You're gonna have to do some serious catching up."

A scream of laughter enveloped the room. "I'll pass on the catching up," Maggie said. "I think someone here might need to stay sober."

"Good idea." The sentiment came from Mike Randall, who sat at the bar with another man who looked vaguely familiar to Maggie. Mike wore his HomeNHearth polo shirt; his companion was dressed in a suit. The men appeared to have come to Junie's straight from work. "Hey, Maggie," Mike said. He winked at her and then motioned to the man next to him. "Don't know if you've met my brother-in-law, Jules Tremblay."

A feeling of recognition clicked in. "Yes, we met once, briefly. Hi, Jules."

Jules mimed tipping a hat. "Miss Maggie." He followed this with a seductive smile. Like Mike, he was a flirt. Unlike Mike, who was flirtatious in an aging ex-quarterback way, Jules exuded the dissipated charm of an ill-fated Tennessee Williams character. Maggie had to wonder about Denise's and Pauline's taste in men.

Gaynell saw Maggie. She jumped to her feet and waved her over. "Excuse me," Maggie said to the air. With neither man getting the response they sought from Maggie, both had already turned their attention back to their drinks.

Maggie navigated her way to Gaynell, who greeted

her with a hug. "You made it—yay!" Gaynell said. "I'm going over the plan for tomorrow. Meet some of your fellow lady Mardi Gras." Gaynell made a wide swoop with her arm. Maggie estimated around forty women filling the tables, many of whom she recognized, which made her happy. She was finding her place in Pelican. "Maggie," Denise Randall called from one of the tables. She was sitting next to her cousin Pauline, who waved hello. Maggie waved back, then saw Ione and Mo sitting together and waved to them as well.

Gaynell banged an empty pitcher with the back of a knife. "Okay, madams and mademoiselles, listen up. Here's what's happening Tuesday morning—on Mardi *Gras*!" The women whooped and hollered. Gaynell gave them a minute to settle down. "We meet up at nine a.m. wearing costumes and masks. About a dozen of us'll be on horseback, including me, your *capitaine*. We'll also have two flatbed trucks that you can jump on and off if you need a break from walking. I've got a map of our route, but it's best just to follow along with the group. I got the okay from about ten houses for us to stop at. When we get to them, we sing our song, beg for gumbo ingredients that'll go into the communal town gumbo, fool around a little—but not too much; we don't want to go overboard and offend the homeowners with pranks like the guys sometimes do—" A loud boo rose from the crowd, and Gaynell banged the pitcher again. "Anyway, once we finish our stops, we march over to the Crozats, who've kindly donated their big, beautiful front lawn for the town's festivities."

Gaynell gestured to Maggie, and the women applauded. A few staggered to their feet in a slightly drunken standing ovation. "My parents get all the credit," Maggie said. "Between us, I think my dad keeps the party close to home so his gumbo doesn't have to travel." Thanks to the high alcohol content of the crowd, she was rewarded with more laughter than her small joke merited.

"*Eh bien*, that's it for now. Any questions, text me." Gaynell banged the pitcher one last time. "Meeting adjourned. Ladies, let's par-tay!" She ran over to the stage and hopped up on it. Members of her all-female band, Gaynell and the Gator Girls, clambered onto the stage and joined her. Gaynell strapped on an accordion and launched into a zippy zydeco tune she'd composed. Women poured onto the dance floor. Maggie took an empty seat next to Eula Banks from the Hall of Records, and poured herself a glass of beer. "Maggie, I was going to call you." Eula yelled to be heard over the music. "I got in touch with the New York Foundling Hospital. They found some records on Jacob Seideman and Bridget Colleary."

"They did?" Maggie yelled back. "That's wonderful."

"It's probably what we had in those missing files— maybe even more information. I'll forward whatever they send me to you as soon as I get it. I'm hoping it'll hold the clues you need to identify Gerard's murderer."

"I hope so too. Thanks so much, Eula. Can I buy you a drink?"

"Sure." Eula held up her stein. "Abita Light."

Maggie gave Eula a thumbs-up and trooped toward the bar. She was distracted by the sight of Pelican PD's Cal Vichet and Artie Belloise coming in through the front door. Both were regulars at Junie's, but the looks on their faces told her they weren't there for some off-duty imbibing. The officers headed straight for Mike Randall and Jules Tremblay. Cal had a hand on his revolver; Artie was holding a pair of handcuffs as he walked. They stopped in front of Mike and Jules, who sensed their presence and turned toward them.

"Mike. Jules." Cal addressed them in a somber tone.

"Hey, Cal." Jules's tone was friendly, but guarded. "What's up?"

Artie put his hand on his partner Cal's shoulder. "I know you go fishing with these two fellas, so I'll take it from here." He opened the handcuffs and readied them as he spoke. "Mike Randall, I'm afraid you're under arrest."

TWENTY-TWO

THE EAR-PIERCING SCREAM Denise Randall unleashed when she saw her husband in handcuffs set off a chain reaction of screams from the other women that made Maggie's ears ring. "My husband's not a murderer!" Denise cried as she ran after the police officers.

"He's not being arrested for murder," Artie said. "He's under arrest for vandalism. He tore up—"

"Allegedly," Cal interrupted, throwing his fishing buddy Mike a sympathetic glance.

"*Allegedly* tore up Doucet's front steps. You can meet us at the station, Denise. Temporary station. Dang, I keep forgetting."

Cal and Artie disappeared through Junie's front door. Denise fell sobbing into her cousin Pauline's arms. "It's okay," Pauline said, stroking the distraught woman's hair. "Jules, give Quentin MacIlhoney a call. Hurry."

"He's probably at Fais Dough Dough," Maggie said. "You can run right over there."

Eula Banks seconded Maggie's suggestion, adding, "His mother-in-law's been living with him, so he never goes home these days. Wouldn't be surprised if he had a cot set up in the Fais Dough Dough back room."

"Thanks, I'm on it," Jules said, and sprinted out the door.

"I cannot believe this is happening," Denise wept. "My poor Allouette. How's she gonna take her daddy being in jail? Now she'll never been be Pelican Mardi Gras Gumbo Queen."

Seriously? was what Maggie wanted to say. Instead, she summoned up the self-control to respond in an even tone, "I wouldn't give that a minute of worry right now. Here's a thought. Why doesn't Pauline go take care of Allouette, and I'll take you to the police station?"

Eula again backed Maggie up. "That's a good idea. Maggie's gotten to know Pelican PD real well, what with all the murders around her."

Maggie gritted her teeth. Eula was starting to bug her. "I know Pelican PD mostly because of my relationship with Bo Durand. But yes, I might be helpful that way."

Pauline and Denise exchanged a look, and then Pauline said, "Thank you, Maggie. I'm going to bring Allouette over to our house. If you need me, I'll be there."

Gaynell appeared at Maggie's side. "I called Ione. She's going to meet us at the station. This is all news to her. She had no idea the police had a suspect."

The word *suspect* triggered another round of tears from Denise. Maggie put a comforting arm around her shoulder. "Let's go. The sooner we get to Pelican PD, the sooner we can clean up this mess."

MAGGIE QUICKLY FOUND a space in the giant parking lot outside Pelican PD's provisional station, which was located in a big box store that had gone out of business. Inside the abandoned building, officers had used empty floor displays as partitions to create everything from offices to a holding area for anyone being transferred to Baton Rouge PD's jail, the closest functional way station for Pelican's small criminal element. This was where she and Denise found a glum, still handcuffed Mike Randall. "Baby," Denise cried out, and ran to her husband. Cal Vichet, stuck with guard duty, made a halfhearted attempt to stop her.

Mike opened his mouth to respond to Denise, but Cal shushed him. "Best not to say anything right now." Abashed, Mike nodded.

Chief Perske emerged from his improvised office, followed by Ione and Quentin MacIlhoney. The defense attorney wore an apron over his pink, perfectly ironed polo shirt and charcoal-gray designer slacks. For Quentin, this was dressing down. "How-do," he greeted the new arrivals. "I was about to frost some cupcakes at Fais Dough Dough when Jules Tremblay zoomed in and sounded the alarm. But this case was so easy, I have half a mind not to charge you for it, my friend. Notice I said *half* a mind."

Chief Perske hovered over Mike Randall, his six-foot six-inch tree trunk of a body casting a giant shadow. "Go buy a lottery ticket, Randall, because today's your lucky day." Perske swung a thumb and a look of disdain at Quentin. "Thanks to this shyster here, Miss Savreau says she's dropping all charges."

"It seems my client did Doucet a favor," Quentin said. "Take it away, Ms. Savreau."

"When we were throwing out the ruined wood from the steps, I noticed something," Ione said. "It wasn't old growth cypress, the original material. Somewhere along the way, the steps were replaced. Probably in the 1950s, when the state first assumed control of the property. They thought they were upgrading the facility, but what they did was replace a good wood with a bad one. Those steps were rotting and termite-damaged. One of our visitors could've put a foot right through them and gotten injured."

"You see?" Quentin said. "Mr. Randall's a downright hero." He blithely ignored the glares emanating from both Ione and Chief Perske.

"Mr. Randall, you still committed an act of vandalism," Ione resumed. "But I'm willing to drop the charges *if*"—Ione placed a large emphasis on the small word—"you replace the Doucet steps with perfect new ones. And do a bunch of other tasks around the old place. Historic sites like ours are always short on money, so we'll take donated labor any way we can get it, including from a vandal."

"Yes, ma'am. I can do that." For the first time since they'd arrived at the police station, Maggie saw a glimmer of life in Mike. "You tell me what you need, and consider it done." Then he looked down at the floor, unable to face Ione. "I'm sorry about the steps. When I was working on the security system, I heard you and Maggie talking about the painting and the treasure and...we could use some money. I got suckered into buying this online course on investing. Turns out the only one making money from it was the guy selling it. From now on, I'll stick to what I'm good at—delivering stuff."

Maggie felt for Mike. She now saw his flirtatious bravado was an act masking his deep insecurity. "What you did was wrong, Mike. But there's nothing wrong with delivering stuff. Where would flood repair be without you?" This earned a slight smile from him. "And remember, you have a wife who adores you and an absolutely extraordinary daughter. So, you must be doing something right."

"Not so sure about the 'wife who adores you' part

right now. Denise?" His tone was tentative. "You still love me? After what I pulled?" Denise responded with a fresh burst of tears and buried her face in Mike's shoulder.

"Now that's what this ol' shyster likes to see, a happy ending," Quentin said. "'Course, I prefer seeing it after a long, drawn-out court case fulla billable hours, but it's Louisiana. Someone's doing something bad somewhere— they just ain't been caught yet."

Like Gerard Damboise's murderer, Maggie thought. She saw Chief Perske scowl. *I bet he's thinking exactly the same thing.*

WHEN MAGGIE RETURNED to Crozat, she discovered the B and B's guests were off being tourists, much to her relief. She was worn out from the events of the last few hours and lacked the energy to make small talk with strangers. Her grumbling stomach alerted her to the fact she had skipped lunch. She retrieved a container of jambalaya from the refrigerator and spooned it into a pot on the stove. When it was hot—but not too hot, Maggie transferred the jambalaya into a bowl and devoured it. She was sopping up the last remnants with a thick hunk of French bread when her cell rang. Bo's name flashed on the screen, and her heart flip-flopped. "Hey." Maggie kept her tone casual, despite her swirling emotions.

"Hey yourself." Bo's tone was warm, but also casual. "Just wanted to check in."

"That's nice. Thank you." *Oh, that was so lame.* An uncomfortable silence followed. Maggie, desperate to end it, asked, "Any progress on the late Mr. Stein?"

"Yes. Took too long, but we did get a search warrant

for the library. Stein was obsessive-compulsive and, according to the head librarian, always did his genealogy searches on one particular computer. Unfortunately, it also turns out the computers are set in a way that erases a patron's history. We'll need a forensic computer expert to retrieve data. I was hoping we'd leave tonight, but now it looks like it won't be until morning at the earliest. There's one nonstop flight that'd get us to New Orleans by around four p.m. We'll miss the Courir and the gumbo contest, but even with the drive from the airport to Pelican, we'll catch the rest of Mardi Gras. Ru's bummed, though. He's gone off to drown his sorrows in pizza and a Broadway show."

"You didn't go with him?"

"No. Wasn't in the mood. There's about a hundred Chinese restaurants around here. I'll grab something from one of them and wait to hear back from the computer expert. NYPD fast-tracked it. I think they want to get rid of Rufus. He's really ticking them off with his constant comments about how New Orleans is so much better than New York. They started calling him 'the Big A-hole from the Big Easy.'"

Maggie had to laugh at this. "I miss New York cops."

"I hope you miss a New Orleans one too." Bo's voice sounded hesitant.

The Crozat doorbell rang. "Someone's here—I need to go," Maggie said, grabbing an excuse to end the conversation. Yes, she missed Bo terribly, but with the future of their relationship a big question mark, there was no point in admitting that. Better to fight off vulnerability than give in to it. "Safe flight home." She ended the call before Bo could respond.

The doorbell rang again, and Maggie hurried down

Crozat's front hall. She opened the door to find Belle and Allie standing there. "Hello," Belle said, polite as always.

"Hello," Maggie responded. "Allie, I'm so sorry about what happened with your dad. How is he? How are *you*?"

Allie, who had looked tense, relaxed. "We're both okay, thank you for asking. It was awful, but in a way, things are better now. It's hard to explain."

"I get it. A traumatic experience can be a wake-up call that reminds you of what's really important in life." The girl nodded in the way teens did when they weren't interested in what an adult was saying but were trying to be respectful, and Maggie suddenly felt her age. There was an awkward moment of silence. "Can I help you with something?"

"We're here to find out who won the pageant and gets to be the new Miss Pelican Mardi Gras Gumbo Queen," Belle said.

Maggie gasped and clapped her hand to her mouth. "Oh wow, I've been so caught up with what all's been going on, I totally blanked on the contest. Come in." She ushered Belle and Allie through the doorway and into the front parlor. "The judges should be here any minute. It won't take long to make our decision. And whatever happens, remember, you're both winners." Allie couldn't contain an eye roll, but Maggie, knowing how fatuous the comment sounded, forgave her.

The doorbell rang again. Maggie hurried down the hallway and let in Constance, Mo, and Robbie. "I don't have snacks or coffee today. To be honest, I forgot about the contest. I got distracted by the drama with Mike Randall."

"Yes, we need to talk about that," Constance said sotto voce as Maggie steered the group past the teens in the front parlor to the back parlor office. The judges took their seats. "This meeting should fly by. It's obvious we should disqualify Allouette due to the controversy with her family. We certainly don't want to seem like we're rewarding criminal behavior."

Maggie wasn't surprised by Constance's reasoning, but it infuriated her. "A child shouldn't suffer because of a parent's misguided actions," she said, steaming. "Our choice should be based solely on the merits of the contestants. The sins of the father should not be visited on the daughter."

"That was both poetic and dramatic, but inconsequential. Let's poll Mo and Robbie and see what they think."

Constance focused on the two judges, who both looked acutely uncomfortable. They exchanged a glance, and then Mo spoke. "I agree with Maggie that we should base our decision on what the girls brought to the table. And given that criteria, I have to go with Belle. She's pageant worthy. Allie's a wonderful kid, but still a work in progress. I don't think being a pageant queen is a fit for her quite yet."

"I agree," Robbie said hastily.

"Let's take a vote," Constance said. "All in favor of bestowing the honor of Miss Pelican Mardi Gras Gumbo Queen on Belle Madeleine Tremblay, raise your hands." All hands went up except for Maggie's. "We have this year's winner. Based on merit, not scandal."

Maggie decided to be gracious in defeat, although she was still angry with Constance. She had to admit Mo made valid points about whether Allie was ready or even wanted to assume the crown. "I've been out-voted, so I bow to democracy. And Allie did win the essay contest. I think she knows how important the title is to her cousin and will be okay with the result. Let's go tell them."

Maggie led the judges into the front parlor. Neither girl was there.

"They probably went to the restroom," Maggie said. "I'll go look for them. Why don't you go back to the office and wait for us?"

Constance, Robbie, and Mo trooped off while Maggie checked the first-floor restroom reserved for day-trippers. No one was there. She went upstairs to see if Belle had utilized the bathroom in the one yet-to-be-occupied guest room. She heard two voices coming from behind the bathroom's closed door. One of the girls was crying, but Maggie couldn't tell whether it was Belle or Allie. She put an ear to the door.

"Are you sure?"

"Yes, I've taken a million tests."

"You didn't use the ones from the dollar store, did you? Because Miranda Phelps did, and it was wrong. She was, like, hysterical, and it was a total false alarm."

"Well, this isn't. What am I going to do?" This plaintive question was followed by a fresh burst of sobs.

"It's okay. I'll help you."

"You can't. You need to go away to college. I want to go too, but now…"

Maggie had heard enough. She knocked on the door, eliciting a gasp and whispers from inside. After a moment, the door opened and Allie peeked her head out. "Um, hi. Belle and I were just talking. We'll be downstairs in a minute."

Maggie gave the door a gentle push and entered the bathroom. She closed the door behind her and locked it. Belle, who was crouched on a small vanity stool, looked up. Maggie could tell the girl had been crying for a while. Instead of being her preternaturally composed self, Belle was a wreck. Her face was blotchy and streaked with tears. Her hair hung in strands. "I'm not feeling well," she said. "Allie was keeping me company."

"I heard some of your conversation," Maggie said. "This isn't about you not feeling well, is it?"

Belle and Allie exchanged a look. Then Belle scrunched her face and shook her head. "No." She burst into tears. "I'm pregnant."

TWENTY-THREE

WHILE BELLE HAD a good cry, Maggie put together the pieces of how she wound up in her "situation," as Gran' would delicately call it. Because Belle's mother Pauline was Lia and Kyle's interior decorator, the teen must have found out about Grove Hall's secret room. Maggie recalled the post-party mess she'd found there. The culprit wasn't Kaity or Jayden or some transient. It was Belle. Perfect, pageant-queen-ready Belle. "I heard you say you took some tests. You're absolutely sure about the results?"

Belle nodded.

"Who's the…"

"His name is Brandon. He was the friend of a friend from another parish. We got a bottle of cinnamon whiskey and brought it to that room my mom and Mr. Bruner found in his new house. My friends and I went there a few times over the last couple of months to party. Sometimes Brandon and I just went. Anyway, one time… stuff happened."

Did it ever, Maggie thought. Belle let loose with more tears. Maggie put her arms around the teen and comforted her. "You need to tell your parents, honey."

Belle pulled away, a horrified look on her face. "No way. We're Tremblays. Nothing can ever, ever mess up our family name."

"I can be with you if that would help. But you have to tell them as soon as possible."

"She can tell them after Mardi Gras," Allie said. "It'll be easier once this whole stupid pageant is over. It only means waiting a couple more days."

More secrets. But Allie did have a point. "Fine. But she has to do it first thing Wednesday morning."

Belle dropped her face into her hands. "Okay," she said, her voice muffled. "Can you both be with me? Please?"

"Of course," Maggie and Allie chorused.

Belle lifted her head. "But I have to drop out of the pageant. You're not allowed to be pregnant."

"No way," Allie declared. "If you drop out, I drop out."

"Then no one will be the Miss Pelican Mardi Gras Gumbo Queen."

"So? That's their problem."

Maggie grimaced and massaged the bridge of her nose. Between the pageant and gumbo drama, she was starting to wish she'd left town for Mardi Gras. "Here's a solution that will get us to Wednesday. I shouldn't be telling you this, but given the circumstances, I think it's okay if I break the rules. Belle, you won the contest. So accept the crown now and wear it tomorrow. Then on Wednesday, you'll withdraw for personal reasons, and Allie will finish your reign. Which probably only means going to a few local events in the sash and crown."

Allie made a face. "I tried on Pauline's crown once. Those things are heavy. I hope I don't have to wear it too much."

"Oh, *chére*, how I wish that was the biggest problem

here. Put on your game faces, girls. It's time to face the other judges."

Maggie extended a hand to Belle, but Allie was already helping her cousin up. She tenderly wiped the tears from Belle's face with the sleeve of her plaid flannel shirt. "It's okay, ma'am. I'll take care of her."

Allie took Belle's hand and led her out of the bathroom. Maggie followed behind. As they walked down the stairs to the back parlor office, she thought of her own close relationship with her cousin Lia. If nothing else came out of this unexpected twist to the Miss Pelican Mardi Gras Gumbo Queen contest, it reinforced a lifelong bond between the teenage cousins.

MAGGIE ENDURED THE celebration of a new Miss Pelican Mardi Gras Gumbo Queen, knowing Belle's reign would be brief and, despite all efforts to the contrary, scandalous. She decided to lay low for the evening, bowing out of a pre–Mardi Gras celebration at Junie's. Instead, she helped her mother make a King Cake for their guests. Gran', a Sazerac in her hand, watched the women work. "I was never one for baking. Maggie, I've told your mother umpteen times she should follow my shortcut recipe using that crescent roll dough from the store or, better yet, those cinnamon rolls that come in a tube."

"And I've told your *grand-mère* umpteen times, I like making my own dough," Ninette said, rolling said dough into a large rectangle.

Maggie grinned as she spooned a rich filling onto the uncooked King Cake dough in big dollops. Her mother and *grand-mère* had this debate every year of her childhood and adolescence, and probably every year she was away in New York. "Both of your King Cakes are delicious," she said. And she meant it.

Several hours later, the house was redolent with the delicious scent of butter, cinnamon, and brown sugar. Maggie sat in the kitchen, waiting for the King Cake to cool off so she could frost it and tuck a small plastic baby inside. Traditionally, whoever got the slice with the baby supplied the next year's cake, but given the B and B's itinerant clientele, this rarely happened. Still, every so often a guest who got the baby would instantly plan a return visit to honor the tradition. Usually, this bold offer came after the guests had washed down their pastry with a few rounds of Tug's Banana Bon Temps cocktail.

As Maggie contemplated the tiny plastic baby, she thought about Belle. An idea came to her. Whitney Evans longed to be a mom again but couldn't conceive. When the time was right, Maggie would bring up the possibility of adoption to both Whitney and Belle.

Her mind then wandered to the missing children from the orphan train. What was it like for them, coming to a world so different from the tenements of New York? Had they run away like Hans Herbig? Or did their new families wipe out their pasts, thinking the foundlings would benefit from a clean slate?

She checked the King Cake. It had cooled off. She pulled her mother's homemade cream cheese frosting from the refrigerator and slathered it all over the top of the cake. Then she liberally sprinkled it with colored sugar, alternating purple, green, and gold. The colors of Mardi Gras: purple for justice, green for faith, and gold for power. "I have faith the power of law will see justice prevail in the murders of Ira Stein and Gerard

Damboise." Maggie said this out loud, as if verbalizing the sentiment would make it so.

She wrapped up the King Cake and refrigerated it. After cleaning the kitchen, she turned off the lights and headed for the shotgun cottage to see if Eula Banks had emailed the promised records from the New York Foundling Hospital. Horn honks, zydeco music, and whoops of pleasure came from cars on the River Road—revelers returning from the pre–Mardi Gras festivities in town.

Once inside the cottage, Maggie changed into a sleep tee and sweats. She checked her laptop and phone. Nothing from Eula and no updates from Bo. Frustrated and nerves on edge, she uncorked a bottle of red wine and poured herself a glass. She heard an odd thumping sound, then saw it came from Gopher's tail slapping against the old wood floor. She bent down to pet him. Jolie, wanting in on the petting action, used her muzzle to bump Gopher out of the way. "It's okay, I can alternate," Maggie told the pooches, and then did so. After a few minutes of petting and wine drinking, she stood up, yawned, and stretched. The wine had made her tired. "Okay, gang, time for bed. I've got a busy day tomorrow, and I need my rest. So no hogging the bed tonight, Gopher."

With that, she padded into the bedroom, the pups on her heels. And when Gopher did hog the bed, she didn't mind one bit. Instead, she snuggled with the basset, taking comfort from his unconditional love.

MAGGIE WAS AWOKEN at dawn by a persistent rapping on her window. She roused herself and looked out to see Gaynell. Her friend was dressed entirely in black, from her sneakers to her fedora. The one pop of color came from her cape's bright red lining. A capuchon hat and a smaller bag hung from the garment bag she held. Maggie jumped out of bed and ran to open the front door.

"Happy Mardi Gras!" Gaynell greeted her, and the two women hugged. Gaynell followed Maggie back into the house. "It's early and I didn't want to wake your Gran'. But I finished your costume. Here."

Maggie took the capuchon and placed it on a side table. She opened the small bag first and pulled out the mask Xander had made for her. She held it over her face, and Gaynell mimed fear like a silent movie star. Gaynell then opened the garment bag, revealing Maggie's completed costume. "You're gonna make a great Mardi Gras."

"And you're gonna make a great *capitaine*." The women hugged again. "I'm really excited now."

"I gotta go; I got so much to do," Gaynell said. "I'll see you at ten in front of the Hebert place. They agreed to be our first victims. Bhua ha ha." Gaynell gave her impression of an evil laugh, which dissolved into a fit of giggles. Then she dashed off to her car.

Maggie, singing the traditional *"Chanson de Mardi Gras"* to make sure she had it memorized, returned to her bedroom for a shower. She had plenty of time before the Courir, so she went to the kitchen and fixed herself breakfast. Her laptop pinged, alerting her to an incoming email. Maggie took her coffee over to the small antique desk that served as her office, and perused her mailbox. The long-awaited email from Eula had arrived. Attached were scans of the New York Foundling Hospital records for Bridget Colleary and Jacob Seideman. Maggie opened both documents and read them thoroughly. Neither were runaways. Both were adopted. And the names of the adoptive families were familiar to Maggie. She closed her eyes and took deep breaths to center herself and clear her mind. After a few minutes, she opened her eyes. She had the names. She had a possible motive.

Now all she needed was proof.

TWENTY-FOUR

MAGGIE SAVED THE documents to a folder she titled "Orphan Train." She was typing a thank-you to Eula when she noticed an email from Constance with the subject line "I Remembered." Maggie finished her note to Eula and pressed "Send." Then she opened the email from Constance and read:

Remember how you said the weather might remind me of when Gerard changed his attitude about the orphan train exhibit? Well, I thought about that, and it came to me that the change happened a day before the floods. Gerard was in a terrible mood, and I thought it was because of all the scary weather reports, but he said no. I brought up some business, including the exhibit, and out of the blue he flat-out shot it down. I was surprised he had soured on the idea, and was going to press him about why he had turned against it, but then the floods came. Hope this helps.

The floods. Which had delivered the body of Ira Stein to the grounds of Crozat. Maggie thought she knew why the old man was killed. But again, the death of Gerard stumped her. He'd delivered exactly what the murderer wanted—a veto of the orphan train exhibit. Then why was he killed? What "lies" and "secrets" did he know that doomed him? Maggie replayed their last few moments together. She knew she'd heard his last two words clearly. But what if she'd made assumptions about whatever else Gerard was trying to tell her?

Gran' emerged from her bedroom. "Morning, *chére*," she said with a yawn. She was clad in a purple satin peignoir set. "Happy Mardi Gras. As you can see, I'm in purple to mark the occasion."

"Purple for justice," Maggie murmured.

"Well, I wear it because it's pretty. What are you doing at the computer? Shouldn't you be off on the Courir, pranking some good-natured neighbors?"

"I don't have to be there for a while. Gran', I need to run something by you."

"Not without coffee."

Gran' exited to the kitchen, and Maggie followed. She waited at the café table while her *grand-mère* poured herself a cup of coffee, then added a splash of cognac. "A makeshift café brulot to celebrate the holiday." She took a seat across from Maggie and sipped her drink. "Better. Now talk to me."

"I think the murders of Ira Stein and Gerard Damboise are all about how the past affects the present. Both Ira and the orphan train exhibit would have revealed a secret the killer was determined to hide, a secret they were convinced could ruin their life. And I think when Gerard said 'I' to me, he wasn't talking about himself. He was trying to name Ira Stein and explain their connection. My one bump is why was Gerard killed when he'd reversed his position on the exhibit? The obvious answer is blackmail. But what was the lure? The Damboises seem financially comfortable. Pelican PD hasn't dug up anything that would show otherwise. He had an important, respected position in town, so a power grab is out. What was missing in his life that might drive him to make a dumb, dangerous move?"

"That's easy." Gran' took another sip of her doctored coffee. "The one thing Gerard could never get his hands on was a home for his beloved Historical Society. He even sniffed around us, dropping clumsy hints about how much work it must be to run a barely functional B and B, especially with me aging and your mama being a cancer survivor. He'd end by saying if we ever wanted to donate Crozat as a home for the Society, he'd do us a favor and take it off our hands. I believe this might have grown into an obsession that drove him to take reckless actions."

"Here's a scenario." Maggie leaned in, her mind racing as she assembled the puzzle pieces of the murders. "The killer offers Gerard a bribe to cancel the exhibit in order to protect a secret about their family lineage. They offer some way to come up with a home for his collection—and I say *his* because I think that's how Gerard perceived everything in the Historical Society—as his, not Pelican's."

"Yes. He became extremely and annoyingly possessive about every last item. That's why I only donated a few things pro forma and made sure they were of little emotional value to us, which is sad because the Society should be of historical value to all in Pelican."

"Agreed. So the floods come, and Ira Stein turns up dead. My guess is Ira contacted Gerard to find out more about the genealogy search that brought him to Pelican. After Ira died, Gerard connected the man's death to the killer. And Gerard turns to blackmail. He'll keep his mouth shut if the killer delivers the ultimate prize—

whatever Gerard needs to create a permanent home for the Pelican Historical Society."

"I'm assuming you have an idea about who our demented murderer might be."

"Yes, but I'd rather not name a name because my theory is so fantastical it could get me in a lot of trouble if I'm wrong."

"It could get you in more trouble if you're right. Please watch out for yourself, *chére*."

"I will. Promise."

Gran' finished her coffee and returned to her bedroom to dress for the day. Maggie forwarded the email from Constance to Bo, with a note to have someone at Pelican PD check Gerard's datebook for all appointments the late Historical Society president had scheduled the week of the floods. She debated texting Bo her theory about who the killer might be, but had a sudden attack of paranoia about putting it in writing. She decided to pick up Bo at the airport and share her thoughts with him on the drive home. In Louisiana, even a killer could be counted on to take Mardi Gras off.

It was a decision that within hours she'd deeply regret.

SHORTLY BEFORE THE Courir de Mardi Gras was to begin, Maggie changed into her costume. The day was cloudy and cool, so she slipped on undergarments that would keep her warm under the cotton fabric. Her slim five-foot four-inch frame still swam in the bright red pajamas. She pulled her brown hair into a high ponytail and then twisted it into a bun she stuffed under the capuchon hat. Just for fun, she put on Xander's spooky, elaborate mask. She giggled when she saw herself in the mirror. An unrecognizable figure stared back, both amusing and unsettling. Maggie shook her arms and twisted her waist back and forth, making the multicolor strips of fabric decorating the outfit dance. Then she left the cottage to begin the celebrations.

Ninette and a group of local women were on Crozat's front lawn, organizing for the community gumbo, when Maggie showed up in her costume. "Happy Mardi Gras!"

Ninette clasped a hand to her chest. "*Chére*, you put a scare in me. With that mask on, I didn't know it was you."

Maggie lifted the mask. Despite the nip in the air, drops of perspiration slid down her forehead. "This thing is hot. I don't know how I'm going to wear it for hours."

"You'll be having so much fun you'll forget it's on."

Ninette kissed her daughter on the cheek and returned to work. Maggie traipsed through the damp grass to where her father and his gumbo-cooking cohorts were setting up for the cook-off. The men—and the contestants were all men, for the Pelican townswomen, confident in their own cooking talent, had good-naturedly ceded this particular contest to the fellows—had to follow strict rules. Cooking would begin simultaneously at one p.m., after the various courirs finished. The only prepared ingredients allowed were precooked meats, foul, seafood, and potato salad, which locals liked to add to their bowls of gumbo.

There were two long rows of tables and twenty butane burners or camp stoves for the contestants; no electricity was permitted. Some men had entered on their own; others built teams from friends and coworkers. Maggie noticed Team HomeNHearth was sans Mike

Randall, who she assumed was lying low after his close dance with jail time. There'd be no Mississippi gumbo this cook-off. She found her father carefully lining up his ingredients in the order he would need them. "Good luck, Dad." She kissed him on the cheek. "I know you'll take home the trophy."

"I hope," Tug grumbled. "Artie and Cal are claiming they have some new secret ingredient." Tug craned his neck to suss out the two officers' setup.

"Uh-uh, no peeking," Artie scolded.

"I'm not peekin'. I'm takin' a mental picture of what a loser's table looks like," Tug shot back.

"Then you best be looking right in front of you, my friend." Artie whooped at his own comeback and high-fived Cal.

Maggie laughed. "I'll leave y'all to your gumbo trash-talking. I got a Run to run."

Maggie drove over to the Hebert homestead, passing the occasional throng of Mardi Gras revelers. Given their general state of inebriation, she was glad they'd chosen to walk—or stagger, as it were—instead of get behind the wheel of a car. By the time she parked and joined Gaynell's Courir, a large group had already assembled. All were costumed and masked, making it impossible to recognize a soul. This made Maggie uncomfortable despite the festive atmosphere. She wondered if some men had snuck into the Courir to prank the women, which she heard had happened in the past.

"Maggie," a female voice said, and a Mardi Gras slapped a hand on her shoulder. The costumed woman lifted her mask, revealing Eula Banks. The grandmother of four had a beer in hand, despite the fact that it was eight thirty in the morning. "Did you get those files on the lost orphans I forwarded to you?"

"Yes, thank you so much."

"*Ce n'est pas rien.* It's nothin'." Eula let out a loud belch, and Maggie got a wheaty whiff of hops. "Here's hoping the files help you lock up the latest murderin' town crazy."

"*Attention, tout le monde,*" Gaynell called through a megaphone. She, along with half a dozen other participants, was on horseback. "Remember the rules. Beg as much as you want, but no stealing. No damaging anyone's property. Keep the roughhousing playful so I don't have to whip ya." She brandished a leather whip, and the Mardi Gras reacted with mock fear. Gaynell used the whip to point out a couple of flatbed trucks sporting Porta Potties tricked out with Mardi Gras decorations. "We got two Andy Gumps on the flatbed trucks, if you need to take care of business. As far as riders go, the trucks can take as many people as can fit on them. But priority goes to those who have trouble walking."

"I gotta ride cuz of my knee replacements," Eula announced to the crowd. A dozen older women chorused, "Me too." Given Pelican's propensity for overweight citizens who'd rather hold onto the extra poundage than cut back on the rice and beans, this came as no surprise to Maggie.

"Are you ready, Mardi Gras?" Gaynell shouted. The group's loud whoop answered the question. "*Allons-y! Let's go!*"

There were more cheers as everyone descended on the Heberts, who were already waiting on their front porch. Mardi Gras fell to their knees, begging in French, and the Heberts responded by tossing bags of celery, onions, and green peppers. Maggie hung back, self-conscious. "Celeste Fontenot is up a tree!" someone yelled. Maggie turned to see a Mardi Gras had climbed into one of the Hebert's trees and was pretending to ignore Gaynell's demands she come down. Gaynell cracked her whip on the grass. Celeste mimed tears, slid down the trunk, and ran back to join the group, which began singing a loud, off-key rendition of *"La Chanson de Mardi Gras"* as they marched away from the Heberts.

The Courir de Mardi continued this way for the next two hours. The crowd grew larger, drunker, and more raucous. Maggie got over her shyness and joined in the festivities. The other Mardi Gras cheered her when she caught a live chicken that had been released as a ceremonial addition to the gumbo. "Run free, little friend," she whispered to it. She released the bird, and it scampered off to join its feathered brethren in the field. Maggie noticed Gaynell was having trouble controlling some of the more inebriated mischief-makers. "Do you need help?" she asked as her friend tried to coax yet another Mardi Gras out of a tree.

"Nope, this is my job as *capitaine*. But thanks. Hey!" With a yell and crack of her whip, Gaynell startled the Mardi Gras, who tumbled off the low-hanging branch.

Maggie returned to the group. Thirsty, she took a gulp of beer from a can offered up by a Mardi Gras who pulled it from a pouch attached to her costume. Many of the costumes had these pouches, which served to store the donated gumbo goods the Mardi Gras scored. The single beer gulp was enough to give Maggie a slight buzz, and she linked arms with a few other women as everyone sang:

Les Mardi Gras s'en vient de tout partout,
Tout alentour le tour du moyeu,
Ça passe une fois par an, demandé la charité,
Quand-même ça c'est une patate, une patate ou
des gratins.

They switched to the English version of "The Mardi Gras Song":

The Mardi Gras come from all around,
All around the center of town,
They come by once per year, asking for charity,
Sometimes it's a sweet potato, a sweet potato or
pork rinds.

Another hour went by, and Maggie's energy was flagging. She'd given in to the party mood and finished the can of beer, which was acting as a soporific. *I might as well have taken a sleeping pill*, she thought with a yawn. She forced a jog to catch up with the flatbed trucks, which were as packed with humanity as a New York subway at rush hour. "Any room for me?" she asked plaintively, to which she received a resounding, "No."

A loud yell came from the front of the group. It was matched by a loud yell from across the street. "The men's Courir," a Mardi Gras shouted. The crowd instantly tripled in size and noise. The men's run featured a local Cajun band on a flatbed truck, which broke into a dance tune. The street quickly filled with dancing, singing, flirting Mardi Gras. Maggie, overwhelmed with the desire to go home and shower before driving to the airport to pick up Bo, stumbled out of their way. Her mask had become a mini furnace, causing sweat to pour down her forehead. She turned her back to the crowd and furtively lifted up the mask, grateful for the unusual midday cool breeze. She was relieved when the crowd began singing and dancing their way back to the Hebert home, where the women's Courir had begun, and trudged along with it.

"You look beat, *chére*."

Maggie glanced around. On one side a couple was singing; on the other, two Mardi Gras were cracking themselves up as they pretended to smooch through their grotesque masks. No one was paying attention to her.

"Y'all like a ride?"

She looked up to see a masked horseback rider beckoning to her. "Yes, thank you."

"Help her on the horse," the rider called to a few roisterers.

Two male Mardi Gras lifted Maggie into the air and onto the horse, their alcohol intake seeming to give them super-human strength. *"Laissez les bons temps rouler!"* they called after her as the horse cantered off with its two riders.

"I really appreciate this," Maggie said to her mystery rescuer, who nodded a response. "I'm Maggie Crozat. Do I know you?"

The rider muttered something in a guttural voice. The singing and imbibing had made many of the Mardi Gras hoarse. Between that, the mask, and the oversize costume, Maggie had no idea if she was clinging to the waist of a man or a woman.

The rider suddenly pulled on the reins, and the horse took off in a new direction...away from the Courir. Maggie watched helplessly as the jerky movement caused her cell phone to bounce out of her pocket onto the road. "My phone fell—do you mind if we go back?"

There was no response. Instead, the horse's canter turned into a gallop. And bile rose in Maggie's throat as she realized she wasn't being rescued.

She was being kidnapped.

TWENTY-FIVE

"Help! Somebody help me!"

Maggie knew screaming was useless, but she was desperate. She debated jumping off the horse, but it was galloping too fast. She might crack her skull or break her neck in the fall. As they rode, her wire mesh mask bounced up and down, creating a map of painful scratches and abrasions on her face.

The horse picked up speed, forcing Maggie to hold on even more tightly to her captor. They made a sudden turn and galloped into the driveway of Grove Hall. The rider pulled on the reins, causing the horse to rear as he came to a stop. Maggie lost her balance and tumbled onto the hard ground. She lay there, dazed, for a minute and then scrambled to her feet. Her plan to run was derailed by the barrel of a gun stuck in her back. It was a small gun barrel—the size of a purse pistol. Like the one Constance Damboise owned. "Scream and I'll shoot you," her tormentor said in a rough voice. "Go into the house."

"It's locked," Maggie said, hoping to thwart whatever plan was being enacted.

"It's not. Go."

Maggie did as she was told. She turned the knob of the massive front door, which opened with ease. Maggie cursed herself for not getting around to telling Kyle he should change the lock.

She and her abductor entered the empty, unfinished front hall. "Go up the stairs," the mystery Mardi Gras ordered. Maggie hesitated as she contemplated making a sudden move that would throw her kidnapper off balance. The gun barrel dug deeper into her back, canceling the potential escape plan. "Now. *Move.*"

Maggie reluctantly walked up the stairs. When they reached the landing, the gun directed her to make a right. She knew exactly where they were going. "You're taking me to the secret room," she said. "Aren't you, Pauline?"

The kidnapper snorted. Then she pulled off her mask, revealing Pauline Boudreau Tremblay. "Ding-ding-ding," she said, making the prize-winning sound of a game show. "I can finally take this thing off." Pauline tossed the mask over the landing rail, and it crashed to the floor below. "So now that you know where you're going, let's get there. *Allons-y.*"

"I don't remember which room it's in," Maggie said, stalling for time.

"No worries. I do."

Again, Pauline used the gun to poke Maggie in a specific direction. She marched Maggie down the hall and into a bedroom, where she pressed on the door hidden in one of the room's walls. The door swung open. Pauline nudged Maggie into the room, which was once more littered with illicit partying paraphernalia. "Here's what's going to happen," Pauline said. "I'm going to load you up with sleeping pills. If you have any 'trouble' swallowing them, this gun should fix that problem. Someday I have to thank Constance Damboise for introducing me to the value of a purse pistol. They're so convenient. Although I'd rather not shoot you. It's too close to the other deaths."

"You mean murders."

"I have no desire to argue with you. I want to get this over with so I can watch my daughter continue the family legacy of being crowned Miss Pelican Mardi Gras Gumbo Queen."

"It's a legacy built on a lie. You're not a Boudreau at all, are you? Or a Favrot. Your great-grandmother was Bridget Colleary and your great-grandfather was Jacob Seideman."

Maggie had come to suspect that, despite her self-deprecating attitude, Pauline Beaudreau Tremblay was deeply invested in her impressive Louisiana lineage and status as a pillar of Pelican society. And thus she had the most to lose if her true background was exposed. Maggie assumed the decorator was behind the theft of the files at the Hall of Records. But Pauline couldn't stop the New York Foundling Hospital's records from revealing her secret—a secret obsessively guarded by generations of the woman's ancestors. Both Bridget and Jacob had been adopted by families determined to hide their birth lineage, so they were raised as Boudreaux and Favrots. They eventually met, fell in love, and married, taking the secret of who they both really were to their graves—if they ever knew, having been adopted as infants. "You found out your true ancestry from Ira Stein, who was obsessed with genealogy," Maggie said. "Ira, whose mother's maiden name was Seideman. A distant relation of yours."

Just hearing the names of her orphaned ancestors made Pauline grimace. "Do you think Jules would have married me if he knew about my real background? Do you think anyone would have?"

Maggie stared at her in disbelief. "Uh, *yes*. Considering it's not the eighteenth century, I think a lot of people would have married you." *They would have regretted it in a big way when they realized you were out of your mind, of course*, Maggie thought, but wisely refrained from saying. She clung to the desperate hope that if she sympathized with Pauline, there was at least a chance of having her life spared.

"Jules never, ever would have proposed. Tremblays marry up, not down." Tears slipped down Pauline's cheeks. "Do you know what it's like to find out your whole past is a farce? Of course you don't, because your background is legitimate." She spit out the last word. "You know who wasn't legitimate? Either of my great-grands. My great-grandmother's mother was a chambermaid, father unknown. My great-grandfather's parents were teenage Jewish immigrants. No wonder Ira was so thrilled to find out he was related to a distinguished Louisiana family. Except being related to him canceled out the distinguished part."

Maggie was revolted by the malignant narcissism of the woman but masked the feeling. "I know it must have been hard on you, and I'm sorry." She stopped herself from adding, *But these are insane reasons for killing people.*

Pauline stared past Maggie. "My father drummed it into me—'Never forget where you come from,' he'd say. He held his status over my mother's head because her family didn't go as far back in Louisiana as his did. He had disdain for Denise's family because her mother married an out-of-stater, and then Denise did too."

Maggie remembered what she'd told Gerard Damboise when he'd declaimed about the impressive bloodlines of Pauline's family. "Names from a hundred years ago shouldn't matter now."

"They do when they're the one thing you're famous for in this town."

Keep her talking, Maggie. Appeal to her ego. "Pauline, you have fantastic taste and style. You're a great decorator. This stuff about your family history being the only thing you're good for—it's all in your head."

"Argh, enough. I got totally off track." Pauline searched the pouch on her costume with her free hand. "Where are those sleeping pills?"

"I'm supposed to pick up Bo at the airport. He's going to figure out something's wrong when I don't show up."

For a minute, Pauline looked worried. "Did you tell them anything about me?"

Maggie's heart sank. She'd figured out Gerard wasn't trying to say *please* when he'd clung to her. If he'd had the strength, the puff of air he'd managed to issue would have formed the name *Pauline*. But in her fear of making a mistake and accusing the wrong person of murder—especially a respected citizen like Pauline— Maggie had never named her as a suspect. "Yes," she lied. "I told him all my suspicions about you."

Pauline snorted. "No, you didn't. You should have seen your face when I just asked you that. Anyway, it doesn't matter. By the time they figure out there's a problem, you'll be in the Atchafalaya Swamp. Where are those flipping pills?"

"Maybe they fell out of your pocket like my phone fell out of mine."

Pauline groaned and let out a string of unladylike profanities. "I've got to go find them."

"See if you can find my cell while you're out there," Maggie said, her tone acerbic.

"You have miserable luck with phones, don't you?"

Something dawned on Maggie. "My first phone. You're the one who broke it. Why?"

Pauline shrugged. "I guess there's no harm in telling you now. Gerard was wearing a Tremblay heirloom tie clasp I gave him, hoping it would get him off my back and make him go away. He mentioned you took photos of the judges, and I didn't want anyone to see the tie clasp and get ideas. Especially you." Pauline stood up, hovering over Maggie. "You can blame your current situation on Eula Banks. I knew you were snooping around, but it wasn't until the Courir meeting at JJ's, where she yelled that she'd sent you records from the foundling hospital, that I realized you were a genuine danger to me."

"I'm guessing Gerard found out about your family's past from Ira Stein and was somehow using it to get something from you. But I can't figure out what."

"Our home, Maggie." There was a catch in Pauline's voice, and for a moment she sounded vulnerable. "He threatened to tell everyone the real story of my family if I didn't sell him Camellia Plantation for his stupid Historical Society. He'd already picked out the furniture he was going to take from us to put on display."

"The pieces at your house marked with red dots. You weren't changing them out with items from your attic. Those were antiques Gerard laid claim to." *Of course*, Maggie thought. *It all makes sense now.* Gerard's own obsession with controlling Pelican's past through the Society had brought about his present-day death.

"I can't let anyone find those pills. I'll have to retrace my steps."

It dawned on Maggie that there was no lock on the secret door. Pauline's hunt for the sleeping pills offered her a chance to escape. Unfortunately, this also dawned on Pauline. "But first…"

Pauline picked up a discarded liquor bottle. Before Maggie could shield herself, she cracked the bottle over Maggie's head, and the world went black.

MAGGIE SLOWLY OPENED her eyes to a blurry world. She was disoriented, her head throbbed, and she felt like she was suffocating. It took a moment to realize the reason for this—her mouth was duct-taped shut. She instinctively moved her hands to pull the tape off, but they were bound with the tape, as were her ankles. She tried to roll onto her feet, but failed. She wriggled up against a wall and using her back, shimmied up it to a standing position. The world swirled and Maggie fought back the urge to pass out. She hopped her way to the room's small window, her head pounding with each step. The window was covered with brown butcher paper. Maggie rotated until her back faced the window, reached for the paper with her manacled hands, and used her fingernails to tear off strips of it. She then rotated around again to face the window and stared through the holes she'd managed to rip. The view stretched over Grove Hall's endless sugarcane fields to the bayou and swamp beyond. Not a soul was in sight. Maggie would have to escape on her own.

She hopped to the room's door, but it swung inward,

not outward. Maggie was desperately trying to maneuver the door open when she heard sounds from below. She froze, assuming Pauline had returned. Then she heard giggling and murmuring from two voices, one male, the other female. She tried to scream, but the tape muffled her voice. Maggie heard footsteps on the manor house staircase and was about to jump up and down, but stopped herself. The sound might scare off the visitors. She'd wait until they got closer and could recognize her muted pleas for help.

"You sure this is okay?" the male voice asked.

"Yeah," the female voice responded. "A lot of kids come here. Nobody's living in this old place yet, so nobody bothers you if you come at the right time, when the workers are gone."

Maggie heard the couple approaching the secret room and hopped backwards. The door flew open and Kaity entered, with Jayden right behind her. All three screamed the instant they saw one another, although the duct tape over her mouth made Maggie's cry sound more like a chicken being choked.

"Miss Crozat, what the…"

Kaity was in such a state of shock she let the sentence trail off. Jayden went to Maggie and ripped the tape off her mouth. She cried out from the pain.

"We weren't going to do anything bad," Kaity, who had found her voice, blabbered. "We were going to hang out, and I'm eighteen so it's okay and—"

Jayden held up his hand and Kaity stopped talking. "Thank you," Maggie said, grateful to the vet. She tensed as she heard the sound of a galloping horse growing closer. "No time to explain. I need your help. Pauline Tremblay will be here any minute."

"Belle's mom?" Kaity exclaimed. "Seriously, what the—"

Jayden held up his hand again. "Go on, ma'am."

"There's a closet in the other room. Hide inside. The minute she comes in, Jayden, jump out and tackle her. But be careful. She has a gun."

"Got it. Kaity, come."

Jayden took Kaity's hand, and they exited to the bedroom. Maggie hopped into the room behind them while the couple hid in the closet. The manor house front door opened and shut. There was the sound of footsteps hurrying up the staircase and onto the landing. Maggie, whose head still throbbed, heard a loud thumping noise. It took a minute to realize the sound came from her own heart.

The bedroom door opened, and Pauline entered the room. She froze at the sight of Maggie standing in front her, hands and feet still duct-taped. "How did you get out of there?"

"Now!" Maggie yelled.

The closet doorknob turned, but nothing happened. Pauline collected herself and pulled the purse pistol out of her costume pocket. She aimed it at Maggie. Suddenly the closet door flew open, and Jayden, with a battle cry, tackled Pauline to the ground. She fought back, but he subdued her. The roll of duct tape rolled out of Pauline's costume pouch. Jayden grabbed it and used the tape to bind the murderess.

Kaity ran to Maggie and began pulling the tape off her hands as the air filled with the familiar, comforting sounds of police sirens. "I texted 911 while we were in the closet," Kaity said. "Sorry we didn't come out right away, but the doorknob inside the closet got stuck."

"Remind me to tell Kyle and Lia to put that on their punch list," Maggie said.

And then she collapsed to the floor in a faint.

TWENTY-SIX

EMTs Cody Pugh and Regine Armitage made Maggie sit up during the ambulance ride to St. Pierre Parish Hospital, where the ER doctor on call diagnosed her with a slight concussion. She was checked in for observation and wheeled off to a hospital room, where, after being hooked up to a variety of monitors, she was deemed not to be at risk. Given the okay by her doctors, Maggie fell into a much-needed sleep.

She woke up a few hours later with a sensation of being watched. It wasn't her imagination. Surrounding her bed were Ninette, Tug, Gran', and Bo. She greeted the group a touch warily. "Hello? You're not on some kind of death watch, are you?"

There was relieved laughter, and then everyone began talking at the same time.

"Thank the Lord Almighty you're all right."

"We were so worried."

"Craziest Mardi Gras ever."

"You need some water, *bébé*?"

Maggie waved her hands in the air. "Stop, y'all are giving me a headache. And yes to the water." Ninette poured her daughter a glass and handed it to her. "First of all, does Pelican PD have Pauline in custody?"

"Yup," Bo said. "She's under lock and key in Baton Rouge."

"How's poor Belle taking it?"

"Her reaction was strange, to be honest," Ninette said. "Jules and Denise broke it to her and asked me to be there for support. When we told Belle, she seemed almost...relieved."

Maggie wasn't surprised by Belle's reaction. The girl was absorbed in her own drama, and in her eyes, a mother being arrested on charges of kidnapping and suspicion of murder trumped news of a teen pregnancy. But since Belle had yet to reveal her secret, Maggie simply said, "She was probably in shock and not quite sure how to respond."

"Probably."

Gran' gave her granddaughter's cheek a fond caress. "Now that we know my beloved *petite fille* will be all right, why don't we leave her and Bo alone for a bit? I think they deserve some time to themselves."

"Hint taken, Mama," Tug said. "No need for the nudge in the ribs." He bent down and kissed Maggie on the forehead. Her mother and *grand-mère* did the same. "Just rest. You're safe now, *chére*. We all are."

The three started for the door. "Wait," Maggie said. "Who won the gumbo cook-off?"

"It was postponed," Tug said. "Everything except the parade was; the kids and tourists would have been too disappointed if that didn't happen. Still, it's hard to go on with Mardi Gras celebrations when one of the town's most storied citizens turns out to be a murderous madwoman."

"The postponement turned out to be a godsend for your father," Ninette said while Tug motioned for his wife to be quiet.

"Dad." Maggie's voice held a hint of admonishment.

"I was so busy trying to figure out Cal and Art's secret ingredient, I burned my roux," Tug sheepishly admitted. "The good Lord taught me a lesson, I'll tell you."

There was a long bout of Southern Door Syndrome as the family's goodbyes stretched out, and then they were gone. Bo took the room's 1950s era Eames chair and pulled it next to Maggie. He placed a hand on hers and kept it there. "How are you feeling?"

"Like someone cracked a liquor bottle over my head."

Bo chuckled. "A little advice from when I had my concussion." Only a few months prior, Bo had also been injured by a murder suspect. "Rest as much as you can. Don't strain your brain, because you'll get a killer headache."

"But I want to know everything, starting with how you made it back to Pelican."

"When you weren't there to greet us and there was no message, I knew right away something was wrong. I called a friend of mine who's an officer with the New Orleans force. Ru took his own car and Jonathan picked me up in a patrol car. He turned on the siren, put the pedal to the metal, and we got here *real* fast."

"Did you find evidence incriminating Pauline in New York? In Gerard's datebook? Is Quentin MacIlhoney her lawyer? Don't bother answering that last one; I know he is."

Bo put a finger to her lips. "No brain strain, remember?"

"But—"

"Shh. Rest."

She nodded and closed her eyes. Bo remained where he was, his hand on hers. *I have no idea what our future is*, she thought as she drifted off. *All I know is I want him here now.*

Tug and Ninette picked up Maggie from the hospital the next morning. It was her turn to recuperate in the Rose Room, which had been vacated by Gran' after her bout of walking pneumonia and was empty of guests post–Mardi Gras. Maggie followed Bo's advice and took it easy for a few days, using the time to heal as well as track the unfolding saga of Ira Stein and Gerard Damboise's murders. She also gave Pelican PD a detailed statement of the conversations she'd had with Pauline while being held captive. The masterful maneuverings of Louisiana's best defense attorney, Quentin MacIlhoney, would be challenged by this case, especially after the NYPD's computer forensics expert came through with what he discovered on a computer in the Upper West Side library.

"He dug up an email thread between Pauline and Ira Stein, laying out a timeline for Pauline's plot," Bo explained during a break from making a test batch of gumbo with Tug. The night air was soft and silky, and the family had convened for cocktails on the manor house veranda. "Once Stein established his genealogical link to orphan Jacob and by default to Pauline, he eagerly shared this information with her—and also the details of the trip he'd already booked to meet his newfound relative in person. Knowing Ira could reveal her real lineage, Pauline tried to talk him out of the trip. When that failed, she arranged a 'reunion' the day before the floods that eventually deposited Ira's body in your backyard."

"But how on earth did Gerard Damboise get involved?" Gran' asked, taking a sip from her second Sazerac of the early evening.

"Ira got in touch with him to see if the Historical Society had any information on Bridget and Jacob. Gerard

didn't, but directed him to the Hall of Records, where
the records just happened to be 'missing.' Our crime
scene guys found evidence they'd been shredded and
then burned in the backyard fire pit at the Tremblay
manse. Anyway, Gerard appears to have been very interested in Ira's story. His datebook showed he was supposed to meet with Ira the day of the flood. Ira never
showed, of course, because he was dead by then. But
the datebook also revealed Gerard had several meetings
with Pauline, including one on the day he died. Now
that Quentin's handling her case, she's not talking. But
putting together that meeting with what Pauline already
blabbed to Maggie, we're guessing Gerard figured out
our John Doe was Ira, and hoped to use this to blackmail Pauline."

"She must have been stunned when she came upon
you and Gerard on the River Road," Ninette said.

Maggie nodded. "She was. I thought she might faint
when she saw Gerard. At the time, I assumed she was
in shock. Which I guess she was, but not because of his
death. It came from realizing Gerard had survived his
gunshot wound long enough to drive and try to get help.
But it's interesting; she never asked me about what happened when I found him, like whether he was still alive
or not. Or whether he said something to me."

"I'm not remotely surprised," Gran' said. "You've
developed a bit of a reputation for nosing around, so
she was probably afraid it would make you suspicious."

Bo grinned. "It wasn't until you started full-metal
nosing that you became a threat to her."

Maggie made a face. "Okay, I think we've all used
the word *nosing* enough for one day." She stared at the
Pimm's Cup in her hand. Her father had made the drink

stronger than usual, so she was consuming it in small sips. "It's so hard to believe anyone would judge Pauline harshly for her family's roots in this day and age. But she believed they would, and that's all that matters. Her identity, her business—she thought everything would be destroyed if anyone discovered the secret of her family tree."

"It does seem an antiquated way of thinking," Gran' acknowledged. "Although it wasn't long ago that no amount of success or money could get your daughter onto a New Orleans Mardi Gras court if she didn't sport an esteemed surname. I know families that didn't have a black pot to pee in, if I may be crass, but took out loans for their daughters' Mardi Gras gowns so they could make their debuts at a Rex or Comus ball."

A pickup truck made a right from the River Road onto Crozat's long drive and meandered toward the house. "I wonder who that might be," Ninette said, peering into the darkness.

The truck parked, and Allie Randall jumped out of the driver's seat, dressed in her uniform of ripped jeans and flannel plaid shirt over a black tank top. She waved to the family and ran up the steps to them. "Hey. Hope I'm not disturbing y'all."

"Of course not, *chére*," Ninette said with a welcoming smile. "Tug, would you get our guest an iced tea?"

"Oh, that's okay. I won't be long. How're you feeling, Miss… Maggie?"

"Very close to a hundred percent better. Thanks for asking."

"I'm… I'm super sorry about my aunt. I knew she was kind of rigid and judgy, even though she hid it well. But seriously, none of us knew she was so messed up."

"No one did, Allie," Maggie reassured the teen.

"Anyway…" Allie hesitated, embarrassed, then summoned up the courage to continue. "Writing the essay for the contest kind of got me interested in history, especially the history here. You know, in Pelican. When I heard about the secret room at Grove Hall, I was, like, wow. What *is* that? So, I did some research at the Historical Society, which is a really cool place, by the way. I found a bunch of old papers and stuff about Grove Hall that someone donated—"

"That was me," Bo said. "Grove Hall belonged to my family, the Durands, for over a hundred and fifty years until we sold it to Kyle and Lia. We cleaned the place out, and my cousins all wanted to toss those old papers, but I thought the Historical Society might get some use out of them."

"Well, I sure did." Allie's excitement was building. "I found a floor plan from when the house was built, and that room was labeled *'la chamber pour Etienne.'* 'Etienne's room.' And I was like, who's Etienne? So I looked through everything, and I found a diary kept by Etienne's mom."

"My dear, I couldn't be more on the edge of my seat if this was an action movie," Gran' said. "Tell us what you learned."

"Okay, so from what I read, Etienne was mentally challenged and maybe autistic. His grandparents built Grove Hall for their son, who was Etienne's father, and included a secret room so Etienne could be hidden away and not bring shame on the family. It turns out some houses had rooms like that back in the olden days. Anyway, Etienne's parents hated the idea, but the grandparents were rich and they weren't, so they were being forced into it. But then the Civil War happened, and Etienne's mom and dad used that as an excuse to leave for 'a safer place' and start their own life without the mean grandparents. They moved up north. To around Shreveport. That's where Etienne's mom's diary ends."

There was silence as everyone took in the story. Then Bo spoke. "Those were my ancestors," he said. "The beginning of the Shreveport Durand clan. I always wondered how my part of the family ended up there. Now I know. They did it to protect a child with issues." Bo's voice was thick with emotion. "A hundred and fifty years ago, Etienne's room could have been Xander's room."

"But it wouldn't have been, because you and Whitney would have done exactly what your ancestors did," Maggie said.

"That's all I have for now, but I can't wait to look at more diaries and stuff at the Society," Allie said. "Ms. Damboise said I could volunteer there. It's weird. I'm always saying how I can't wait to get out of here. Now I can't wait to find out more *about* here. I'm going to apply to Louisiana State University and Tulane next year. That way I'd be away from home, but not too far away. Besides, with what all's happened to my family... well, they might need me. Especially Belle. She's having a hard time, between her mom and...everything else. She's good at making it look like she's okay, but inside she isn't."

"Poor thing," Maggie said. "I feel for her. We all do."

"I'm hoping when everything is over and settled, she can come to school with me. I know she wants that too, so... Anyway, I better get going. I just wanted to tell you about what I found out."

"You're amazing, Allie," Maggie said. The others nodded in agreement, and Allie simultaneously blushed and beamed. "I'll tell Lia and Kyle what you uncovered. They'll be fascinated. And let your family know if they need anything, we're here for them."

"I will."

Allie scampered down the stairs and, with a wave, took off in her truck. The others watched her go. "We shouldn't ignore the past. We should study it and use what we learn to build a better future," Maggie said.

"What's that?" Tug asked.

"I'm paraphrasing a line from Allie's contest essay. The sentiment really stayed with me. And with her too, obviously." Maggie's phone vibrated with a text alert. She looked down and read it. "Speaking of the past, Ione got permission from the Doucet Board to excavate under the nursery hearth. Anyone up for some treasure hunting in the morning?"

"Yes," everyone chorused.

Maggie laughed. "I thought so."

TWENTY-SEVEN

AT SEVEN A.M. the next day, Ione shepherded Maggie and her family into the nursery at Doucet, along with Bo and Gaynell. Maggie snapped photos of the hearth. Then she, Bo, and Tug began the painstaking task of chiseling its centuries-old bricks. As a brick was removed, Maggie numbered it. That plus the photos would ensure the hearth was accurately restored post–treasure hunt.

For forty-five minutes, Maggie, Bo, and Tug dug out one brick after another. The group was beginning to lose hope when Tug took his chisel to a chunk of mortar and they heard the unmistakable sound of metal on metal. "I hit something that's not dirt," he said.

Maggie shone a flashlight into the area where her father was working. The others peered over her shoulder and saw the corner of an old metal box. Tug lifted loosened bricks off the hearth, revealing the whole of the box, which was a deep green, pocked with rust, and about two feet long, a foot wide, and a foot deep. Bo and Tug extricated the container from where it had been hiding for over a hundred and fifty years. "There's no lock," Bo said.

"Denis Doucet must have thought hiding it here was protection enough," Ninette said. "He didn't want his family to worry about finding a key too." Maggie heard the catch in her mother's voice as she spoke of her ancestor, and put an arm around Ninette's shoulder.

"Oh my goodness, I can't stand the suspense." Gran' nudged Maggie. "You found the treasure—you get to open it."

"Okay," Maggie said. Bo handed her the box. "Here goes."

Everyone held their breath as Maggie lifted the lid. A parchment envelope lay on top of stacks of currency. Maggie handed the letter to Gran' and picked up one of the stacks, which were in remarkably good shape. "These are from the New Orleans Canal and Banking Company." She perused the top layer of bills. They were larger than current money. Each denomination featured intricate lettering and designs, black on one side, a faded red on the other. A distinguished gentleman with a serious expression stared out from the center of the twenty-dollar bills; once important, his identity was now lost to time. "They're dated 1860. Before Louisiana joined the Confederacy. What does the letter say?"

Gran' gently broke the envelope's wax seal and removed the letter inside. The brittle edges of the paper crumbled. "It's in Latin... Give me a minute." She furrowed her brow as she examined the letter. Then she read, *"'The war is here. Nothing and no one is safe. If you have found this, I have met my fate. Care for my beloved family. Denis Doucet. January 1861.'"*

The room was silent, absorbed in the history of that moment. "Denis died in February of 1861," Maggie said. "He was mortally injured in a fall from a horse spooked by gunfire. He must have buried this just a few weeks before he passed away."

Gaynell held up her cell phone. "I just looked up that bank. It changed its name a bunch of times and closed in the 1930s."

"These bills went out of circulation long before that," Tug said.

Gaynell looked disappointed. "So they're worthless."

Maggie shook her head. "Not to collectors. They love this stuff. I'll research some online sites where the bills could be put up for auction or sale. It would be a great way to raise money that would help preserve Doucet."

Ione picked up a stack and examined it. "Any money raised by the sale of this currency would be divided between Doucet and the surviving descendants of the original family."

She smiled at Ninette, who seemed nonplussed. "Me? Really? Oh my."

"You don't need to think about that right now, *chére*," Tug reassured his wife. "First order of business is putting this hearth back together."

"Yes, thank you." Ione took the box from Maggie and closed it. "Our tours start in an hour. I'll lock up the box in the Doucet safe."

"And I'll mix cement for resetting the bricks." Bo picked up a small bag of cement he'd brought with him to the nursery. He addressed Grand-mère. "By the way, Charlotte, nice job on that Latin translation. I'm impressed."

"The nuns at the all-girls Immaculate Heart Academy assumed if they kept our heads in the books, we wouldn't think about boys," Gran' said. "They were wrong."

Two WEEKS LATER, on a brisk winter day, locals celebrated Second Mardi Gras in a big way, which was no surprise to anyone who knew Pelican's propensity for partying. For the second time, gaily decorated floats rolled up the village main street, its masked krewe members rewarding the young and young-at-heart with beads, doubloons, and the occasional small plush alligator. "It's amazing how fast you move when there's a free anything in your sights," Cal Vichet commented as his hefty fellow officer Artie Belloise deftly managed to catch a toy gator.

Post-parade, the Crozat front lawn was once again abuzz with activity. Purple, green, and gold decorations hung everywhere, perhaps more than for Mardi Gras itself. In one tent, Gaynell and the Gator Girls played Cajun tunes to a packed dance floor. In another, contestants were deep into making their gumbo for the rescheduled cook-off, with new entrants filling in the slots of the few who couldn't reschedule. A cloud of cooking steam hovered over the tent, perfuming the air with ingredients ranging from meats to seafood to those found in *gumbo z'herbes*, also known as green gumbo, which was made with garlic, bay leaves, herbs, spices, and almost a dozen different vegetables. Working the crowd were the dozen teenagers who'd originally competed for the title of Miss Pelican Mardi Gras Gumbo Queen, each wearing a tiara featuring a rhinestone gumbo pot.

"Look how happy they are," Maggie said as she and Gran' watched Kaity, Belle, Allie, and a few other contestants pose for pictures with a group of giggling tweens.

"I know. It's lovely to see, considering everything that's happened. Using some of the treasure money to buy each of those girls her own crown was a wonderful idea, *chére*."

Maggie had guessed right about collectors' interest in the tin box's treasure trove of defunct currency.

When she posted one of the twenty-dollar bills on an online auction site, a wealthy numismatist specializing in paper currency from nineteenth-century Louisiana banks snatched up the whole collection. The generous proceeds of the sale were divvied up between the non-profit foundation tasked with maintaining Doucet and Ninette Doucet Crozat. A family conference split most of the money the Crozats received between Pelican's flood relief efforts and continued construction of the B and B's spa facilities. The tin box and one bundle of bills were donated to the Pelican Historical Society, along with a generous financial contribution to help fund the Society. Maggie's suggestion to use another chunk of the earnings to buy crowns for all the pageant contestants was approved with a unanimous vote.

"I love how they sparkle in the sunlight," Maggie said. "They really are beautiful."

"Oh my, do I hear longing in your voice?" Gran' teased.

"I have to admit, I get them now," Maggie said sheepishly. "I can see why a girl would covet the crown. It's gorgeous. But I was never comfortable with the idea of judging teens, having been one myself." She and Gran' helped themselves to small sample cups of gumbo, then used golf pencils to rate the blind taste test on scoring sheets. "This way, Belle doesn't have to reveal her secret yet, but she's also not living a lie because *all* the girls are Miss Pelican Mardi Gras Gumbo queens. And by the time she starts to show, there won't be so much attention on her."

"Have Whitney and Zach committed to adopting her baby?"

"Yes. They couldn't be more thrilled. Xander will have a sibling soon."

"And eventually, perhaps, more than one."

Gran' gave Maggie a knowing look. Maggie ignored her. She and Bo had hardly seen each other in the last couple of weeks. Whether this was due to legitimate scheduling issues or passive-aggressive avoidance, Maggie didn't know. What she did know was that post–Second Mardi Gras, she and Bo would be having The Talk.

Gran' surveyed the crowd, and Lee Bertrand caught the octogenarian's eye. He did a brief two-step and beckoned to her. "Lee wants to take me for a spin on the dance floor. If you don't mind…"

Maggie grinned. "Go for it. At least this time it won't be behind my back."

"Consider me chastised."

Gran' blew her granddaughter a kiss and wended her way through the festival crowd toward her beau. Maggie walked over to a row of tables set up for local merchants to promote their wares. Mo Heedles was busy handing out skin-care samples to a bevy of interested customers, which included Rufus Durand. "How's the sunblock coverage in this?" he asked, holding up a lotion bottle. He patted his thinning scalp. "I'm tired of getting iffy growths removed from up here, and don't want to spend all my off hours wearing a baseball cap."

"That's got an SPF of seventy," Mo said. "And it's non-greasy, so it won't oil up your hair."

"Sold. Dang it, Mo, I can never say no to you."

"Few can, honey. Few can."

Rufus pulled out a credit card. As he and Mo became engaged in their transaction, Maggie saw Stacy Metz perusing the display of Veevay items for sale. Stacy picked up a small pink and gray container of moisturizer, then hesitated and placed it back on the table. She caught Maggie's eye. "I'm trying," she said, flushed with embarrassment.

"I know," Maggie said with a sympathetic smile.

She continued her stroll through the festivities. Jayden and Kaity had made themselves comfortable on the veranda rocking chairs. Kaity took off her gumbo pot tiara and mischievously put it on Jayden's head. Jayden burst out laughing, and for the first time since Maggie met him, the vet looked like the boyish twenty-two-year-old he was. Gin had thrown a fit about the relationship, but Kaity pointed out to her grandmother that, being eighteen, she was an adult and legally free to date whomever she wanted. More importantly, her chosen beau was someone who'd put his life on the line for their country, and who could argue with that? Gin couldn't, and gave up. Jayden also had a new home and a steady job on top of his freelance construction work, which helped Kaity sell the relationship to her grandmother. Lia and Kyle hired the former Marine to work as a security guard at Grove Hall. Once they moved in, the plan was to transition Jayden to estate manager. He'd live inside the plantation until renovations were completed, and then move into the restored overseer's cottage on the property.

Someone tapped Maggie on the shoulder. She turned around to find Mike Randall. The change in him was apparent. Gone was the arrogance born of insecurity, replaced by a kind of gravitas. They exchanged polite greetings. There was a pause as Mike cleared his throat and stared at the ground. Then he lifted his head and looked Maggie in the eye. "I want you to know I thought a lot about what you said to me at the police station. You know, how basically the best way to measure a man is by his friends and family. Jules and Belle are gonna be moving in with us. For as long as they want. I don't know if you heard, but Constance Damboise is using a portion of the insurance policy from Gerard's death to buy Camellia Plantation from him."

"No, I haven't heard that."

"Yeah, neither Jules or Belle want to be there anymore after what happened with Pauline. Constance is gonna live in part of the house and turn the rest into a home for the Historical Society. She's got a bunch of displays planned. Mo's gonna help her with one about the history of Creole Africans in Pelican. And my Allie's gonna help set up the orphan train exhibit." Mike shared the last piece of news with great pride. "Constance is even adopting Houmas and Pepin, and letting the girls take care of them. She knows how much they love those horses. Jules and Belle will eventually find a place to live nearby, maybe in Ville Blanc. In the meantime, Jules doesn't have to give up his job to look after his daughter. He can travel as much as he needs to for work, and she'll be with us. I plan on taking real good care of my girls. All of them."

Mike put an arm around Denise, who had joined him. Dressed in jeans, sneakers, and a navy tee shirt, her hair back to its natural blonde, she no longer looked like a fifth-generation copy of her killer cousin, Pauline. She greeted Maggie with a hug, then told her husband, "They're about to judge the gumbo contest. If you want more free samples, we best get over there."

"'Bye," Mike said, and took off with his wife, leaving Maggie to contemplate the irony that it took death to get Gerard Damboise what he connived for in life—a home for the Pelican Historical Society at Camellia Plantation.

THE RUSH ON gumbo samples delayed the final tabulation of scores, so a winner wasn't determined until early evening. As everyone gathered around the concert stage to hear Mayor Beaufils announce the results, Maggie searched for Bo. Rufus and Sandy walked by, hand in hand. Rufus held a half-eaten oyster po' boy in his free hand. "Ru, do you know where Bo is? I haven't seen him all day."

Ru shook his head and chomped down on his po' boy. "No idea. He did say something about running an errand in New Orleans. Maybe he's there."

"Maybe," Maggie said with a shrug, trying to hide her disappointment.

"Hey, everyone, listen up," Mayor Beaufils called to the crowd. "I want to give out these results before the ice melts in my bourbon. Coming in third today—the gumbo stylings of Cal Vichet and Artie Belloise."

The onlookers whooped as Cal jumped onto the stage. Artie lumbered up the stairs to join him. They took their trophy and held it high. "In second place," the mayor continued, "Got-to-go-gumbo himself, Tug Crozat."

Maggie cheered as her father took to the stage and faked a humble bow. Then he grabbed the trophy and kissed it. "It ain't first place, but it's first place's first cousin," he yelled to the crowd.

"And the grand prize trophy for this year's annual

Mardi Gras Gumbo Cook-off goes to a last-minute entrant… Ninette Doucet Crozat!"

Ninette, who'd decided to break with the unspoken men-only tradition of the contest, sauntered onto the stage and waved to the assemblage, which roared its amused approval. She graciously accepted a giant trophy topped with a plastic gumbo pot and then motioned to Maggie and Gran' to come onstage, which they did. The entire family posed for a group shot.

"I hope you're not disappointed, *chér*, but I did warn you about my gumbo," Ninette said to her husband.

"At least the trophy stays in the family," Tug replied, and embraced her.

"Congratulations," Artie said, slapping both Tug and Ninette on the back. "I got a confession to make. We didn't really have a secret ingredient. We were just trying to throw you off your game."

"Well, it worked with me," Tug said. He gazed affectionately at his wife. "But I don't think anything would have thrown this champ."

"Ya got that right," Ninette responded with a mischievous grin.

The gumbo cook-off winners exited the stage, and Gaynell and the Gator Girls replaced them. They picked up their instruments, launching into a zydeco dance number that had partygoers spinning and two-stepping. "Second Mardi Gras is so successful, I think we need to make it a new holiday in Pelican," Gran' said, yelling to be heard over the music. "I already have ideas for Crozat B and B Second Mardi Gras getaway packages."

"I'm sure you do," Maggie called after her as Lee swept Gran' back onto the dance floor.

Maggie roamed aimlessly for a few minutes and

then decided to retreat to the shotgun cottage. She was greeted with doggy kisses from Gopher and Jolie. "Who wants a nap?" she asked. The pups responded with enthusiastic barks and followed her into the bedroom. She lifted both onto the bed and snuggled between them. "I do love my furbabies," she murmured. Maggie yawned and then fell asleep.

EPILOGUE

Maggie awoke a few hours later to a quiet, pitch-dark world. "I guess Second Mardi Gras is over," she said to her sleeping companions. "I might as well go back to sleep."

She was about to do exactly that when she heard a gentle tapping at the front door. She put on slippers, padded into the living room, and opened it. Bo stood in front of her, wearing the black leather bomber jacket she'd bought him for Christmas.

"Did I wake you?" he asked.

"No. Come in."

"Actually... I wondered if you were up for a walk."

"A walk?" Maggie was puzzled. "Okay. Let me put on some sneakers."

"You might want to put on boots. I thought we'd go up on the levee, and the grass is wet there."

Maggie did as Bo suggested, and the two left the cottage. They walked by the tents, which were still a mess from the party. Cleanup had obviously been postponed until the next day. Bo and Maggie crossed the River Road and hiked to the top of the levee, high above the Mississippi. "I kind of feel like this is our special place," Bo said.

"You do?" Maggie said, touched. "Me too."

They were both quiet for a moment. "We never finished our talk about babies," Bo finally said.

"No. We never did." Maggie tried to tamp down the sick feeling in her stomach.

"I'm afraid. I admit it. The thought of starting with kids again...anything could happen. Good, bad—I don't know. I don't want to be a coward..."

Maggie closed her eyes and steeled herself for the 'but' she knew was coming.

"So I decided I'm not giving in to that fear."

Maggie's eyes popped open. "Wait. There's a *so*? Not a *but*?"

"No *buts* except for the pain-in-one I was being by dodging the whole issue. I've been thinking about my ancestors and how they took a chance and sacrificed everything for Etienne. And how I ended up in Pelican because I knew it would be better for Xander. What I didn't know is how much better it would be for me. Look at my life now. I've got a happy, thriving kid. New friends and a great job. And a great, great love."

Bo took a small box out of his jacket pocket. "I've been wanting to ask you something for weeks, but I had to wait until this was ready. And today it was. That's why I wasn't at Second Mardi Gras. I was down in the city, picking it up."

Bo began to bend down on one knee. Maggie, over-come, put out a hand to stop him. "Don't, it's wet—you'll get grass stains."

Bo burst out laughing. "Seriously? That's what you're thinking right now?"

"No. Yes. I don't know." Maggie wiped tears from her face and waved her hands in the air helplessly.

"Alright, I'll do this standing up." Bo opened the box. Inside, resting on a bed of satin, was a gold band, and perched on it, in chocolate diamonds and yellow topaz, was a tiny replica of the gumbo pot gracing the crowns Maggie had given each pageant contestant. "Your very own crown, *chére*. Magnolia Marie Crozat, artist, innkeeper, and light of my life…will you do me the honor of being my forever Miss Pelican Mardi Gras Gumbo Queen?"

Maggie took a deep breath to regain control of her emotions. Then she gave a simple response. "Yes. Yes, I will."

Bo slipped the tiny gumbo pot on Maggie's ring finger and kissed her. The embrace turned passionate. After a minute, they separated. "We're going to need our own real gumbo pot," Maggie said.

Bo laughed. "Let's make that the very first thing we buy together."

He pulled her close to him, and she stayed in his arms, her head resting on his heart, her breathing in rhythm with its soft beat. The wide river lay below them, empty of boats for a change. Behind Bo and Maggie, the lights of Pelican's village twinkled in the distance, a Cajun brigadoon nestled between bayous and sugarcane fields.

Pelican… Their home. Their future.

* * * * *

LAGNIAPPE

I KNEW OF the orphan trains that brought children out West. But I had no idea there was an orphan train specific to Louisiana until a friend gave me a book about the subject. Between 1854 and 1929, the New York Foundling Hospital sent over two thousand children to the state. Many were orphans; others were homeless, illegitimate, or surrendered by poverty-stricken parents in the hope they'd find better lives away from the overcrowded, disease-ridden tenements of the city.

My mother came to this country with her parents from Italy in 1930, only a year after the orphan train ceased its journey. Through her stories, I learned of the hardships immigrants to New York faced. Although the difference between city and rural life was extreme, most of the children who were adopted by Louisiana families adjusted and prospered. My story is fictional, of course. But you can learn more about the real orphans thanks to the Louisiana Orphan Train Museum in lovely Opelousas. A visit to the museum is now on my bucket list.

NEW ORLEANS' MARDI GRAS, with its over-the-top parades and festivities, is legendary. But small towns throughout Cajun Country celebrate Mardi Gras with a completely different tradition—Courir de Mardi Gras.

Courir de Mardi Gras translates to "Fat Tuesday

Run." On Mardi Gras morning—or the prior weekend for some runs—people meet at a central location. Some walk, some ride horses. Others travel along the run on flatbed trucks. All are masked and dressed in vibrant costumes sewn together in patchwork style, sporting fringe and appliqués. Many of the Mardi Gras—yes, for the Courir, Mardi Gras also refers to the people who participate—wear *capuchon*, pointed hats resembling dunce caps. The face masks, usually created from wire mesh, are a study in folk art with their creative "found" decorations. Bottle caps become eyes. Look closely and you'll see the hooked nose on a mask is a recycled milk jug handle—just like in *Mardi Gras Murder*.

Led by a *capitaine*, who's unmasked and uncostumed, the revelers party their way from house to house, pranking agreeable homeowners and begging them for ingredients to use in a communal gumbo. Musicians are an important addition to the runs, and Mardi Gras often break into a chorus of *"La Chanson de Mardi Gras,"* also known as "The Mardi Gras Song." At some point in the courir, a homeowner may release a live chicken that the Mardi Gras trip over themselves trying to catch. Many runs are men only, due to the drinking and carousing. But over the last twenty years, male-and-female runs, all-women runs, and family runs have sprouted up, and their ranks grow every year.

The courirs culminate in communal gumbo parties featuring more music, dancing, and booze. Some Mardi Gras unmask; others don't. These days, the gumbo is usually premade, and the ingredients gathered from the run are saved for the future. Being that this is Louisiana, the partying usually doesn't end with the gumbo festivities. Many communities have *fais do-dos*—dances—

in the evening, where the Mardi Gras continue their playful charades. Courir de Mardi Gras generally take place in towns west of the Mississippi like Mamou, Eunice, and Iota. I cheated geography in the interest of sharing this fascinating tradition with my characters and readers.

LOUISIANA MAY BE the only state in the union where there are more festivals than days in the year. And each festival seems to have its pageant queen. The idea for Miss Pelican Mardi Gras Gumbo Queen came from meeting the lovely winner of the Teen Miss Festival of the Bonfires a couple of years ago when I was researching the tradition of building bonfires on the Mississippi levee up river from New Orleans, for the third book in this series, *A Cajun Christmas Killing.* I fell in love with the girl's pageant crown, which featured the recreation of a bonfire and flames in rhinestones.

An online search revealed more fantastic tiaras, and I made it my mission to write them into one of my Cajun Country Mysteries. And no, I didn't make up the rule disqualifying a pregnant contestant. Here's an example from an actual pageant application:

A contestant cannot be married at the time of the contest and must never have been married. She must not have or ever have had a child. Nor may she reside with any male not of blood relation. Marriage, pregnancy, or cohabitation with a male of no blood relation during her reign will result in automatic revocation of her title and all prizes and privileges of the same.

TO ME, THIS RULE seems dated, and I hope one day it will be expunged from pageant applications.

OYSTER SOUP

Here's the recipe for Ninette's classic Oyster Soup—one of Maggie's favorite dishes.

Ingredients

8 tsp. butter
1 bunch scallions, chopped
½ cup finely chopped parsley
2 celery ribs, chopped
3 tsp. flour
1 cup oyster liquid, strained to remove any shell pieces
1 qt. milk
3 dozen oysters, cut in thirds (you can buy them in jars at the grocery store and use the liquid for the recipe)
  Salt and pepper to taste

Instructions

Sauté scallions and celery in butter. Add parsley and cook for two minutes. Blend in flour, stirring constantly. Don't let it brown!
Add oyster liquid and milk, and stir, stir, stir. Cook slowly over low heat for 30 minutes, and again, stir! Before serving, add the oysters and cook for five more minutes.

Serves 6–8.

BANANA BON TEMPS COCKTAIL

Here's the recipe for what the Crozats would call a dessert cocktail.

Ingredients

2 oz. dark rum
2 oz. banana liquor
1 tsp. brown sugar
1 cup milk
1 cup ice
1 ripe banana

Directions

Blend everything together in a blender except ½ tsp. brown sugar. Pour in (highball) glasses, and sprinkle each serving with the remaining brown sugar.
Serves 2.

BANANA PANCAKES WITH BROWN SUGAR BUTTER

Here's another recipe centered on what may be NOLA's most popular fruit.

The Butter

Ingredients

1 stick (8 T.) unsalted butter, softened
½ cup brown sugar
2 T. milk
1 tsp. vanilla (or rum, if you're not serving kids)
¼ tsp. salt

Instructions

Combine ingredients in a mixing bowl and mix until thoroughly blended. Set aside.

The Pancakes

Ingredients

2 cups Bisquick flour
1½ cups milk
1 ripe banana, cut up
1 tsp. cinnamon
2 egg whites
Chopped raw pecans (optional)

Instructions

Combine all ingredients in a clean mixing bowl. Using a mixer, mix slowly at first to gently combine the ingredients, and then increase speed until the ingredients are well blended.

Pour in ¼ cups onto a hot griddle. Flip when the pancakes start to bubble. Press down on them if you need to in order to make sure they cook through.

To assemble, take one pancake and slather on the brown sugar butter. Top with another pancake and do the same. If you want a third pancake, follow the previous instructions. Sprinkle with chopped pecans.

Serves 4–6.

Note: You'll have lots of brown sugar butter left over. It stores for a couple of weeks if you want to wait until your next batch of banana pancakes. Or here are a few bonus recipes:

1. Spread on toast and sprinkle with pecan pieces.
2. Mix a ½ cup brown sugar with a ¼ cup rum, and melt in a skillet or frying pan. Add a cut banana to the butter, and cook until the banana is soft. Serve over vanilla ice cream. Voila! Your very own Bananas Foster.
3. Blend ¼ cup with a ¼–½ cup of light cream cheese, and serve as a dip with cinnamon pita chips.

EASY-PEASY BUNDT KING CAKE

The Crozats generally leave the baking to Ninette or order delicious treats from Fais Dough Dough. But if Maggie's called upon to make a King Cake, she follows Gran's advice and takes a tasty shortcut, using cinnamon roll dough. Gran's super-easy King Cake recipe will have all your friends thinking you made one from scratch. Tradition dictates whoever gets the baby in their slice of King Cake has to provide the cake for the following year's Mardi Gras celebration.

The Cake

2 17.5-oz. cans jumbo cinnamon rolls (reserve icing packets)
3 T. brown sugar
½ tsp. cinnamon
Pinch of salt

The Frosting

3 oz. whipped cream cheese
Both frosting packets from cinnamon cans
½ tsp. vanilla
2 T. milk (you can add more if it's needed to make the frosting spreadable)
Purple-, green-, and yellow-colored sugar
1 tiny plastic baby

Instructions

Preheat the oven to 350 degrees.

Mix together the brown sugar, cinnamon, and pinch of salt.

Layer the cinnamon rolls, one by one, in the bottom of a Bundt pan so they overlap. Sprinkle the brown sugar mixture over the top, pressing it into the uncooked buns gently with the back of a spoon or a spatula.

Bake for 30–35 minutes, until cinnamon rolls are done. Let cool. When the cake is completely cooled, poke the plastic baby inside it, then flip the cake over onto a plate or cake plate.

Blend the cream cheese, icing packets, vanilla, and milk together. Frost the cake.

Once the cake is frosted, sprinkle it with alternating rows of purple-, green-, and gold-colored sugar.

Serves 8–16, depending on how big you cut the slices. *Note:* Alert guests to the baby so that it doesn't become a choking hazard!

If you're interested in an authentic King Cake, bakeries around Louisiana will ship them during the weeks prior to Mardi Gras.

CINNAMON ROLL KING CAKE

Here's another easy way to make a delicious King Cake.

The Cake

Ingredients

2 cans regular-size cinnamon rolls (reserve icing packets)

The Frosting

Ingredients

8 oz. whipped cream cheese
Both frosting packets from cinnamon cans
1 tsp. vanilla
¼ cup powdered sugar
Purple-, green-, and gold-colored sugar
1 tiny plastic baby

Instructions

Preheat the oven to 350 degrees.

Cover a baking sheet with a piece of parchment paper. Overlap the cinnamon rolls one by one on the paper until they form a circle.

Blend the cream cheese, icing packets, vanilla, and powdered sugar together. (*Note:* if the frosting is too thick, thin it with a little milk. If it's too thin, add more powdered sugar.)

Using clean fingers to gently separate the rolls, insert a tablespoon of the frosting mix between each of them, reserving the rest of the frosting.

Bake 15–17 minutes, until the cinnamon rolls are done. Let cool. Frost the cake when it's completely cooled, and then sprinkle with alternating rows of purple, green, and gold colored sugar. Poke the baby inside the cake.

Serves 8–16, depending on how big you cut the slices.

Note: Again, make sure the plastic baby isn't a choking hazard!

GUMBO RECIPES

Gumbo is possibly Louisiana's most famous and popular dish. Open any Cajun or Creole cookbook, and you'll find a great recipe for it. Given this easy access, I decided to try something new in *Mardi Gras Murder*. Rather than create my own gumbo recipes, I asked my dear friend, Gaynell Bourgeois Moore, to share hers. Gaynell is one hundred percent Cajun, and these recipes have been passed down through generations of her family. For Gaynell, making gumbo is an intuitive skill without precise measurements. To ensure the recipes are authentic, I've kept them in Gaynell's own words.

Gaynell's Chicken and Sausage Gumbo

First, make a roux in a big black iron pot. (You can use a stainless steel pot, but things tend to burn quicker in it.) Place a half cup oil and a half cup flour in the pot, and continue stirring until it's about the color of peanut butter. If it burns just a little, you may as well throw it out because it will give the gumbo a bad taste.

In another large pot, put in a cut-up fryer chicken and brown it. (An old hen is better for flavor.) In a separate pot, brown about a pound of cut-up sausage. I use andouille, a smoked sausage made with hunks of smoked meat.

Remove the sausage and add it to the chicken. Add a little oil to the pot where the sausage was, and brown one large, cut-up onion. Be careful it doesn't stick. Some people add tomatoes, celery, and bell peppers. I put those in my seafood gumbo.

Add the chicken, sausage, and onion to the roux. Then add two quarts of water, Creole seasoning to taste—I use Tony Chachere's—and simmer. How long you simmer depends on the chicken; an old hen takes longer. Make sure you have the heat on a low fire to prevent sticking, and stir often. I would simmer for about an hour and a half if it's an older chicken.

Some put filé powder directly in the pot. If you choose to do that, I'd put in a couple of tablespoons, but scatter it out over the gumbo at the end of cooking. Most of the time I put the filé powder out on the table and let people add it in on their own. Not everybody likes it.

Serve the gumbo over rice.

Note 1: You may substitute a quarter of a jar of Savoie's Old-Fashioned Roux (dark) and a rotisserie chicken to save time, but it won't have the flavor you get from a raw chicken.

Note 2: Years ago, my grandparents fried okra and added it to the pot for a thicker gumbo. It was cooked down so much that you could hardly know okra was in it. I fry okra because if you put it in the gumbo without frying it first, it's going to get slimy. So I fry it on a low fire and stir it a lot until it quits sliming. You can also bake it in the oven on a flat baking pan. Individuals may add it to their gumbo bowl if desired, but nowadays many people don't like okra.

Gaynell's Seafood Gumbo

First make a roux from scratch (see the recipe above), or substitute a quarter cup Savoie's Old-Fashioned Roux (dark) that comes in a jar.

Sauté two large onions and one bell pepper in the same pot. Some people add celery—that's the holy trinity of Cajun cooking, onions, bell pepper, and celery—but I don't because I have family members who don't like it.

Add a quart of water and stir often. You'll have to add more water as you go. It depends on how thick you want your gumbo. I add oysters at this time, about a dozen large ones and their juice, after I make sure the juice doesn't have any shells in it. You can add okra too, but make sure you fry or bake it first so it's not slimy.

Add Creole seasoning to taste, and more water until it's about four inches above your ingredients. Cook on a low fire for about 45 minutes.

Add small crabs and cook about half an hour more. We use the small crabs we catch in the bayous for our gumbo, about six of them. You can add the whole crab or the meat of it. It's mostly just for flavor. Make sure lots of liquid still remains at this point, then about a pound of shelled, deveined shrimp. You can also add a pound of crawfish tails if you like.

Cook a little longer, making sure there's plenty of liquid. I cook for about an hour, simmering and stirring. I want it to have some substance.

ELLEN'S CAJUN COUNTRY POTATO SALAD

One thing I love about Cajun Country is that I learn something new every time I visit. Last year, when I was in Baton Rouge for the Louisiana Book Festival, a friend introduced me to the delicious gumbo served in the state capitol cafeteria—which could also be ordered with a side of potato salad to add to the gumbo, much as you'd add a cup of rice. I'd never had potato salad in my gumbo before, and I loved it.

I've created a potato salad recipe that complements a bowl of gumbo. Add it to your gumbo with rice or instead of rice. Or serve it with burgers at your next cookout. However you use it, *laissez les bons temps rouler*!

Ingredients

3 lb Yukon Gold (or red) potatoes, cooked, chilled, and cut into chunks. Whether you peel the potatoes or not is up to you. I generally don't, especially with the Golds. I also cut them up before I cook them, because the smaller pieces cook quicker.

3 hardboiled eggs, diced

1 cup low-fat (or regular) mayonnaise

¼ cup minced stuffed green olives

¼ cup minced green pepper

¼ cup minced celery

¼ cup sweet relish
2 tbsp. minced scallions
1 tbsp. plus 2 tsp. Creole mustard—or a stone ground
  mustard if you can't find Creole
1 tbsp. minced fresh parsley
1 tbsp. minced dill pickle
1 tbsp. white wine vinegar
1 tbsp. juice from the jar of green olives
½ tbsp. Worcestershire sauce
¼ tsp. black pepper
Paprika for garnish.

Instructions

Combine all the ingredients *except for the potatoes and diced eggs*. When the other ingredients are all well blended, gently fold in the potatoes and diced eggs. *Gently* is the operative word here, in case the potatoes are a bit overcooked. You don't want your potato salad turning into mashed potato salad!

A BONUS RECIPE: GAYNELL'S POTATO SALAD

Says Gaynell: "Some people do put potato salad in their gumbo. I don't. I always have mine on the side."

Here's her recipe:

Boil about 6 medium potatoes until they're tender and boil about 8 eggs. (I like plenty of eggs in my potato salad.)

Drain and place the potatoes in a large bowl. When they've cooled, cut them into small chunks.

Peel the eggs, cut them up, and place them in a separate bowl. Add 1 cup mayonnaise, ¼ cup mustard, ½ cup sweet relish, salt, pepper, and Creole seasoning to taste. (I use Tony Chachere's Creole Seasoning.)

Add this mixture to the potatoes, mixing everything together well.

Note: Recipes for Jambalaya can be found in "Body on the Bayou." Recipes for Holiday Brandy Pain Perdu and Shrimp Remoulade can be find in "A Cajun Christmas Killing."

ACKNOWLEDGMENTS

I OWE A debt of gratitude to my neighbor and pal Julia Bricklin, who inspired a plot when she turned me on to a wonderful book, *From Cradle to Grave: Journey of the Louisiana Orphan Train Riders*, by the Louisiana Orphan Train Society; editor, Neal Bertrand.

As always, I have to thank my fellow Chicks at chicksonthecase.com—Lisa Q. Mathews, Kellye Garrett, Mariella Krause, Vickie Fee, and Cynthia Kuhn— as well as my GoWrite gals, Mindy Schneider, Kate Schein, and Kathy McCullough. And, of course, a thank-you to all the friends I've named in the books preceding this, plus a couple of new ones: Debra Derbyshire Burnette and her husband, NOPD officer Jonathan Burnette, who offered valuable research assistance when I needed it, and all-around general support. *Merci*, you two! A thank-you to author Marni Graff for connecting me with Jevon Thistlewood, art conservator at the University of Oxford's Ashmolean Museum; he gets both my appreciation for his help and an award for the best name ever. Maureen "Mo" Heedles, thank you for your generosity at the Malice Domestic Convention, and I hope you enjoy being in print.

Without my agent, Doug Grad, there would be no Crooked Lane connection; and without Mathew Martz, Sarah Poppe, and Jenny Chen, there would be no Crooked Lane books or Cajun Country Mysteries.

And then there's the amazing cover design team, including the artist responsible for the brilliant artwork on my covers, Stephen Gardner.

I'm blessed to belong to Sisters in Crime and Mystery Writers of America, specifically the chapters SinCLA and SoCalMWA. A special shout-out goes to chapter presidents Rochelle Staab and Elizabeth Little for shepherding an amazing California Crimewriters Conference, which led to a desperately needed breakthrough on this particular book; and keynote speakers Hallie Ephron and William Kent Krueger, whose workshops inspired me, as did workshops with Jeffrey Deaver and Jess Lourey.

As I mentioned above, so many friends have supported me through this fabulous journey—rather than list you all, just know how much I value each and every one of you. My darling daughter Eliza, your love and humor inspire me every day. And Jer…words can't express my love and appreciation for everything you've done to encourage me.

On a deeply personal note, there was a time when I feared for the life of my mother, Elizabeth Seideman. So, I want to give special thanks to everyone at Phelps Memorial Hospital in Tarrytown, New York, for saving her. Those of us who know and adore this remarkable woman are forever in your debt.